THE CAVENDISH HOME FOR BOYS AND GIRLS

THE CAVENDISH HOME FOR BOYS AND GIRLS

CLAIRE LEGRAND

ILLUSTRATED BY SARAH WATTS

SIMON & SCHUSTER BOOKS FOR YOUNG READERS

New York London Toronto Sydney New Delhi

SIMON & SCHUSTER BOOKS FOR YOUNG READERS
An imprint of Simon & Schuster Children's Publishing Division
1230 Avenue of the Americas, New York, New York 10020

For information about special discounts for bulk purchases, please contact Simon & Schuster Special Sales at 1-866-506-1949 or business@simonandschuster.com.

The Simon & Schuster Speakers Bureau can bring authors to your live event. For more information or to book an event, contact the Simon & Schuster Speakers Bureau at 1-866-248-3049 or visit our website at www.simonspeakers.com.

Book design by Lucy Ruth Cummins
The text for this book is set in Goudy Oldstyle.
The illustrations for this book are rendered digitally.
Manufactured in the United States of America
0712 FFG
2 4 6 8 10 9 7 5 3 1

Library of Congress Cataloging-in-Publication Data
Legrand, Claire.
The Cavendish Home for Boys and Girls / Claire Legrand.—1st ed.
p. cm.
Summary: Practically-perfect twelve-year-old Victoria Wright must lie, sneak, and break the rules when her investigation of the disappearance of her best—and only—friend, Lawrence, reveals dark secrets about her town and the orphanage run by the reclusive Mrs. Cavendish.
ISBN 978-1-4424-4291-7 (hardcover)
ISBN 978-1-4424-4293-1 (eBook)
[1. Fairy tales. 2. Best friends—Fiction. 3. Friendship—Fiction. 4. Perfectionism (Personality trait)—Fiction. 5. Orphanages—Fiction. 6. Missing children—Fiction.]
I. Title.
PZ8.L4758Cav 2012
[Fic]—dc23
2011028405

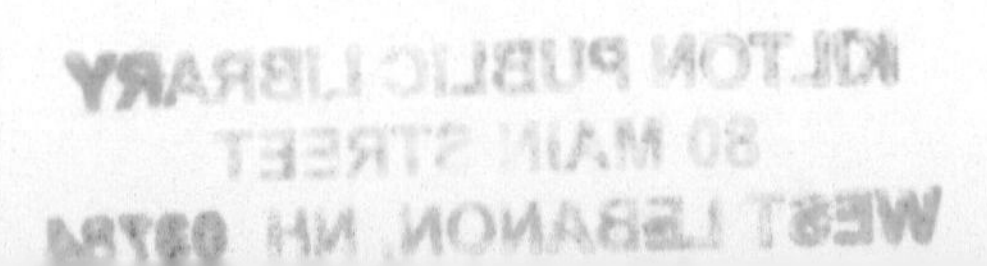

For my sixth-grade lunch table, who loved my scary stories

ACKNOWLEDGMENTS

Many people are involved in the making of a book, many more than one might originally think. "Is writing a book not simply a writer sitting at a desk and writing said book?" one might ask, befuddled. "Is that not how it is done?"

Why, yes, that is how it is done—but much more happens after that, and even before and during that, and it is those people, those doers of the *much more*, that I would like to take a moment and thank.

First, I must thank my agent, Diana Fox, who is much more than an agent and in fact could be considered superhuman. I am more grateful than I can say for her belief in me and my stories. Similarly, I would like to thank Pouya Shahbazian and Betty Ann Crawford.

Secondly, thank you to my brilliant editor, Zareen Jaffery, for so precisely and so vividly understanding my book and how to make it even better. Thanks must also go to the tireless team at Simon & Schuster Books for Young Readers, who helped bring *The Cavendish Home for Boys and Girls* to life: the intrepid Julia Maguire, Katrina Groover and Michelle Kratz, Justin Chanda, Michelle Fadlalla, and Lydia Finn and

Paul Crichton. Especial thanks must go to designer Lucy Ruth Cummins and the outrageously talented Sarah Watts for making everything look so very pretty.

My first readers, Kendra Highley, Kait Nolan, Susan Bischoff, Lauren Hild, Amanda Johnson, and Malika Horton, encouraged me and, just as I knew they would, made me a better writer. Thanks to Joanna Volpe, as well as to Veronica Roth, Victoria Schwab, Nova Ren Suma, Leigh Bardugo, Stephanie Burgis, Kody Keplinger, Serena Lawless, the relentlessly supportive Apocalypsies, and all the other writers on Twitter and in the blogosphere who support, inspire, and amaze me.

Over the years, several teachers have taught me how to better read and write: Judy Young (first grade), George Uland (sixth grade), Susan Addy (ninth grade), Mike Crivello (twelfth grade), and Ian Finseth (college). And I cannot forget my music teachers, considering how important music became to Victoria and Lawrence in their adventures: Ellie Murphy, who made up stories with me, Dr. Marty Courtney, who taught me discipline, and John Holt, who understood when I needed to leave music behind.

My stepsister, Ashley Mitchell, and my cousin, Emily Jones, are voracious readers and exemplary fangirls. My family—all my aunts, my uncles, my cousins, my stepbrothers—cheer me on every day. I must specifically thank Grandpa, for deeming me "Scribbles," and Grandma, for always having paper and colored pencils handy.

The warmest of thanks go to Brittany Cicero, who never let me give up; to Jonathan Thompson, who always believes and never judges. And to Beth Keswani, Melissa Drake, Amanda Tufano (of the aforementioned sixth-grade lunch table), Chris Siefken, Starr Hoffman, and Maureen Murphy, who have tolerated much radio silence on my part and still remain the dearest of friends. To Matt, who loves me—please never stop whirling me about in the air.

Thanks to Anna and to Dad, my very own WD, who love and support me in every way possible, even when that involves reading a manuscript so immense that it takes up two enormous three-ring binders.

For Drew, who is the most loving brother I could imagine, for Mom, who is my best friend and the ultimate heroine, and for Amos, who is a most excellent cuddler despite his overabundance of hair—thank you, always.

WHEN VICTORIA WRIGHT WAS TWELVE YEARS OLD, she had precisely one friend. In fact, he was the only friend she had ever had. His name was Lawrence Prewitt, and on Tuesday, October 11, of the year Victoria and Lawrence were twelve years old, Lawrence disappeared.

Victoria and Lawrence became friends shortly after Lawrence's first gray hairs appeared. They were both nine years old and in fourth grade. Thick and shining, Lawrence's gray hairs sprouted out from between his black, normal hairs and made him look like a skunk. Everyone made fun of Lawrence for this, and really, Victoria couldn't blame them. Victoria decided that these hairs were a cosmic punishment for Lawrence's inability to tuck in his shirt properly, use a comb, pay attention in class (he preferred to doodle instead of take notes), and do anything but play his wretched piano. Not that Lawrence was bad at piano; in fact, he was very good. But Victoria had always thought it an incredible waste of time.

After a few weeks of watching Lawrence's gray hairs sprout thicker and thicker, and hearing everyone's snickers, Victoria put aside her general dislike of socializing with, well, anyone, and decided that Lawrence would be her personal project. Obviously, the boy needed help, and Victoria prided herself on telling people what to do with themselves. Sacrificing her valuable time to fix Lawrence would be a gift to the community of Belleville. "How *charitable* of you, Victoria," people would say, and beam at her and wish *their* children could be like her.

So, at lunch one day, Victoria marched from her lonely table to Lawrence's lonely table and said, "Hello, Lawrence. I'm Victoria. We're going to be friends now."

Victoria almost shook Lawrence's hand but then thought better of it because she feared he might very well be infested with lice or something. Instead, she sat down and opened her milk carton, and when Lawrence looked at her through his skunkish hair and said, "I don't really want to be your friend," Victoria said, "Well, that's too bad for you."

Over the years, Victoria pushed herself into Lawrence's

life and was pushed out of it when he decided that enough was enough, and then pushed herself back in, and finally they were really, truly friends, in an odd sort of way.

Every weekday morning, they met at the crossing of Silldie Place (Victoria's street) and Bourdon's Landing (Lawrence's street) and walked together to school. Most mornings, their conversation went something like this:

"Honestly, Lawrence," Victoria would say, leading him briskly down the cobbled walk, for Victoria never walked anywhere without extreme purpose, "can't you tuck in your shirt?"

Sometimes it would be, "Can't you comb your hair?" or "How do you manage to get past your parents with those ugly shoes?" or "Did you finish your essay on the Byzantine Empire for extra credit like you were supposed to, or did you spend the entire weekend playing that silly piano?"

And Lawrence would roll his eyes or cuff her on the shoulder and say, "Good morning to you, too, Vicky," which Victoria hated. She abhorred nicknames, especially that one. She also abhorred how Lawrence was always chewing on something, like a toothpick or pen or whatever nasty things he pulled from his pockets.

Nobody liked Lawrence, because he never really bothered to make friends. He lived in a dreamer's world of ivory keys and messy shirts, unconcerned with the people around him.

"Honestly, Lawrence," Victoria would say, . . . "can't you tuck in your shirt?"

Those gray hairs of his didn't help matters. He didn't seem to mind what anyone thought of him, though. He didn't seem to mind about much at all except for his piano—and Victoria. For Victoria's twelfth birthday, Lawrence had written her a long letter and read it aloud right in front of her. It was full of jokes and funny stories, at which Victoria tried not to laugh *too* loudly, and that was all well and good, till the end happened.

". . . and so what I really mean is," finished Lawrence, his face turning quite red, "sometimes, the counselors or professors or Mom and Dad say, 'Don't you care that you don't have many friends?' And I say, 'Not really. Because I have Vicky.'"

Then Lawrence had folded up the letter and shoved it in his pocket. "So . . . you know. I mean, I really like that we're friends is what I'm saying. Happy birthday."

Victoria had been so embarrassed that she had said, "Well . . . you . . . I . . . that's very nice," and then ignored him for the rest of the week. She never allowed herself to think about why she'd felt so embarrassed. Such thoughts were messy. *Friends* were messy, which was why Victoria avoided them at all costs (except for Lawrence, but he was just a charity case, a project, and certainly—*certainly*—nothing more than that). Victoria hated messes. She hated distractions. Friends were the worst distraction of all.

Victoria began every day with a plan, and friends were simply not a part of it.

The Monday before Lawrence disappeared, Victoria awoke at half past six, just as she did every weekday—not one minute before, and certainly not one minute after. Tardiness was an offensive concept. She showered and dressed in her Academy uniform, white blouse and gray pleated skirt pressed stiff and straight. She sat at the vanity her parents had ordered custom from Italy, and brushed her blond curls till they gleamed. Everything about Victoria gleamed.

On her way out, she paused at the bedroom door, as she so liked to do, and inspected everything—vanity and desk; glittering chandelier, white canopy bed; a wall of mirrors and a ballet barre for practicing her exercises; a wall of shelves opposite her bed, floor to ceiling, containing pretty, labeled boxes where Victoria kept all her bookmarks and books and lotions and paper and pens and postcards and ribbons, because that way she never had to see even the tiniest bit of clutter. Her pride and joy were the spotless white walls and white carpet, marred by neither pictures nor smudges.

On most days, Victoria would gaze upon all this and feel a hot swell of satisfaction in her chest. But the Monday before Lawrence disappeared, Victoria felt no such satisfaction. Everything looked just as it should, shining with perfection.

Morning bathed the room in clean, white light. Victoria's schedule hung above her desk, clearly marking her tasks and lessons for that week. Piano lessons, ballet lessons, painting lessons, and French lessons filled her evenings with blocks of orderly color.

But below that schedule sat her academic report, and when Victoria forced herself to look at it, nausea overwhelmed her. On the crisp manila paper, in black text as immaculate as Victoria's own handwriting, she saw the three A's in Letters and Literature, History of the World, Intermediate French—and the one grotesque, intolerable B. She received a B in *music* class, of all things.

Victoria had never received a B in her entire life. She knew that some of her classmates yearned for B's. They were glad for B's. They jubilated at B's. But to Victoria, a B was even worse than mud on her carpet or a tangle in her perfect blond curls.

She walked to the desk, her breath trembling, folded the report into its envelope, pressed the golden Academy seal over the flap, and shut the report away in the bottommost drawer. It had a keyhole she had never seen the point of using before now, for she had never had a secret worth hiding. She found the appropriate key in the box labeled MISCELLANEOUS along with the other things she hadn't much use for, locked the drawer, and put the key back in its proper place.

She turned and stared at the closed drawer. She was supposed to get her parents' signatures and return the report by the following Monday morning, but the idea of admitting this catastrophe to anyone horrified her.

"Just breathe, Victoria," she said, putting a hand to her heart.

She caught the time on the silver clock beside her bed. 7:04. She had dawdled.

She hurried down the staircase, past her father's art collection on one side and the sweeping view of her mother's rose gardens on the other. She arrived at the kitchen in a bit of a flurry. Her father looked up from his newspaper, and her mother looked up from her magazine, for Victoria was seldom in a flurry.

"Good morning, Mother, Father," Victoria said. She could not look at her parents; if she met their eyes, they might see the B on her face. They would be disappointed in her, which they had never been before. Victoria didn't know what it felt like for anyone to be disappointed in her, but she could imagine it based on what she had heard others say. Mr. and Mrs. Wright would sigh and shake their heads, and when they went out for dinner, they would not brag to the next table about their perfect daughter. They would not even go out at all; they would be too ashamed.

Victoria swallowed hard. When she said, "Good morning, Beatrice," it sounded a bit funny.

Their old housekeeper, Beatrice, raised a slender white eyebrow and passed Victoria a bowl of fruit and a slice of toast with jam.

"Good morning, Victoria," said her mother.

Miranda Wright did not work in the conventional fashion, but she supervised Beatrice and the gardener who tended the roses, and was an expert shopper. She kept her magazines in pretty, labeled boxes in her closet. She wore fancy aprons in the kitchen even though she didn't cook, because she looked lovely in aprons, and that's what one is supposed to wear in the kitchen, after all. Miranda Wright was beautiful and stylish with penny-colored hair. She lunched with important Belleville ladies and knew everyone in town, even those about whom she would whisper to Victoria as having "questionable taste." Her high heels clicked just *so*. A member of the neighborhood homeowners' association, she loved making everything around her just *so*, too. Whenever Victoria looked at her mother, she felt almost as proud as she did when adding another medal to her MEDALS box, which held years' worth of honor roll pendants and spelling bee ribbons and "Top of the Class" certificates.

But she could not look at her mother today.

"Good morning, Victoria," said her father.

Ernest Wright was a successful, middle-aged lawyer, and he looked exactly like a successful, middle-aged lawyer should look. He drank mild mint tea, spent thousands of dollars on dental work so that his teeth would be perfect and white and gleaming, and shared his wife's fascination with trendy diets. His most triumphant success in life was the sleek, modern swimming pool he'd had installed in their backyard, although no one ever used it. He was considering tearing it out and putting in another one, because the Nesbitts' new pool was even sleeker and more modern than his. Mr. Wright knew everyone in town, too, and was one of the richest men in Belleville, and some people were even afraid of him because he was so rich and perfectly toothed. Few things could impress him, but Victoria had always managed it.

And now she had failed him. She had failed them both. The realization filled her belly with ice.

They must never find out, Victoria thought.

With the good-mornings said, Mrs. Wright flipped another page in her magazine, and Mr. Wright returned to his newspaper. To them, everything was just as it should be in the Wright house. Flushing with shame, Victoria returned to thoughts of the B in music class. She thought about it so much that she couldn't finish her breakfast and excused herself despite Beatrice's protests. Grabbing her book bag from the coat closet, she rushed out the front door.

Like every other street in Belleville, Silldie Place boasted cobbled walks, large trees, tall hedges, lampposts, and iron gates. Houses had high, peaked roofs and pretty white gables and impressive brick chimneys inlaid with stone birds. Yards were luxurious and groomed and spotless. If someone's yard began to wilt, they heard about it at once. Mrs. Wright would leave a crisp, red warning note in their mailbox.

The largest house and grounds in the whole town lay at the end of Victoria's street, on a rolling estate with trees so old you could hear them creaking two streets over, and a pond and a long, gray brick garden wall. This was Nine Silldie Place, the Cavendish Home for Boys and Girls. Victoria didn't like to think about the Home. She didn't even like to go near it. Orphanages held a distinctly untidy connotation. Although she had to admit she had never actually *seen* any orphans doing such things—or any orphans near the Home at all, for that matter—she couldn't help imagining a passel of them, dirty-fingernailed and smelly, running amok and knocking all her labeled boxes to the floor.

Shoving that horrifying image out of her head, Victoria marched along, growing angrier about her B with every step.

Surely Lawrence hadn't gotten a B. Surely Lawrence had received not only an A in music class but also another of old Professor Carroll's glowing essays about *talent this* and *prodigy that*, urging Mr. and Mrs. Prewitt to send Lawrence to the city for more advanced study.

By the time she reached the Prewitt house at Two Bourdon's Landing, Victoria found herself wishing, rather viciously, that Lawrence would go live somewhere else for a while. Every time she saw him now, she would be reminded of her failure.

She rapped with the knocker till the door opened to reveal Lawrence, hunched over and frowning. Of course his shirttails hung loose. Of course his tie wasn't tied.

"You're early," Lawrence said, flicking his gray eyes back over his shoulder, into the dark house.

Victoria scowled and stalked past him into the living room, where the Prewitts kept their ancient piano. It wasn't good enough for Lawrence. On her reasonable days, Victoria knew this. On her reasonable days, Victoria wondered if perhaps Lawrence should go to the city to study his music, even though the Prewitts would never let him. They were dental surgeons and wanted Lawrence to follow in their footsteps. Music was supposed to have only been part of a well-rounded education. All Belleville children needed culture, after all.

But when Lawrence's piano lessons turned into an obsession and he spent hours practicing Mozart sonatas and Chopin preludes and Gershwin solos till the neighbors complained, the sensible Prewitts realized they had a serious problem. They had never meant for *this* to happen.

However, today was not a reasonable day; Victoria had an academic report sitting at home with a B on it, for goodness' sake. There was no time to listen to Lawrence whine and sigh about how he wished his parents understood him and his stupid music better. Victoria slammed open the piano and rummaged through Lawrence's untidy stacks of music.

"Where's the Fauré?" she snapped. "Let's play it."

Lawrence blinked. "The Fauré?"

"Yes, the duet. We've got an exam on it next week, don't we?"

Lawrence sat on the piano bench beside Victoria, looking around from beneath his hair. The house was much darker than usual. The air sat strangely quiet and heavy around their shoulders.

"I don't know if that's such a good idea," he said.

"Well, I don't care." Victoria put her fingers on the keys and glared at him. "Come on, play."

"What's the matter with you, anyway?"

Victoria didn't answer. She started playing the bottom

part of the duet. Her anger made the notes choppy and clumsy, but she kept going, her cheeks flaming. All she could think of was that awful B mocking her.

Lawrence joined in after a few measures, and even in the dark house and despite Victoria's fury, once Lawrence began to play, everything seemed better. His fingers flew across the keys, delicate and confident. Music came to him as easily as order and structure came to Victoria. Lawrence's eyes glazed, and he got that tiny secret smile that he always got when playing. When they ended the duet with four bouncing chords, Victoria sat in angry silence. She glared at the piano.

"I got a B," she said.

"I figured."

"Oh, don't act like you know me so well."

Lawrence grinned. "Can't help it. That's what happens when you've got only one friend."

"You're lucky you have even that," Victoria said.

"You aren't bad at piano, you know. You just need to relax."

Victoria scoffed. "People who relax don't get anything done."

"Oh, that's right. For a second, I forgot who I was talking to."

"Make fun of me all you want, but don't come crying to me when you're working in a dump someday, all smelly and rumpled with only your lousy music to keep you company, when I'm at some big, fancy office somewhere, making lots of money and . . . and . . ."

Victoria stopped. Lawrence watched her from beneath his hair, the silver strands bright in the light of the piano lamp. He looked pathetic and hopeless. Victoria's stomach sank with shame, but she tightened her mouth and refused to look away.

"That's really what you think of me, huh?" said Lawrence.

"It's not like I ever made a secret of it," said Victoria, wincing inside even as the words popped out. It wasn't what a friend was supposed to say. She couldn't help saying it, though; her anger was too great. *I have a B, for goodness' sake*, she thought. And anyway, Lawrence could use a harsh word or two, to snap him out of his piano world and into the real one.

Lawrence frowned and closed the piano. "Let's just go to school."

As they passed through the foyer, Lawrence grabbed his tattered book bag from the floor by the door. He kept tripping over himself as he pulled on his shoes. Victoria watched, her nose wrinkling.

"What in the world's wrong with you?" she said.

"Nothing," said Lawrence, but Victoria noticed for the

first time that his normally sleepy gray eyes seemed a bit funny, like a rabbit's eyes—scared and stupid.

Upstairs, someone stalked across the floor, toward the stairs. Victoria jumped at the sudden noise. Lawrence flinched.

"Let's get out of here," he said quickly.

Victoria stared at him. "Shouldn't we wait to say good-bye to your parents? It sounds like they're coming right down."

"No. Let's go."

When they reached the front gate, Victoria sniffed and said, "Look, I'm sorry about what I said before. I didn't mean it. Your music isn't lousy." She hated apologizing, especially when she knew she was right in the first place. All right, so his music wasn't lousy; anyone could tell that much. But if Lawrence didn't start trying harder at school, he would go on probation, or he might be dismissed, and then he would have to attend one of the public schools outside Belleville, and that would ruin him forever. What good would music do him then? It wasn't practical; it wasn't profitable.

Victoria opened her mouth to tell Lawrence all these things in the hopes that he might actually listen to her this time, but before she could, Lawrence grabbed her hand and tugged her through the gate.

"What're you—?"

"Hurry, Vicky," he said, looking back over his shoulder again.

"You act like you're scared or something," said Victoria, shaking him off.

But then she looked back over her shoulder too and saw Mr. and Mrs. Prewitt watching silently from the front door. She was too far away to see their eyes, and their faces were only blurred, white disks, but for some reason, the sight of them chilled her.

"Don't look at them," said Lawrence. "They're . . . not feeling well. They're acting so weird lately."

"What does that matter? You're being ridiculous."

"I heard them talking about me, after supper one night. They didn't know I was listening, but they were talking about my music, and . . . I don't know. Maybe I heard wrong. They didn't sound like themselves, if that makes sense."

"It doesn't."

"Well, it's true."

Victoria sighed. "So, they were talking about your music, and . . . what?" But Lawrence shook his hair into his face and only said "Never mind. I don't want to talk about it anymore."

As they hurried on to school, between clipped hedges and towering black gates, Victoria kept looking behind them, but she saw nothing out of the ordinary except a big black bug on the walk, waving its feelers in the air. Even so, she couldn't shake the feeling of being followed.

A CLUSTER OF ANGRY RED BUILDINGS SAT HIGH ON a hill on the western edge of Belleville, overlooking the entire town—Impetus Academy: Where Tradition Meets Innovation.

Victoria and Lawrence approached the Academy up the familiar cobblestone streets, which were lined with iron-framed black signs saying things like INSPIRATION. Upon the Academy's construction, the town planners renamed the surrounding roads with appropriately educational words: INTEGRITY. CURIOSITY. MOTIVATION.

Victoria's chest pricked with satisfaction upon seeing those signs. DISCOVERY. KNOWLEDGE.

VICTORY.

That one was Victoria's favorite. It was as though her parents had always known she would be a winner. Her very name spoke of trophies, medals, and honor rolls. She thought of that ridiculous B and imagined it was that ugly bug she'd seen earlier on the walk. Then she imagined stepping on that bug, feelers and all, pop and crunch, its unacceptably mediocre guts splattering beneath her shoe.

The image helped. Victoria thinned her lips against the strange memory of Mr. and Mrs. Prewitt at the door of Lawrence's house, and what Lawrence had said afterward. They'd been talking about his music, he said. That didn't seem so awful—unless the Prewitts had finally grown tired of Lawrence doing nothing but pounding away at the piano. She couldn't blame them for being angry, if that was the case; together, Lawrence and his music could drive anyone out of her mind.

Victoria glared over at him. Other students were joining them from the surrounding neighborhoods. "Tuck in your shirt," she hissed at him. "For heaven's sake."

Lawrence shivered as they passed beneath a tree. "No," he said, and when Victoria opened her mouth to say more, he cut her off. "Don't, Vicky. Not today."

Victoria paused at that. Lawrence shoved his hands into his pockets, his lanky shoulders so hunched they almost brushed his ears. He kept glancing around them from beneath his hair. When another student bumped into them, Lawrence jerked back like someone had smacked him.

Victoria looked closer, narrowing her eyes into that awful, cutting look that Lawrence called her demon dazzle because it both terrified and paralyzed its victims. Lawrence hadn't ever been truly scared of it, but he often humored her by staggering back, collapsing, and gasping for mercy. Victoria secretly found this incredibly amusing and gratifying but never told him so.

But Lawrence didn't do anything like that this time. In fact, he hardly seemed to notice the dazzle. He ducked farther down between his shoulders and squeezed his book bag till his knuckles turned white.

The whole effect left Lawrence looking rather like a terrified skunk. But as odd as this was, Victoria was in no mood to pity him. He and his music and his understandably frustrated parents were not her problems. Her B burrowed into her brain till she could see nothing else.

"You're hopeless, Lawrence Prewitt," she snapped, and stalked away.

At the circle drive in front of the Academy's entrance, silver cars lined up one after another. All the doors opened at once, and all the satellite radios were silenced with a voice command from their drivers. All the children stepped out of their cars and onto the curb. All their parents waved good-bye and said, "Have a good day, Madison," or Brooks, Avery, Harper, and on and on.

The cars zipped away in silent, orderly lines, over and over, circling through the Academy drive like busy metal creatures until more took their place. As Victoria passed their open doors, she heard the parents chatting and chirping about fancy soaps and organic tomatoes, diets and weight-loss something-or-others, salons and massages, the maid and the nanny. Their children filed into the Academy between mighty pillars. Then the next set of shining cars glided into place in a triumphant mechanical ballet till the first bell rang at seven forty-five.

Victoria marched straight into Building One, Room Seven, for Round Table. For half an hour each day before first period, everyone in her year gathered to discuss current events and Academy business. But what really happened, to Victoria's disgust, was that the professors on Round Table rotation gossiped over yogurt, and the students played stupid truth-or-dare games, kissed their girlfriends and boyfriends, and snuck over to Room Eight, where the older kids were. Victoria caught bits of conversation from here and there, about who was going out with whom, the dress Bailey

Hightower had bought for the fall dance, and lip gloss.

Victoria turned up her nose in disgust at them all. *Doesn't anyone talk about anything important?* she wondered.

"Oh, look. The Skunk's in top form today," Victoria heard someone whisper as she took her seat. She turned and saw Lawrence scurry in. He didn't join her at the front table, where they usually sat alone—Victoria ready with her notebook open just in case one of the professors got ambitious, Lawrence scribbling in his composition notebook or doing something equally pointless.

Instead, Lawrence darted into one of the back corners and sat down as close to the wall as possible. He clutched his bag to his stomach and stared at the floor, his face set in grim lines.

Victoria frowned—at first because she wanted to slap Lawrence upside his head, and then because something cold slithered through Room Seven like a slow breeze. Victoria crossed her arms and shivered, but no one else around her seemed to notice.

The older, senior professors standing around the room stopped talking to watch Lawrence. Their eyes flickered over to him, and their posture sharpened. Some of their eyes flashed, and some of them seemed frightened for some reason, and some of their faces twitched with tiny, sharp smiles. The smiles and twitches passed from one to the next and the next.

They seemed like wolves eyeing Lawrence as a possible snack.

Then the cold vanished. *Maybe it was only a little chill from outside*, Victoria thought.

The professors started talking again. Their eyes stopped flashing, and they looked normal once more.

"I think the Skunk's finally losing it," someone whispered, and Victoria turned to see Jill Hennessey leaning toward the others at her table. She stared right at Victoria, smirking.

"What do you think, *Vicky*?" Jill said, louder. She batted her eyelashes and flashed her perfect teeth. Some of the girls around her laughed. "You'd know, wouldn't you? You two being so . . . *close*."

Victoria hated a lot of things about the world. She hated when Beatrice didn't iron the pleats in her skirt right. She hated Mr. Tibbalt and his evil red lapdog, both of whom lacked any sort of personal hygiene and unfortunately lived just down Victoria's street. She hated things that didn't make sense.

She hated the B on her academic report.

She even hated Lawrence a little bit right now, what with how strangely he was acting.

But she hated none of that more than she hated Jill Hennessey, her nemesis, the one person in all the seventh-year students who cared about school as much as Victoria did. Jill, who fought with Victoria to be the first to answer questions, to write the longest papers, to be top of the class.

Jill, who could never, *ever* know about Victoria's B.

Victoria stared at Jill and her frozen smile. Jill tossed her shining red hair and let it slide around her neck. Immediately, her friends all did the exact same thing.

"I don't know what you're talking about," said Victoria. She tossed her curls, which were the best in their year because she had made sure of it. It was part of the plan—perfection, achievement, the top, the best. Victoria's face burned with pride and hardened into a fierce dazzle.

The other girls blinked, but not Jill. She kept staring at Victoria, her eyes sharp like all those professors glaring at Lawrence, and Victoria felt a tiny bit sorry, but she just couldn't keep it in: "I don't care anything about the Skunk," Victoria said. The words came out without her permission and twisted her chest uncomfortably, but she shoved the feeling away. This was not the time to feel sorry for anyone.

Jill laughed. "What's it like, *Vicky*? Being a Skunk's girlfriend, I mean?"

Victoria tried to stop herself from blushing, but it happened anyway. *Girlfriend?* Her mouth dried up, and she suddenly had no idea what to do with her hands. They would not stop fidgeting. Lawrence's smiling face popped into her head, and she scowled. "I'm no one's *girlfriend*," she snapped.

"He's always creeping around like a bug," said Tate Gardiner. "Like a—like a *skunk*." Obviously, Tate thought herself very clever.

Victoria gave her a withering look. "Brilliant. No one's ever come up with that before." Turning away to her notebook, she began copying out *-er* verbs for that afternoon's French quiz. She tried to push all thoughts of Lawrence and girlfriends and stupid Jill Hennessey out of her head.

Manger. To eat.

But it was no good. Victoria heard them still whispering. She felt Lawrence sitting in the corner of the room and felt a little bad for calling him the Skunk, but, well, there was such a thing as hair dye, after all. His face popped into her head, this time looking sad and pathetic. She ignored it and kept working.

Je mange. I eat. *Tu manges*. You eat. *Il mange*. He eats.

Behind Victoria, Jill cleared her throat.

Victoria frowned and pressed her pencil harder.

Nous mangeons. We eat.

The words left indentations in the paper. The graphite tip snapped off Victoria's pencil.

"Oh, by the way, Victoria," said Jill, her voice smiling.

Victoria didn't even have to turn around. She knew what was coming. She heard it in Jill's tone. Bile churned in Victoria's stomach and throat. A sick feeling raced down her arms. She got goosebumps and tried to will them smooth. Her heart had never pounded with such anger and fear.

"I heard," Jill said, leaning forward, "that you got a B."

The others gasped. Some of them laughed. Tate blurted, "Ha!" The sound echoed, and others turned.

Victoria turned too. She kept her face cold and raised an eyebrow.

"You got a *B*," Jill repeated, grinning. "In music class."

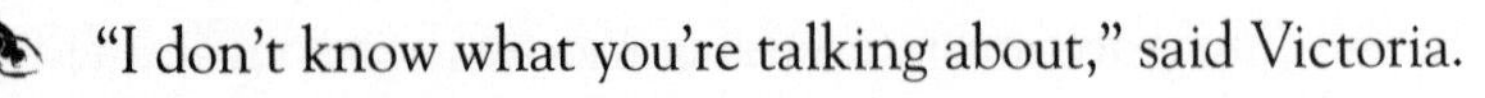

"I don't know what you're talking about," said Victoria.

"Yes, you do. On your academic report."

Lots of people were watching now. Inside, Victoria raged. Outside, Victoria rolled her eyes.

"Oh, I'm sure," she said.

"*I'm* sure," said Jill. "I saw it in Professor Carroll's gradebook. Victoria Wright, B. I got an A minus." Jill widened her eyes and whispered, "You know what that means, of course?"

Oh, Victoria knew what that meant, and it made her ill.

She couldn't contain her mortification any longer. A flush crept up her cheeks. Tate hid her mouth and giggled.

"It means," Jill said slowly, relishing her triumph, "that now *I'm* top of the class."

Victoria's world heaved. Her mind rebelled against the very idea. Top of the class was hers and always had been. She owned it. She had fought from infancy for it. It was her blood, it was her soul, and everyone knew it. Victoria had never made a secret of her ambition. It was her identity: Victoria, the best.

Jill, the second best.

Lawrence, the Skunk.

Jill looked ready to burst out laughing.

"Oh, poor little ice queen, turning all pink," Tate said, giggling.

Victoria grabbed for the only weapon she could find; it popped out from her mind in a rush of fury. That Jill dared gloat like this, in front of everyone, and make Victoria look stupid, when in fact she was the exact opposite of stupid, enraged her. That Professor Carroll had dared give Victoria a B enraged her. That Lawrence had dared to be born with the kind of musical talent that would earn him an A while Victoria was given a B enraged her.

Anger rushed from her head to her arms and the tips of

her toes, until Victoria could feel and see and think about nothing else. She glared at Jill and said, through clenched teeth, "And where's your sister Jacqueline today, Jill?"

Jacqueline, the freak.

It was a sloppy move, to bring up Jacqueline, but Victoria needed time to gather herself. Normally she enjoyed arguing with Jill, because she liked making Jill look stupid. But now that people knew about the B, Victoria had no more wit. So instead she used Jacqueline, Jill's ugly, strange, hated twin sister and the shame of the Hennessey family, as a distraction. Jacqueline, who talked to herself, who drew on her arms in class, who scribbled gruesome drawings in her notebooks. Jacqueline, who had splotchy, bumpy skin and hunched over when she walked and hid behind her tangled hair.

Jill laughed. "Jacqueline?" she said. Beside her, her friends looked just as confused. Their eyes looked a bit fuzzy. "Jacqueline who?"

"What do you mean, Jacqueline who?" Victoria said. "Your twin sister, you idiot."

A rush of cold slid past Victoria. Jill's eyes hardened into sharp little points. Her face sharpened like the professors' had—all wolfish and watchful. This close, it was even more striking. Victoria blinked and looked at the others to see if they noticed, but they had turned away, laughing and chatting to themselves with bright eyes and bright smiles.

"Jacqueline's home sick for a while," Jill said, but her voice sounded different now, lower and quieter. It matched her new, wolfish face. She smiled a small smile. "What do you care about Jacqueline, Victoria?"

"I don't," said Victoria. She didn't know what to make of Jill's strange behavior and decided she was imagining things. It was Lawrence's fault; if he hadn't been acting so weird earlier, Victoria would not be so out of sorts. She stood up in a huff. "As far as I'm concerned, you're both idiots. I just thought maybe if you went to find her, between the two of you you'd have enough IQ for it to be a fair fight."

The bell rang. First period would begin in ten minutes. Victoria spun away from Jill, slammed her books together, and marched toward the door.

Someone shoved ahead of her, hard.

"Be careful, Victoria," Jill murmured in that low voice, rushing past, her hair rippling blood, her purse gleaming silver coins. Victoria watched her glide away into the crowd of students. At the corner, she saw Jill's face, and it looked normal again.

Victoria pushed the fanciful images from her head. Surely, logically, Jill ran into her on purpose and said "careful" just to be the awful witch that she was. But Victoria couldn't help thinking Jill meant something else by that. Lawrence's frightened eyes and how he had talked so fearfully about his parents, the wolfish professors, the wolfish Jill, the cold room—it all left an uncomfortable knot in Victoria's belly.

"Don't be ridiculous," Victoria said to herself. Instead, she focused on the clicks of her shoes and on the gloss of her ribbon and curls in the courtyard windows. She held her head high and smiled. "Time for work."

In algebra, when everyone traded quizzes for grading, Victoria scrawled blistering corrections all over Henry Calvary's pathetic excuse for mathematics. He turned green when he saw it.

In biology, when her lab partner, Catie Vassar, got queasy and started to cry because she simply *couldn't* cut up the poor dead froggie, Victoria snatched the scalpel, sliced everything open, pinned all the organs to their appropriate labels, and sat in disdain while Catie ran to the girls' restroom to vomit.

By the last class of the day—History of the World, Building Four, Room Nine, Professor Alban—Victoria was back in her element.

She took her seat in the front row, folded her hands, and waited for Professor Alban to begin his lecture. She very much approved of Professor Alban. The other students complained about him because he was new. "He assigns too much work to make up for the fact that he doesn't know what he's doing," they said.

But Victoria thought Professor Alban knew exactly what he was doing. He did give them too much work, but it was a challenge, and Victoria liked nothing better than a challenge.

Nothing better, except for the sound of her name being called out at the year's-end ceremonies. Every year since kindergarten: Victoria Wright, top of the class.

VICTORY.

Abruptly, Victoria remembered that perhaps she wouldn't hear her name this year. What if she never recovered from this B? What if instead she heard, "Jill Hennessey, top of the class"?

Unacceptable. That wouldn't happen. It *couldn't.* She would find a way to win.

All during class, Victoria took such fervent notes that her hand froze into a claw. Professor Alban kept glancing at her like he feared it would snap off. At the end of his lecture, he passed out a short quiz. Victoria snatched her paper. Behind her, Jill Hennessey snatched *her* paper. Their pencils scratched harder now, and it hurt a bit, but it was all worth it.

Victoria finished first, Jill just after. The bell rang. Victoria ran to Professor Alban's desk and slammed down her quiz. Jill did the same, shoving Victoria out of the way.

"Whoops." Jill laughed. "You'd better watch out, Victoria. You'll get run right over." Then she vanished out the door.

Victoria glared after her, seething. Professor Alban stared after Jill too. Victoria noticed for the first time that he looked a bit ill. His skin was pale, and his forehead was all furrowed like he was thinking about something really hard.

That same coldness crept through the air again. Victoria had never been one for fantasizing about things, but the cold had a skinny, stinging feel to it, like the cord of a whip or a snake on the prowl.

Victoria shivered.

Professor Alban shivered.

Their eyes met. Professor Alban took off his glasses and cleaned them, put them back on, and forced a smile. "How's your hand, Miss Wright?"

Victoria said sharply, "It hurts," and left.

That day, she didn't wait for Lawrence at the front of the school as she usually did. Basking in the satisfaction of beating everyone at everything all day, she walked right past their usual meeting spot and didn't even think about it. Later, once Lawrence was gone, she would remember this and feel sick to her stomach.

But it wasn't later yet, so she happily walked home alone, making sure to click her shoes just *so* on the cobbled walk down INSPIRATION, away from the prim silver circus of cars in front of the Academy.

Finally, it felt like autumn. It had arrived late this year, summer stretching into late September. Now the air had that firewood chill to it. The sky seemed muted, burrowing into its own gray, waiting. The angry wind yanked red and gold and dying leaves down the street. It yanked Victoria and her curls along with them. Finally, at the corner of Silldie Place and Bourdon's Landing, the wind yanked out Victoria's hair ribbon.

She watched in horror as it flew down the road, a sensible satin pink mixed up in all the leaves.

"Oh, no you don't," she said to the wind.

She ran after it, dodging clumps of mud and dirty puddles. For a moment Victoria wondered about that because it hadn't rained lately, but then a gust zipped her ribbon even farther away, and she was running too hard to wonder. The wind pushed her on, keeping the swirl of leaves that had her ribbon just out of reach. She passed Six Silldie Place, where Mr. Tibbalt's little red dog snapped at the gate. She paused to glare at its ugly, mashed-in face. It stared right back for a moment and then, just when Victoria's eyes started to burn, the dog backed away, whining.

"Yes, that's right, you'd better run away from me," said

Victoria, and she kicked Mr. Tibbalt's gate for good measure.

Finally, Victoria reached the end of the street, where the road curved and circled back. The mass of leaves holding her ribbon rushed into a gray brick wall with a black iron gate and crashed apart into whirling pieces.

Victoria stopped to find her breath. She peered past the gate's iron curls of leaves and petals. Beyond the gate, a long drive wound back from the road into shadows and swaying tree branches. In front of the gate, white and yellow flowers bobbed in the wind. A brass plate on the wall read NINE SILLDIE PLACE and another, darker plate read THE CAVENDISH HOME FOR BOYS AND GIRLS.

A pale flicker caught Victoria's eye—her ribbon, stuck in the brambles of a red-berried shrub near the gate. She grinned in triumph, bent to grab it, and heard someone say, "It looks like a tongue."

Victoria froze. She turned and saw a man at the open gate. She blinked. The gate had been closed before, and she hadn't *heard* it open, and there hadn't been a man before.

"Excuse me?" she said.

The man smiled. He wore dark work clothes and held a rake in one hand. His brown hair was perfectly combed. His eyes moved quietly in place like he was seeing too many things at once.

"I said that it looks like a tongue. Don't you think?" He took off one of his gloves, and clumps of dirt fell from it. His naked hand was large and white. He plucked the ribbon and held it out, towering over her. "Is it yours?"

Victoria snatched it from him, frowning. She should have been more polite, but she had tolerated enough strange people for one day, and this man was the strangest of all. It was something in the expression on his face, and how strangely he moved, and how the skin on his face and neck and hands bulged out all puffy.

"Yes, it's mine," she said. "I lost it in the wind."

"The wind can be tricky," said the man, smiling. "Especially this time of year." He held out his ungloved hand. "I'm Mr. Alice."

"It's nice to meet—"

"And you're Victoria."

Victoria leaned in for a handshake and a demon dazzle so she could see just what, exactly, was going on with this man. But she couldn't see anything except his darting eyes.

"How do you know who I am?" she said slowly.

"Oh, Mrs. Cavendish makes a point of knowing all the children in the area," said Mr. Alice. "Professional interest, you know."

Victoria pinched Mr. Alice's hand and dropped it. She

hoped it hurt him. "Well, anyway. I have to go now. And thank you for getting my ribbon." She started to walk away, smoothing her curls back into place.

"Maybe you can meet her someday," Mr. Alice called out after her.

Victoria looked back. "Meet who?"

But Mr. Alice was gone.

The gate stood open. Victoria stepped closer and squinted beyond it. The pebbled drive circled back through a clean woodland park of oaks and pines and lampposts, already lit for the evening. At the end of the drive, far back in the estate, Victoria saw the faint shape of a wide, shallow house with three chimneys.

Victoria shivered. *It's just the wind*, she scolded herself as the autumn chill swept her home. When she reached Three Silldie Place, she squinted back down the street. The Cavendish Home's gate was now closed.

That night, as Victoria fell asleep, something tapped on her window. Her half-asleep mind imagined that the tapping came from the prongs of a rake, and she dreamed of gardens that came alive and had hands and mouths.

LAWRENCE DISAPPEARED THE NEXT DAY, TUESDAY, which had always been Victoria's least favorite day of the week because it had no point to it. Monday was the beginning. Wednesday was the middle. Thursday was a prelude to Friday. Friday was the end. Saturday and Sunday were for studying, cleaning, getting ahead on everything, and sometimes shopping, if Mrs. Wright found herself in a buying frenzy, which she did quite a lot. Given all that, Tuesday was simply a placeholder.

(Later, Victoria would have quite a different reason for hating Tuesdays, and she would think about how fitting it was that all the trouble had started on what had always been her least favorite day.)

So, Victoria awoke the morning of Tuesday, October 11, already miffed due to the nature of the day. Then she remembered three things:

1. her imperfect academic report;
2. Lawrence skunking about school yesterday (and Jill teasing her about being his *girlfriend*, for goodness' sake); and
3. Mr. Alice holding out her ribbon in the wind with his bulging white hand.

Victoria's mood darkened even more. After allowing herself the customary extra one minute to stew about Tuesdays, she remembered the *tap-tap* on her window from the previous night and got out of bed to peek outside. She saw only her street and a wet, leafy autumn day. There was no rake, and the flower gardens below her window had no mouths or fingers as she had dreamt.

"Well, of course the gardens don't have mouths or fingers," she muttered, fluffing her curls into place. "Don't be stupid." She could not afford to let such ridiculous thoughts distract her; she had to think about more important things, like what to do about that awful B.

Obviously, she couldn't give the report to her parents to sign, because that would mean admitting her failure to them. Obviously, she had to turn in a signed report because otherwise she would receive a demerit on her otherwise perfect record.

It was a dilemma.

Victoria pondered it at breakfast while her father stirred his mint tea and watched the morning news stream on the television. Mr. Wright nodded at the shouting newscasters and said, "Isn't it all a shame?"

"Yes, dear," said Mrs. Wright, poring over a catalog of facial creams and hand creams and foot creams. She marked the good ones with circles. "It really is."

Beatrice set down Victoria's breakfast, and Victoria pushed the plate away. "I'm not hungry."

"You should eat your breakfast," said Beatrice. "It's good for you. Got to stay strong, don't we?"

Something about the way Beatrice said that last part made Victoria look up. She met Beatrice's eyes, which were old and tired and gray in flawless skin. Beatrice got facials every week. Mrs. Wright wouldn't hear of having an ugly housekeeper.

Beatrice nodded at Victoria's breakfast as if to say, *Well, eat up*—but then Victoria saw a slip of paper wedged beneath her plate. She looked up in surprise, glanced at her parents, and looked back to Beatrice, who shook her head. Mr. Wright kept sighing at the state of the world. Mrs. Wright found a new eye cream and clicked her pen in triumph.

Victoria pulled the hidden paper to her lap and unfolded it to see two simple words in Beatrice's handwriting:

BE CAREFUL.

Victoria glared at Beatrice, who stood at the island chopping shallots. That same inexplicable coldness from the day before swept through the room. Victoria's parents didn't notice; they tended not to notice out-of-the-ordinary things. Beatrice, however, kept glancing over at Victoria, pointing to the note with her eyes.

Victoria got up and slammed in her chair, wondering why everyone felt the need to be so *strange* lately, even Beatrice, who was normally more no-nonsense than even Mr. and Mrs. Wright. And now here she was passing strange, secret notes at the breakfast table. It infuriated Victoria.

"Not so loudly, Victoria," Mrs. Wright murmured distractedly, but Victoria was already out the front door.

Be careful. Twice in two days, someone had said that.

"And what, exactly, am I supposed to be careful of?" Victoria said to herself.

It must have stormed overnight, because Victoria kept having to step around puddles. The street was even dirtier than it had been yesterday, with black mud piled here and there between the cobblestones, like something had been digging around. The sky churned. The sick black and yellow light made it impossible to tell the hour. It could have been dawn or dusk or noon. The only color on the street was a dot of red by Six Silldie Place. Victoria frowned to see Mr. Tibbalt's dog and started to turn away, but then she noticed that the dog was sitting in utter silence *outside* Mr. Tibbalt's yard, which he had never done before. He stared down the street toward the Home. The wind blew dirty leaves at him, but he didn't even twitch an ear.

Victoria paused, scolded herself for being stupid, and walked toward the dog anyway. She stopped beside him, curling her lip in disgust His scruffed neck all bristly, he looked up at her and growled, almost as though *he* were disgusted with *her*.

"Yes, I hate you too," said Victoria.

The dog turned away and pricked his shaggy ears down the street.

Victoria followed his gaze toward the Home's gate, which stood half open. The open part swayed in the wind and banged against the latch, over and over in a pool of black light. A particularly harsh gust of wind slammed it shut at last. The bang rattled Victoria's nerves.

The dog jumped to his feet and yapped down the street at the gate, bouncing around like a toy. Victoria frowned at his ugly, whiskered face and turned away.

"Stupid dog," she muttered, and resumed walking toward Lawrence's house, thinking about her dilemma.

Maybe she could forge one of her parents' signatures, but that thought made her palms sweat. Forging was lying, and Victoria didn't lie. Lying was breaking the rules. Besides, to forge a signature, she would have to sneak into her father's study, find a signed document, and trace it and copy it over and over till she got it right. The Academy had devices to tell a fake signature. They took forgery very seriously. And Victoria wasn't used to sneaking anywhere. In fact, she pointedly avoided it. Sneaking was for people who did wrong things, people who, for whatever reason, couldn't just do as they were told. And this Victoria just could not understand.

At least, she had never understood it *before*. Now, however . . .

No. She shook her head. *No. I do as I'm told. I follow the rules. That's how I'm the best.*

Maybe she could talk with Professor Carroll and ask him to change her grade. She would do a year's worth of extra credit, she would clean the pianos using a toothbrush, she would recopy every piece of music in the Academy archives by hand and in her own blood, if that's what it took.

She needed that A more than she needed the beautiful colored schedule above her desk, more than her lovely wall of boxes, more than family or friends.

Victoria thought about that last one. *Friends*. Well, she only had one, but it was something. Maybe Lawrence could actually come in handy in this situation. He could go with her to speak to Professor Carroll, and Professor Carroll would quite possibly do anything Lawrence asked. He doted on his little prodigy in a way Victoria considered pretty sickening, really.

Why hadn't she thought about this before?

Feeling much better about things, Victoria reached the Prewitt house and rapped with the knocker. A minute passed and no one came. Victoria tapped her foot against the porch. Lawrence had probably overslept or something. Of course.

She knocked again. She knocked three times. She knocked *four* times.

Victoria frowned at the door. She tried to look in the side windows, but the drapes and blinds were closed. She looked around the corners of the house into the ivy gardens. A hose had been left on, streaming water into a soggy mess of ruined flowers and overturned gnomes. Victoria wrinkled her nose at the smell of gook and slime, and turned off the spigot.

She went back to the porch and shouted, “Hello.” She ignored the knocker and pounded on the door with her fist.

The door glided open, and the person standing there stared down at Victoria in silence.

Victoria raised her eyebrows. “Mr. Prewitt?”

Mr. Prewitt smiled at Victoria like someone had pins in the corners of his mouth and was slowly pulling them back toward his ears. It looked just like a smile should look. In fact, it looked better—wide and bright and shining.

“Hello, Victoria,” Mr. Prewitt said. “How nice to see you. What can I do for you today?”

Victoria blinked. “What do you mean?”

Behind him, Mrs. Prewitt appeared, stirring something in a bowl.

“Hello, Victoria,” she said, in the same crisp, cheerful tone as Mr. Prewitt. “How nice to see you. What can I do for you today?”

Victoria took a step back and narrowed her eyes. “I’m supposed to meet Lawrence and walk to school, of course.”

Mrs. Prewitt nodded and stirred. Mr. Prewitt said, “I’m sorry, Victoria. Lawrence isn’t here.”

“Well, where is he?” said Victoria.

Mrs. Prewitt paused her stirring. Mr. Prewitt tapped his

finger against the door. Cold raced past Victoria, and she couldn't tell if it was from outside the house or inside the house. Either way, she pulled her coat tighter.

"He's visiting his grandmother upstate," said Mr. Prewitt at last. "She's gotten sick. Pneumonia, you know. Poor thing. She loves little Lawrence."

"She *loves* him," added Mrs. Prewitt, smiling. She started stirring again.

Victoria tried to inspect their faces, but they looked pretty normal: Mr. Prewitt distinguished and bald, Mrs. Prewitt, striking and dark headed. Victoria couldn't put her finger on what, exactly, made her think something was very wrong.

"Well, when will he get—?" Victoria said, but before she could finish, Mr. Prewitt took her by the shoulders and helped her off the porch. His hands pinched her skin.

"Off with you," he said, flashing his grinning teeth. Behind him, Mrs. Prewitt smiled and stirred. "You wouldn't want to be late for school, now, would you?"

"But—"

"Be good," Mr. Prewitt said, patting her head. The last things Victoria saw before the door clicked shut were the Prewitts' flashing smiles.

Victoria stood there for a long time, frowning at the doorknob.

"What was that about?" she said, but no one answered. It was quiet. It was *too* quiet. The porch gleamed with fresh white paint and bright red flowers, and for some reason, Victoria didn't find it pretty at all.

"Good-bye," a muffled voice said—Mr. Prewitt, tapping on the window over and over. Beside him, Mrs. Prewitt smiled and waved.

"Good-bye," said Victoria, waving back. She walked away quickly, a sharp, sick feeling tickling her insides. *Why* she didn't know. Mr. and Mrs. Prewitt *looked* normal, except perhaps for those too-bright, too-perfect smiles. But they could have just been very happy today. Maybe it was nice to have some peace and quiet without Lawrence banging around with his Mozart and Bach. Victoria wouldn't blame them for that.

All the same, an unsettled feeling rolled around in her stomach. It felt like when Beatrice stacked one of Victoria's boxes the wrong way after dusting; Victoria could always tell something was off, the moment she stepped in the room.

At the street corner, she looked back over her shoulder. The Prewitts hadn't followed her; Mr. Tibbalt's dog must have gone inside; the Home's gate remained shut. Nothing was there except for a pair of those same big black bugs, skittering across the street toward the Prewitt house. Victoria wrinkled her nose and turned away.

On the way to school, Victoria thought about what the Prewitts had said. Old people *did* get pneumonia. Victoria seemed to remember something about a grandmother a couple of Christmases ago. It all added up. Mostly.

So, she had to walk to school alone. Well, there had been days before when Lawrence was sick or something. It was nothing to worry about.

Soon enough, she stopped wondering about the Prewitts and how long Lawrence would be upstate. Instead, for the rest of the week, she thought about her dilemma.

On Wednesday, when she allowed herself to reconsider forgery, she had to spend lunch trying not to be sick in the restroom. *Forgery*. The word sounded dirty. She had never thought she would turn criminal. It was messy to be a criminal.

On Thursday, Victoria noticed two things:

1. Professor Alban's hair seemed more frazzled each day, like he had been experimenting with electrical currents. (Normally Professor Alban looked very *together*. Victoria wrinkled her nose to see him so decidedly *apart*. His eyes kept darting all around like he was trying to hide from something.)
2. Donovan O'Flaherty was absent.

To most of the students, this was particularly tragic.

Donovan defied the Academy's zero-tolerance policy on sweets to sneak in Mallow Cakes on Thursdays and cram as many into his mouth as possible during seventh-year lunch. Everyone thought it a spectacle of grand and entertaining proportions (except for Victoria, who thought it merely repulsive). The administration had tried every form of discipline, but nothing fazed Donovan. He got chubbier and chubbier every year till bits of flesh had recently started poking out of his clothes, but he still crammed the cakes in every Thursday. The seventh-year students laughed and cheered him on as sugar and icing dribbled down his face, but not because they liked him.

But at lunch that Thursday, no one said, "Where's O'Flabby?" or made disappointed noises because they had no disgusting display to watch and laugh about.

In fact, no one said a word about Donovan O'Flabby's absence. No one seemed to notice, except for Victoria.

Probably ate himself to death, she thought savagely. *And good riddance*.

A small part of Victoria's mind thought it a bit of a coincidence for Lawrence and Donovan to be absent at the same time. Donovan never missed a Thursday, after all. Victoria knew that because every Thursday, she would sit stewing in fury as everyone made fools out of themselves to give him the Mallow Cakes *they* had snuck in, to make sure he had enough.

Then Victoria thought about Jacqueline being gone too. The more she tried to focus on these thoughts, however, the fuzzier they became. She could not quite remember what Jacqueline looked like. And Donovan—what did he like to eat again? Who was Donovan? The harder she tried to think about them, the faster she lost her grip. It was like trying to hold on to a slippery bar of soap.

But when Lawrence's face popped into her mind, it was clear and steady. She had no trouble focusing on the memory of his face and how he shuffled alongside her when they walked together in the mornings and how he hummed to himself when he was happy.

After thinking about Lawrence, she found that she could think about Jacqueline and Donovan better too—Donovan with his white, shiny face and crumby lips, and Jacqueline with tangled hair in her eyes and pen ink scribbled across her arms.

I'm just nervous because of the report, she told herself firmly, frowning at her lunch tray and trying to ignore the panicky feeling in her throat. *I'm not losing my memory, I'm only stressed is all. That stupid B is making me lose focus.*

All the same, a niggling bother of a thought kept scratching at the corner of Victoria's mind as she chewed her sandwich. She scanned the room, past the table where she sat alone. It seemed to Victoria that the cafeteria was emptier than usual, at least by a few heads. Of course, she couldn't say for sure; she'd never really paid enough attention to who sat where and with whom and all that foolishness, and anyway, it was too noisy for her to concentrate.

Still, something was not quite right. It was that same box-stacked-the-wrong-way feeling. Victoria put down her sandwich and pushed it away. *Bad batch of lunch meat today*, she decided.

On Friday, Victoria knocked on the Prewitts' door just like she had for the past three days. Again Mr. Prewitt opened the door with a smile and patted Victoria's head. Again Mrs. Prewitt stood smiling and stirring. And again Lawrence was upstate.

"But—" Victoria said, getting frustrated. She needed Lawrence to go with her to Professor Carroll's office that morning. If Professor Carroll didn't change her grade, she would have to show her parents the report. She couldn't forge their signatures; she just couldn't commit a criminal act. It had kept her up the last few nights, as had the tree outside her window with its strangely metallic taps.

"Lawrence's grandmother loves him so much," said Mrs. Prewitt reassuringly.

"But when will he be back?" Victoria insisted, and she stamped her foot before she could stop herself.

The stamp must have triggered something. Cold rushed in, blowing the door open. For a flash of a second, Mr. and Mrs. Prewitt's pretty smiles changed into enormous, wolfish grins. Mrs. Prewitt's fingers clutched her bowl so hard that it smashed into pieces. Hundreds of fat black berries rolled across the floor like bugs. Victoria stared and wondered if they really were bugs, because some of them seemed a bit . . . *leggy*.

"Lawrence will be back as soon as he's ready," said Mr. Prewitt, his voice strangely quiet, his smile stiff and bright. Mrs. Prewitt stepped next to Mr. Prewitt, her shiny shoes squashing the berries. They stank like food gone bad, burning Victoria's nose.

"It's so nice of you to ask, Victoria," said Mrs. Prewitt. She smiled, folding her hands at her waist. Her face and eyes were sharper, harder. "Lawrence is lucky to have such a caring friend."

Victoria refused to be frightened by them and their rotten berries and their strange, wolfish smiles. Instead, she said, "Thank you *so* much, I'm *so* sorry to be a bother, please *do* tell Lawrence I miss him," and smiled and shook their cold, hard hands just to be extra polite. Then she walked away with her head held high.

"Such a nice girl," Mr. Prewitt whispered to his wife.

Victoria pretended not to notice the goose bumps down her back. She tried not to think about how she had been afraid just then. She tried not to think about Lawrence. She thought only of her B. *Focus, Victoria,* she told herself over and over till her hands stopped shaking. *Focus.*

Later that day, the lunch bell rang at eleven forty-five. Victoria rushed from biology to the restroom and waited for traffic to die down. Then she peeked out and snuck across the south courtyard to Building Five, where the music rooms were. This almost sent her into fits. Sneaking around during lunch was definitely not allowed.

Lawrence loved Building Five. He often said it felt more like home than his own home.

Victoria had always thought that a silly thing to say, but now it seemed strangely endearing. Lawrence's face popped into her head—his lazy eyes, his messy hair, his crooked smile. She missed his humming.

At Building Five's front doors, she said to herself, "What? I don't miss his *humming.*" She tugged hard on the doors and stepped inside.

As she walked, she hid her report behind her back, even though the halls were empty. The idea of what she was about to do terrified her so completely that she couldn't bring herself to care about the scuttling black shapes following her in the line where the floor met the walls. The whole town could be infested with bugs and it wouldn't matter. As long as she could get her A, she'd put up with a thousand bugs a thousand times over.

She knocked on Professor Carroll's door. No one answered. Before she lost her nerve, she set her jaw and let herself in.

Sunlight streamed through dirty windows into the main classroom, where pianos lined the walls and stood in rows across the room—black baby grands, open and waiting, keys shining. Sheet music covered everything in teetering stacks, strewn across keyboards, trailing between bench legs.

Victoria wrinkled her nose at the unseemly chaos. After picking her way through fallen music stands and frayed violin bows, she found Professor Carroll in his office. The nameplate on his door hung crooked.

"Professor Carroll?" Victoria said.

He sat at his desk with his back to Victoria, facing a window overlooking the Academy lawn.

She tried again, her palms sweating. She hoped the report's ink didn't smear. "Professor Carroll?"

Professor Carroll turned slowly around in his chair.

"Miss Wright," he said in a voice much cheerier than

Victoria had ever heard him use. "What can I do for you today?"

"Well, I—" began Victoria, but she had to stop and stare, because Professor Carroll's too-wide, too-bright smile was just the same as the Prewitts' too-wide, too-bright smiles. The smile had frozen with his teeth just slightly apart. His eyes gleamed like they had been freshly polished.

Beneath the reams of paper scattered across Professor Carroll's desk, something rustled. Three pens rolled off the desk and hit the floor.

Victoria jumped back.

Professor Carroll's hand whipped out and smacked the moving paper.

The paper fell silent.

"Well?" Professor Carroll said, tilting his head at Victoria. "Do speak, Miss Wright."

Victoria leaned in closer for a good, hard dazzle. "Are you all right? Because you don't seem like it."

"I'm doing quite well, thank you, Miss Wright. What about you?"

Victoria thrust the report at him before she could talk herself out of it. "I got a B this quarter."

Professor Carroll slowly looked down at the report. "Ah, yes, I see that."

Victoria took a deep breath, ignoring the cold in the room and the papers on the desk, which had started rustling again and clicking and scratching.

"I was wondering if I could do any sort of extra credit to—"

"No need to worry about that, Miss Wright," said Professor Carroll as he delicately took the report from her. He used the Academy deblotter to erase the horrid B and stamp an A in its place. He uncapped his pen and scribbled new comments about Victoria's dedication to her craft.

"Such a good, well-behaved girl," Professor Carroll went on. As he spoke, he changed her grade in his ledger from B to A. "Good girls who do as they're told get all sorts of treats. Remember that, won't you? Remember how I helped you."

It seemed too easy, but Victoria didn't dare interrupt. Staring at the A, she could hardly breathe. Her heart soared. It was done. She stared at the fresh black A. Everything should have been perfect. With this A, her future was now safe. She could show her parents a spotless report, and they would smile proudly and show her off to their friends, who of course had much less remarkable children. And best of all, Victoria could now look Jill Hennessey right in the eye and gloat—tastefully, of course. One mustn't be obnoxious.

But that same sick feeling churned in Victoria's stomach

as she took the report from Professor Carroll. He sat there, staring at her and smiling. It wasn't right, that smile. They weren't right, those hard, gleaming eyes.

"Really, is something wrong?" she said.

"Now, now," said Professor Carroll, "off with you. Leave me alone." He turned back to the window, tapping his fingers on the papers, which rustled happily. He bobbed his head from side to side and hummed a minuet. It reminded Victoria of Lawrence, and she couldn't seem to move her feet to leave.

Suddenly, Professor Carroll said, "I'm sorry, I didn't mean it!" His voice sounded more normal that time—not as cheery, and more like the professor who drilled them on scales. He jerked around in his chair and fell silent.

Victoria stared at him. "Sorry for what?" she whispered.

But Professor Carroll only smiled and sighed, much calmer now, and said, "Ah," as if welcoming home an old friend. His smile stretched even wider.

Several sets of gleaming black feelers poked out of the rustling papers to curl around Professor Carroll's petting fingers.

Horrified, Victoria turned and ran.

THAT FRIDAY AFTERNOON, WHEN THE LAST BELL rang at three o'clock, Victoria rushed home through the beginnings of a storm, the sky tinged a sick, yellow color. She dodged piles of wet autumn leaves, slammed open the gate, and raced up the front steps of her house. With each step, she pushed the memory of Professor Carroll's buggy fingers further out of her mind. *Don't think about it, Victoria, don't think about it.*

"Victoria?" said Beatrice, from the kitchen.

"What's all that awful noise?" said Mrs. Wright from her parlor.

But Victoria didn't stop till she reached her bedroom. She shut the door, sat on the edge of her bed, and took out the report from her book bag.

She stared at it, breathing hard, her throat stinging from the stormy air. There it was: A. "Victoria is one of my best students" read Professor Carroll's new, scrawled comments.

Victoria's fingers trembled as she read those words over and over. They were a lie. She wasn't one of Professor Carroll's best students. Lawrence was.

Lawrence, who hummed while he walked. Lawrence, who laughed and told Victoria she was funny, even though she certainly never tried to be.

The words began to blur. Soon they were a soup of black and beige. Victoria let the report float to the ground and began to cry.

All her life, Victoria had never been one for tears. When people cried, it made her uncomfortable. People who cried couldn't handle their lives, and Victoria could always handle everything. Plus, crying messed up your face. It was disorderly and inconvenient.

But she couldn't help these tears. She didn't miss Lawrence. She couldn't. Victoria Wright had only one friend, and he wasn't even a real friend; he was a project, someone to fix and whip into shape. Nevertheless, she could not stop thinking about him. Even with the beautiful A in her hands, which should have been all that mattered, Victoria could only wonder where Lawrence had gone and what those bugs had been doing on Professor Carroll's desk and what the reason for this insufferable feeling in her chest was, this feeling of everything being *not quite right*. She wiped her cheeks till they hurt and balled her hands into fists and dazzled the floor in front of her, but the awful feeling wouldn't go away.

Someone knocked on the door. Victoria quickly cleaned her face with a blanket and smoothed her wrinkled uniform flat. She smiled brightly at the door.

"Yes?" she said.

"I've got your snack" came Beatrice's voice.

Victoria hesitated. She hadn't forgotten the little slip of paper Beatrice had left under her breakfast plate, days ago: *Be careful*. The memory sat strangely in her body after the events of the past week. Before, she hadn't cared about Beatrice's odd note; but that was before, and now she found herself wondering . . .

"Come in," she said, tugging her shirt straight and tossing back her curls.

Beatrice brought in a tray with cut-up fruits laid out in a row—tomato slices, apple wedges, strawberry halves. She shut the door and put the tray on Victoria's bedside table, chattering about her day.

"I picked up your new tights for ballet tomorrow. I think you'll like the penne with salmon I'm cooking for supper tonight. Did you have a good day at school?" said Beatrice, on and on, dusting off surfaces that didn't need dusting. Between Beatrice and

Victoria, this room was always the cleanest in the house.

Victoria watched her but didn't really pay attention. She chewed on a tomato slice. The skin tore and the meat melted on her tongue. As she chewed, she mulled over things: Professor Carroll and Professor Alban; Donovan O'Flaherty and Jacqueline Hennessey being absent for days; Mr. Alice and his rake; Beatrice's note; Jill saying, "Be careful, Victoria." Separately, they were little things; but put all together, they seemed somehow more.

"What did you mean by that note the other day?" Victoria said.

Beatrice froze. "Note?"

"The note that said, 'Be careful.' What does that mean? Be careful of what?"

"I'm not sure what you mean," said Beatrice. Then she knelt in front of Victoria and whispered, "I can't say too much. I don't want anything to hear."

Victoria said, "*Anything?* You mean you don't want Mother and Father to hear? Why not?"

Beatrice wiped her hands on her apron. It was the latest in housekeeperly fashion. Mrs. Wright made sure of it.

"Just go on about your business," Beatrice said, looking around the room as though she expected someone to be there listening. "If we're lucky, everything will soon be back to normal. Sometimes it's worse than others, you see. Like the weather." Beatrice shook her head. "But you just have to pretend like nothing is happening."

"But what *is* happening?" Victoria said. "Something is, isn't it? The teachers at school are acting weird. And Lawrence—" She stopped, swallowing hard. "Lawrence is gone."

"He's not gone," said Beatrice. "He's visiting his grandmother upstate." She didn't sound like she believed her own words.

"Fine," Victoria said. "I don't believe you, but fine."

"You have to believe me," said Beatrice. "If you start misbehaving—" She cupped Victoria's cheek. Her mouth trembled, making her look ancient and exhausted. Then her eyes went a little fuzzy, like something had wiped them blank. "I . . . I don't . . ." She shook her head. When she opened her eyes again, they still had that blurry look about them. "Just do as you're told. Please?"

Inside, Victoria's heart hardened suspiciously into its own version of a dazzle. Outside, Victoria smiled and had a strawberry.

"I will," she said, and after Beatrice left, Victoria paced her room for a long time and finally stopped at the window to look outside.

Mr. Tibbalt's dog bounced at the corner of the street, yapping down Bourdon's Landing, Lawrence's street. Something about the sight of him stabbed Victoria with a jolt of dread. For some reason, deep down in her stomach, she knew she had to follow him.

Victoria grabbed her coat and snuck downstairs. She almost made it outside, but then her mother called out, "Victoria? Where are you going?"

"Um," said Victoria. She wasn't used to lying. Lying meant secrets and things all out of order and possibly getting into trouble.

Beatrice looked at her from the kitchen and shook her head frantically, but Victoria ignored her.

"Mr. Tibbalt's dog got out, Mother," said Victoria. "I'm going to take him back."

"Mr. Tibbalt?" said Mrs. Wright, her voice angry, but Victoria was already outside and didn't hear.

She wanted to run but made herself walk instead, Victoria-style—with purpose, briskly, as if people weren't in fact going crazy all around her. She didn't know why it was so important to act normal, but she knew that it was. Walking instead of running, like she wanted to, made her skin feel like it would burst open.

When she reached Mr. Tibbalt's dog, he stopped yapping and looked up at her. His tail wagged uncertainly.

Victoria wasn't used to talking with animals. "Well?"

The dog tilted his head.

"I don't know what I'm doing out here," said Victoria, looking around. The intersection pulsed with the oncoming storm—or was it going rather than coming, or had it always been there, stewing? In the yellow-green light, the cobbled streets shone. The air smelled bitter and sharp-sweet, like rotten food. Victoria's heart pounded. "I should be inside doing my exercises, but I've got such a weird feeling all the time now. Like something's not quite right."

The dog sat down. His shiny black nose twitched.

"You're no help at all," said Victoria.

The dog got up and walked a little ways down Bourdon's Landing, stopped in front of Lawrence's house, sat down, and looked back at Victoria.

Victoria's skin prickled, and she headed toward him. When she passed him, he didn't get up to follow her.

"Aren't you coming?" she said.

The dog's ears perked, but he stayed put. He panted in the direction of the Prewitts' house.

"What? Why are you doing that?"

The dog whined. Victoria followed his gaze through the gate to the Prewitts' front door. They would be home by now; their dental practice closed early on Fridays. She squared her shoulders, tossed her curls, and opened the front gate.

"Don't be stupid," she muttered to herself. "The dog's only a stupid dog, and you're only going to peek in and make sure everything's all right, simple as that." She followed the damp stone walk and picked up the cold brass knocker. She knocked so many times, she thought the Prewitts' neighbors might call the police, but no one opened the door. All the blinds were shut.

"That's odd," said Victoria. She went around to the side of the house and leaned off the porch but saw nothing except one dim light in an upstairs window—and in the window, a person watching her.

Victoria's mouth turned dry. *It's only Mr. or Mrs. Prewitt,* she told herself. A brush of wind against Victoria's hand pulled her back around the corner of the house. When she tried to put her hands in her pockets and walk away, she realized it hadn't been wind at all.

It was a roach, glossy and black with long feelers, sitting on the back of her hand and clicking glossy black eyes at her.

Victoria screamed and flung it away.

The roach or beetle or whatever it was landed on its back with a wet smack and waved its legs around to turn itself over. It scuttled off into the garden.

Victoria wiped her hand on her coat to clean off bug germs and hissed when something stung. She looked down and saw ten little red marks in her skin where the bug's legs had been.

"Ow," she whispered. She tried to remember everything she knew about roaches and beetles, which wasn't a lot. But surely their feet weren't supposed to cut you like that. And didn't they only have six legs?

"Evil bug," she said. Then, she thought, *How strange*, because as much as she didn't want to think about it, this bug's feelers had looked an awful lot like the feelers poking around on Professor Carroll's desk. She shuddered to remember that. Was Belleville under attack by some sort of roach infestation? But how could it be? Belleville was the cleanest, loveliest town around.

Gritting her teeth, Victoria said, "I . . . *hate* . . . nonsense," and marched back to the Prewitts' front door and prepared to knock again, angrier this time—but the door was already open a crack.

Victoria pushed it open the rest of the way and stepped inside. She left it open in case she needed to make a quick exit. The fact that she had to think about things like quick exits infuriated her.

"I just want things to be normal again," she said, to herself and to anyone who might be listening. She took a few steps and stopped.

Music. Specifically, piano music.

Her heart lifted, and she didn't care that it was silly, being so happy to see Lawrence again. She grinned and ran for the lounge, but when she got there, the piano stood closed. The music wasn't coming from the piano, which already looked gray with dust, like no one had touched it for years.

Victoria turned to find the source of the music and almost screamed.

Mrs. Prewitt sat in the high-backed chair across the room, holding a bowl and spoon in her hands once more, stirring and stirring. Flies buzzed around whatever sat in the bowl. Mrs. Prewitt stared at the piano and swayed along with the music, which Victoria realized was coming from a radio on top of the piano, and not the piano itself.

"Isn't it lovely?" said Mrs. Prewitt, smiling that same too-bright smile, although now it seemed strained, like she was too tired to smile but had no choice in the matter.

Victoria listened and recognized the music at last—a Chopin nocturne, one of Lawrence's favorites. E-flat major, opus 9, number 2. She could almost picture his dreamily smiling face as he said how playing it made him feel like he was floating.

Fists clenched, Victoria said, "Yes. It's beautiful."

Mrs. Prewitt nodded, staring at the silent piano. "One of his favorites."

Victoria's eyes narrowed. "One of whose favorites?"

"Lawrence's."

"I miss him," said a new voice—Mr. Prewitt, who stood silently in the shadows at the top of the stairs.

Victoria backed away, right into the piano. "Mr. Prewitt, I didn't see you there."

"Yes," said Mrs. Prewitt, nodding. "We do miss him. But he'll be back." She turned slowly to face Victoria, plucked a stinking ball of something from her bowl, and took a crunchy bite. "He'll be back before you know it."

"I, er, I have to go," Victoria breathed, stumbling back toward the door.

"Oh, stay a while," said Mr. Prewitt, walking slowly down the stairs. He smiled and put out his hand. "You can stay with us and have supper."

"No, really, it's all right, thank you," Victoria said, and she turned and ran and didn't stop till she was safely down the walk. Looking back over her shoulder, she saw nothing but an empty black street with lamps blinking awake.

Mr. Tibbalt's dog met her at the corner where she'd left him. His fur stood up straight in a growling red poof. He started following her, his claws clicking on the walk.

"I'm going to find out exactly *what* is going on here," Victoria said, her voice shaking, the image of the Prewitts' tight, frozen, perfect faces making her heart race. The rotten smell from Mrs. Prewitt's bowl filled her nose and mouth. "I'll knock on every single door if I have to." She turned the corner and pressed the buzzer on Two Silldie Place's gate.

Mr. Everett answered. He and Mrs. Everett were very old and collected porcelain figurines of African animals.

"Yes?" said Mr. Everett, through the intercom.

"Mr. Everett, it's Victoria. May I come in, please?"

"Virginia?"

"No. Victoria."

"What now?" said Mr. Everett.

Victoria heard Mrs. Everett sigh and say, "It's *Victoria*, darling," and the gate clicked and started opening. "Victoria Wright."

Mr. and Mrs. Everett let Victoria in and gave her tea, which Victoria only pretended to sip at.

"Have you seen my latest giraffe?" said Mrs. Everett, and she held out a giraffe with a neck twice as long as its stub of a body, painted in pinks and blues. "It cost one thousand dollars. It's an antique, you know."

All the Everetts' figurines were antiques. Victoria couldn't believe something so ugly was so expensive. She also couldn't believe that a pink and blue giraffe was an antique.

"Yes, it's nice," said Victoria. "Now I have a question."

"Why, ask away!" said Mr. Everett, looking over their shelves for another figurine to show off. His hand was reaching for a smiling crocodile when Victoria said, "It's about the Prewitts."

The Everetts paused. They looked at each other and then

at Victoria. They didn't say a word. Mrs. Everett poured Victoria more tea and dumped four spoonfuls of sugar into it.

"The Prewitts," Victoria said. "You know."

"Yes, of course," said Mrs. Everett.

"Are they sick or something? Do you know? And Lawrence—"

"He's out of town," said Mr. Everett. "Visiting his grandmother. That's what we heard."

"That's right," said Mrs. Everett. "We did hear that, didn't we? Just the other day."

Victoria said, "Yes, yes. But—" She paused. "Did you hear when he'll be back?"

The Everetts looked at each other again. Mrs. Everett held out her giraffe and smiled. "But don't you want to see the rest of our collection?"

"Look at this croc," said Mr. Everett, his pointy white teeth matching the crocodile's grin. "Priceless, you know. We have only the best in our collection."

Oh, they knew something, all right. Victoria could see it with her dazzle eyes. They were only pretending they didn't know what she was talking about. They weren't going to help her. This realization enraged her. She forced herself to smile the sweetest smile she had ever worn.

"I'm so sorry, but I have to go," she said at last, stopping just short of slamming down her teacup. "Thank you ever so much for your time."

She tried next door at Four Silldie Place, but no one answered, even though Victoria could see shapes watching her from the upstairs windows.

"Well, what about your Mr. Tibbalt?" she said to the dog, who still followed her. The gate to Six Silldie Place stood just open enough for Victoria to slip inside. The dog ran after her to the front door.

"What do you want?" someone growled.

Victoria stopped just before the porch. Mr. Tibbalt stood at the front door with his dog in his arms. The dog seemed perfectly happy, but Mr. Tibbalt did not. He frowned down at Victoria from beneath a rumpled wool cap. It was as patched and worn as the rest of his clothes. His glasses glinted in the lamplight, blocking out his eyes.

"Excuse me, Mr. Tibbalt," said Victoria, hiding her disgust at his messy clothes and the awful state of his lawn. Her mother's red notices flapped all along his porch. "I hate to bother you, but I have a question."

"No more questions," muttered Mr. Tibbalt. "Too many questions."

Victoria couldn't believe his nerve.

"It's about the Prewitts," she persisted.

For an instant, Mr. Tibbalt straightened and came alive. He said something Victoria couldn't quite hear, except for one word: "*Vivian* . . ."

The wind slammed the gate open. Mr. Tibbalt jumped and waved his arm at Victoria. "No more questions," he cried. "Get out of here. Go away!"

Victoria scoffed, glaring at his messy clothes. She should never have bothered with this crazy old man. "I will, but not because you told me to." She turned and left, ignoring the dog's indignant yaps.

"Why, Victoria, how nice to see you," said Mrs. Baker at Eight Silldie Place. She was young and pretty and held her new baby. Her small, pretty children ran in circles behind her.

"Victoria," said handsome Mr. Baker, wiping his hands on a towel. "We just made supper. Would you like to join us?"

"No, thank you," said Victoria, still so furious at Mr. Tibbalt that she didn't bother with small talk. "I've come to ask you about the Prewitts and what's wrong with them and what they've done with Lawrence."

The Bakers stopped moving. Their smiles froze in place.

"What they've *done* with him?" said Mr. Baker, suddenly much cheerier than a moment ago.

"Something's wrong, I know it is," said Victoria. "And no one will tell me."

Mrs. Baker chuckled. "Sounds like the storm's giving you crazy ideas, Victoria."

"I don't get crazy ideas."

"Well," said Mr. Baker, his smile widening. His and Mrs. Baker's heads tilted strangely, as though they were birds. "I think you should go home now, Victoria."

They tried to lead her out the door, but Victoria dug in her heels. "But wait! I want to stay and eat supper with you after all."

"Oh, I'm sorry, Victoria," said Mrs. Baker. "It's getting so late, you see." Together, the Bakers pushed Victoria out, shut the door, and locked it.

Victoria stood alone on the porch, the wind whipping her hair around. Her curls were falling out, which added insult to injury.

"Fine," she said. Clearly, everyone around here knew more about what was going on than they were telling her, and nothing about any of it made any sense. And things were *supposed* to make sense in Belleville. The entire situation was unacceptable.

"So rude," Victoria said, straightening her coat with a snap. "Maybe Mrs. Cavendish will be more polite." She walked to the end of the street, stopping right at the Home's gate. The gray brick wall disappeared into the woods on either side. There wasn't a buzzer or anything.

"How do I get in?" Victoria muttered.

The gate clicked open.

Victoria glared at the gate as she passed through. "It's just the wind," she told herself.

The stone drive wound from the front gate through a huge, freshly cut lawn of black trees and bright white flowers and lamplight. On occasion, Victoria saw a black bench glistening with raindrops, or a rope swing hanging from a tree branch.

"If any of those dirty orphans touch me, I'll tell Father to give Mrs. Cavendish a citation," she said. The thought of her father punishing people and putting things in order cheered her heart. She looked back over her shoulder and saw the gate standing open, far away, with lamps on either side like two yellow eyes.

The Home was gray brick like the wall, three stories tall, and slender from back to front but wide from side to side, with a black roof and black trim and great columns along the porch. Behind the Home, Victoria saw two small cottages and towering tangled gardens. Rows of windows spilled soft light onto the grass.

Victoria knocked on the front door with a huge brass knocker shaped like a rose. No one answered. She sighed and crossed her arms.

"If one more person doesn't answer their door for me . . . ," said Victoria.

"Looking for someone?"

Victoria whirled to see Mr. Alice at the bottom of the front steps. He held a hoe this time.

"I wanted to speak with Mrs. Cavendish," said Victoria.

Mr. Alice smiled. "Of course. Right this way."

He led Victoria around the house, up a smaller set of steps to a door with an awning over it. A paper doll hung in the window and swung happily as Mr. Alice opened the door.

"Someone wants to see you, Mrs. Cavendish," said Mr. Alice. "I didn't think you'd mind."

"Of course not," said a woman at the stove, her voice soft and kind and clear. She was stirring something in a shiny metal pot. It smelled so delicious that Victoria's mouth started watering.

"Hello, Mrs. Cavendish," said Victoria, stepping into the clean, white kitchen. "I'm—"

"—Victoria," said Mrs. Cavendish, setting down her spoon and turning around. "Of course. I know you."

"You do?" said Victoria, staring, for Mrs. Cavendish was really quite pretty and not at all what Victoria had expected. She had dark brown hair that curled at her chin and bright blue eyes and red lips.

Mrs. Cavendish smiled. "I make a point of knowing all

the children in the area. Professional interest, you know."

Victoria remembered when Mr. Alice had said exactly that. "Oh. Right."

"What can I do for you?"

"Well," said Victoria, but she couldn't find her words. The delicious smell of supper, Mrs. Cavendish's lovely smile, and the warmth of the kitchen made her sleepy and fuzzy. She frowned. "I don't remember. Hold on."

"Perhaps you'd like a candy while you think?" said Mrs. Cavendish. She opened a jar of yellow candies by the stove, pulled out two, and folded them into Victoria's hand. Her fingers were warm. "They're butterscotch. My own special recipe."

Victoria popped one in her mouth. It immediately began to melt, thick and warmly sweet on her tongue.

She popped the other in her mouth too.

The texture was chewier than butterscotch usually was. And juicier.

Laughter drew her attention through the kitchen door to the hallway beyond. She heard children running and saw vague shapes that she couldn't quite get a fix on. A paper plane floated through the door and landed at Victoria's feet.

Mrs. Cavendish picked it up and put it on the counter. "Can I get you anything else? I'd invite you to stay for supper, but we have so many mouths to feed here."

Mrs. Cavendish smiled. "I make a point of knowing all the children in the area. Professional interest, you know."

Victoria blinked, struggling to remember why she had come. "No, I think I'm all right. I should go. I'm sorry I bothered you."

"Such pretty curls," said Mrs. Cavendish. She came closer to Victoria and pet her hair with long, warm fingers. "You're a good girl, aren't you, Victoria? You always do as you're told."

Victoria couldn't look away from Mrs. Cavendish's kind blue eyes. They drew her in like jewels. "I like to be the best."

"Yes, of course." Mrs. Cavendish smiled. "And the best way to do that is to do just as you're supposed to. Right?"

"Yes. I've always thought so."

"Your parents love you very much, Victoria." Her stroking fingers sent warm, curling rushes down Victoria's back.

Victoria thought about that. Love was not something she and her parents ever talked about, but it seemed the proper thing to say. "Yes, and I love them."

"Such a good girl. Now run along home." Mrs. Cavendish went to the cupboards on the far wall to get some jars. "We're about to eat supper. Mr. Alice, if you would?"

Mr. Alice took his hoe and walked down the hall toward the laughter.

As Victoria turned to leave, she saw the paper plane on the counter. The sight of it woke her up a bit, like snapping out of a half dream right before falling asleep. She checked to make sure no one was looking, grabbed the plane, and stuffed it in her skirt pocket.

"Thank you for the candy," she said over her shoulder, hurrying outside.

Once out of the Home's light, she ran toward the gate as fast as she could, staying in the trees to muffle her footsteps.

Ahead of her, the gate seemed to be closing, but it was probably a trick of the wind. Victoria ran faster and managed to get out before the gate clicked shut. The storm chased her home.

Beatrice met her in the foyer.

"You're late for supper," Beatrice said. She seemed terrified as she took Victoria's coat and helped her out of her muddy shoes. "Go change and clean yourself up."

"Is that Victoria?" said Mr. Wright, from the dining room.

Victoria raced upstairs. Once alone in her bedroom, she pulled out the paper plane and unfolded it.

Thick red letters scrawled across the paper read:

HELP US.

AT SUPPER THAT NIGHT, VICTORIA TRIED TO explain to her parents why she had been late.

"I told you, I was taking Mr. Tibbalt's dog home," she said, over and over. "He got out." But her parents didn't seem to believe her. It was a silent dinner. When Beatrice refilled their drinks, the clinking ice cubes were the only sounds in the dining room. Every now and then, Mrs. Wright would pat her lips with her napkin. Mr. Wright cut his meat into squares. Neither of them looked at their daughter.

Victoria went to bed early, claiming that her head hurt. She shut herself away in her room and turned off all her lights. Her academic report still lay on the floor. Distracted, she put it on her desk so she would remember to get her parents' signatures on Monday morning.

She put on her pajamas and got into bed. Then she pulled out the crumpled paper plane from beneath her pillow. She unfolded it and read the words by the light of the storming moon:

HELP US.

Help who? And from what? Was there something in the Home that the orphans didn't like? It could have been a joke, she supposed—but thinking that didn't get rid of the uneasy feeling in her belly. And there was still the question of where Lawrence had gone. She could not—*would* not—believe that nonsense about him visiting his grandmother. No, Lawrence was somewhere else and could quite possibly need her help too. The only problem was, she had no idea where to start searching for him. He could be anywhere, he could be hidden away. She stared at the note in her hands. Someone had flown it into Mrs. Cavendish's kitchen so that Victoria would see it. Someone wanted her to help. And maybe helping whoever "us" was would lead her closer to Lawrence.

As quietly as possible, Victoria found the key in her MISCELLANEOUS box and hid the paper in the drawer with the keyhole.

Then she put the key at the very bottom of not the MISCELLANEOUS box but the PENS box. Ignoring the boxes' labels went against all her principles, but she couldn't risk her parents finding that paper, although she couldn't have said why, exactly.

She climbed back into bed, lay down, and folded her hands over her stomach. As the storm rumbled outside, never quite beginning, Victoria thought about everything that had happened till she fell asleep with a frown on her face.

In the morning, as she did every morning, Victoria awoke with a plan.

This time, however, it was a different sort of plan from her usual ones.

It was a plan of investigation.

It was also a plan of deception.

Victoria swallowed down her fear as she wrote the note to her parents:

Dear Mother and Father,

I'm sorry for the short notice, but I have to miss ballet class today, and I also won't make lunch. I've got to work on a paper for my History of the World class. Professor Alban expects ten pages, but I want to turn in twenty and really impress everyone. I need to go to the library. So that's where I'm going. I'll be home for supper.

Sincerely,

Victoria

The house was quiet when Victoria crept downstairs at eight o'clock, which was unusual because Mrs. Wright got up early on Saturdays to drink her diet drinks and do her stretches before brunch. Victoria was used to coming downstairs on Saturdays and seeing her mother all twisted up in knots in the exercise room.

But this Saturday, Victoria could hear her toes curl in her shoes, the silence was so complete. Her parents' bedroom door stood closed. The air thrilled between night and day, between bad things and good things. Victoria hated that feeling, and any *between* feelings, for that matter. Things should be one or the other, not somewhere in the middle, and lately, everything was very *in the middle*. For example, Victoria felt like she could hear the walls holding their breath, watching her. It was a ridiculous, very *in the middle* sensation.

Her skin broke out in goose bumps. Victoria glared at them. "Stop that," she told her arms, and marched outside.

Outside, the streets glistened. Storm clouds sat fat, black, and heavy all along the sickly yellow sky. Victoria wondered if they would ever break or if they would just keep spitting bits of rain forever when no one was looking. She tightened her grip on the umbrella beneath her raincoat and tried not to think about how it felt like the trees were watching her.

Town Square on a Saturday morning was a glorious place. Everywhere whirled shining silver cars, gliding doors, trickling fountains, and stylishly dressed Bellevillians clicking their heels and flashing their smiles at everyone in crisscrosses between shops, salons, and banks. Everything smelled of clean, crisp money.

Victoria breathed easier once the crowds pulled her into their clockwork. In the midst of these gleaming, happy people, there were no strange men with rakes, missing Lawrences, or bowls of bugs. She heard whispers about how "well, you know, rather *large*," so-and-so had gotten, about losing this-many pounds, surgeries for wrinkles and unfortunate spots, and catalogs of pretty things to help get one's life in order.

In *order*.

It was a beautiful word.

Victoria smiled and walked with renewed purpose, her shoes clicking up the marble steps of the library. *This is how things are supposed to be*, she thought.

"Well, then. Hello, Victoria," said Mr. Waxman, the librarian. He stepped in front of her and blocked her way with a wide, white smile. "What can we do for you today?"

Victoria paused to think because for some reason she couldn't quite remember why she was here. The shiny gear-turns of Town Square had, for a moment, made her forget why she had come. After all, how could anything be wrong in the midst of all that gleaming perfection?

"Well, I'm—" Victoria started to say, but then she saw how Mr. Waxman looked rather like the Prewitts, with their

bright, frozen eyes and that too-happy smile. The realization woke Victoria out of her Town Square trance. A rush of cold swept around her, even though the library doors had closed.

In a flash, she remembered the red, scrawled words: "Help us." In another flash, she saw Lawrence's yawning, gray-eyed face. He would be yawning, so early on a Saturday.

Yes. Yes, that's why she had come here. A note like that required investigation. It was a very *between* sort of note. A missing friend also required investigation. And there was no better place to begin an investigation than the library. It was all about order and answers and things filed in labeled boxes; it was the farthest thing from *between.*

"I've just come to do research for a school paper," Victoria said at last. Her heart jumped to hear the lie. She wasn't used to this business of lying to grown-ups. Children who won trophies and made the honor roll did not lie to grown-ups.

Mr. Waxman's face relaxed a tiny bit. "Well. Well, I suppose that's fine, isn't it? How responsible of you."

He stepped out of the way, his eyes bright and still. He licked his lips.

"Just as long as you don't take anything that isn't yours," Mr. Waxman said as Victoria walked away. "We have to behave, don't we?"

Victoria smiled politely and walked away as fast as she could without seeming suspicious. Her heart turned frantic somersaults, the happiness she'd felt outside long gone. Mr. Waxman's eyes followed her into the stacks of books, just as the Academy professors' eyes had watched Lawrence.

"Calm down, Victoria," she said to herself. "You're just seeing things."

She poked around in the reference section, pretending to look through encyclopedias. After a half hour, she decided it was safe to move.

What she really wanted was in the Records Room—

newspapers. They seemed the most logical place to start an investigation.

Victoria crept across the first floor. She stopped here and there to flip through books and scribble things in her notebook. The library seemed too quiet even for a library. Sharp, invisible sensations, like reaching fingers, scratched at Victoria's heels. She tried to hold her head high as she walked, but she felt like all the books had eyes and would report on her to Mr. Waxman.

Finally, she reached the Records Room. She slipped in and closed the door. The room was empty, small, cold, and dim. She looked back over her shoulder, through the frosted window of the door. Beyond it, the library shone white.

"Don't be stupid," she reminded herself, tugging her raincoat straight. She found a computer in the corner and sat down, refusing to hide behind it like part of her wanted to. She took out her notebook and typed in respectable research topics like "Aborigines" and "the Declaration of Independence" and "zoology."

"Just in case," she murmured. "One can't be too careful."

Then, looking around once more just to check, she searched for the *Belleville Bulletin*. It was an old newspaper because Belleville was an old town.

Victoria paused, her fingers hovering above the keyboard. She wasn't really sure what she was looking for, exactly. Usually when she came to the library, it was for an assignment, with a checklist of items to complete. But this time, it was different; this time, she didn't quite know what the assignment was.

Think, Victoria, she scolded herself, and she did, combing over her memories of the last few days:

1. Orphanages that employed strange, bulging-skinned men with rakes.
2. People who smiled so wide and perfect it was like they were ready to pop out of their skins.
3. Roaches with ten legs that stung you.
4. Missing children.

Ah.

Victoria started with the latest issue and searched for missing children. She found a lot of things, sadly, because sometimes the *Bulletin* ran stories from other, bigger newspapers. But she didn't see anything about Lawrence, Jacqueline Hennessey, or Donovan O'Flaherty. And she found nothing about strange roaches or perfect smiles, except for an advertisement for the Prewitts' dental practice, which made her shiver and frown and hunch over the keyboard with renewed determination.

She also searched for the Cavendish Home for Boys and Girls, and Mrs. Cavendish herself.

"What's her first name?" Victoria wondered aloud, but she didn't know. The more she thought about it, the more she realized how very little she knew about the Cavendish Home. It had been there forever, and yet Victoria couldn't recall anyone in town ever talking about it, which seemed stranger and stranger the more she thought about it. Orphans were children without parents, and wouldn't people talk about Belleville parents dying and their children being sent to the Home? Wouldn't people be shocked and upset, and perhaps visit the children with flowers and candy and condolences? And did these orphans all come from Belleville, or did Mrs. Cavendish bring in children from Grandville and Uptown and the poor towns in between?

Victoria shook her head. She did not know the answers to these questions. She had never even thought to *wonder* these questions before. *And isn't that odd, Victoria?* she asked herself. *Isn't it odd that you* wouldn't *wonder?*

What Victoria *did* know, however, was that when she had stood in Mrs. Cavendish's kitchen, in the warmth of the cooking stew, with the orphans laughing just down the hall, she'd forgotten why she went there in the first place. It was almost like a spell from the fairy stories Victoria had always thought so silly. In that kitchen, Mrs. Cavendish was all Victoria knew—till she found the paper plane that held the message "Help us."

The *Bulletin* didn't include many things about the Home,

other than a few blurbs about festivals, tours, and generous donations from Mrs. Cavendish to the library, the Academy, and the hospital.

Victoria frowned. "Well, that's nice of her," she said. She remembered Mrs. Cavendish's pretty face, clean dress, and red lips. The memory made her smile before she could stop herself, only the smile didn't seem like her own. It felt like someone had hands on her face, forcing her lips gently back.

She searched for a long time and found nothing helpful, even years and years back. Then she went back even farther. Missing children bulletins. Letters to the editor about such-and-such. Advertisements: THE CAVENDISH HOME FOR BOYS AND GIRLS IS HOSTING A FIELD DAY FOR ALL AREA CHILDREN THIS SATURDAY, APRIL 14. BEETLE-B-GONE EXTERMINATION OFFERS FREE CONSULTATIONS.

None of this meant anything. They were random pieces of many different puzzles.

In these old papers, Victoria saw the construction of the Academy, her street, and the streets around it.

The *Bulletin*'s oldest issues were on microfilm. Victoria found the right cabinet on the wall. She thumbed through the tiny pockets of film, took out the first *Bulletin* one, put her hand on one of the microfilm readers to turn it on—

Behind her, the door opened.

The white light of the library illuminated a dark figure.

Victoria reached for her umbrella but couldn't find it. She had left it beside the computer.

"What do you want?" she said, trying to sound brave.

The door shut. The figure melted into the room's darkness.

"Miss Wright?" said a voice.

"Professor Alban?" said Victoria. She squinted and saw the frazzled hair. In the computer's glow, his glasses blinked white.

"Are you—" said Professor Alban. He opened the door a bit, peered outside, shut it, and wedged a chair beneath the doorknob. "Why are you here?"

Victoria backed away. "What are you doing with that chair?"

"They've caught on to me, I think. I don't have much time. This might be the last time I can come here."

"Who's they?"

Professor Alban took off his glasses to clean them. Victoria heard the lenses break.

"I don't really know," he said. "But people—*things*—have been following me, ever since I started looking around, searching through files at the Academy, town hall, here. At least, I think something's following me. I can't be sure." He wiped his face. "Why are you here, Miss Wright?"

"I'm writing a paper," said Victoria. She hid the microfilm behind her and wished she had closed the drawer.

"You're here because of the missing children, aren't you?" whispered Professor Alban. "I noticed it a few weeks ago. There's a dozen gone by now. I should have noticed sooner, but I'm only just now getting settled, you know. I've only been here a couple of months."

Victoria felt more afraid than she had since this whole thing began. What, exactly, was Professor Alban trying to say?

She said, "I don't know what you're talking about," and was pleased to hear how crisp and cool her voice sounded.

"Miss Hennessey. Mr. O'Flaherty." Professor Alban paused. "Mr. Prewitt."

Lawrence. His name stuck in Victoria's throat, and an unfamiliar pang ripped through her chest. Professor Alban had included Lawrence's name with Jacqueline's and Donovan's. He'd said it *out loud*. Were they really all gone together somewhere, like Victoria had wondered but never wanted to believe? For the first time in her life, she wished she had been wrong. She didn't know what to say.

"Yes, I've noticed that they're gone, too," said Professor Alban, moving to the computer. He leaned over to read the screen. He read. He looked up.

"The Home," he said. "Mrs. Cavendish's Home."

Victoria gritted her teeth. "And?"

"I think I can trust you," said Professor Alban. "You've always been a good student. And I know Mr. Prewitt was your friend."

"*Is* my friend."

Professor Alban's face was bleary and sad in the computer light. "Yes, of course. What do you have behind your back?"

Victoria didn't move. "Weird things are happening around here."

"Yes."

"How do I know you don't have roaches up your sleeves or something, like Professor Carroll?"

"Roaches?" said Professor Alban. "What do you mean, roaches?"

Victoria tapped her fingers on the microfilm. Professor Alban had always been one of the good ones, one of those professors who actually did things. He made them work.

She decided to trust him and held out the packet. "I was looking at this. The *Belleville Bulletin*."

Professor Alban sighed. "That's what I've been looking for, every time I come here. Something's been keeping it from me, though. I look in the right spot, but it isn't where it should be. I don't understand it. It's like someone's playing a game with me." He laughed sadly. "You know, sometimes I can hardly remember what I'm looking for anymore. I have such a hard time remembering what they looked like. Sometimes I forget they were ever there."

"Lawrence has black hair with a lot of gray hairs, too," blurted Victoria, clenching her fists. "And he's got gray eyes, and he hums when he's happy."

Professor Alban stared at her. "Yes . . . yes, I remember now . . ."

Victoria heard a scuttling near her, and also farther away in the walls, behind the cabinets, underneath tables. A patch of dark approached her.

She put on a dazzle, lifted her boot, and stomped the dark patch once it was close enough. It squished and crackled, and the stink filled the room. Victoria heard a tiny, furious scream like from a tiny pocket person or from somewhere far away.

The other scuttlings rushed away to the corners of the room and fell silent.

Professor Alban got to his feet. "What was that?"

"One of those roaches. There are lots of them. I've seen them all over." Victoria patrolled the room, glaring into the shadows for more things to stomp. "They're evil or something, I think. They've got ten legs, and they pinch you with them. I saw some under the papers on Professor Carroll's desk. Well, I saw feelers. But you know. I saw one at Lawrence's house, too." Victoria scraped the bottom of her boot against the floor, but her boot was clean. All the guts and crushed feelers were gone. It was like there had never been a bug at all.

"I don't know what they mean yet, but they're *something*," said Victoria.

"Well," said Professor Alban. He crossed his arms over himself like he was very small. "I don't know how much time we've got."

"Is someone going to come after us?"

Professor Alban shrank even farther into his own arms. "I think so."

"But *who?*"

"I'm not sure. It's so hard to think." Professor Alban pulled at his collar. His eyes looked funny. "Shadows. Dark things. I haven't been sleeping. Eyes in the walls."

"I was searching the newspapers," said Victoria slowly, forcing herself to focus. *Eyes in the walls*. Were there eyes in these walls, watching them even now? "I want to learn about the Home. It's strange, right? I have a bad feeling about it, and I don't usually have bad feelings about things."

Professor Alban adjusted his glasses. "How so?"

"Well, there's Mr. Alice. He's the gardener. He has weird, twitchy eyes, and his skin is all bulgy and swollen, but the Prewitts and Professor Carroll, they have weird, *still* eyes now. They don't even look real, they're so bright and happy. And Mr. Waxman, too. They're always smiling really big, *too* big." She paused to think about that. "I went to the Home, you know. I was looking for Lawrence, and when I went there, it all *looked* nice, and Mrs. Cavendish gave me some candies. But it *felt* weird. You know, that *in the middle* feeling? It's hard to put into words, but you know something's off all the same."

"I think I know what you mean," said Professor Alban. "Go on."

Victoria began to pace. "And all the missing kids. I wonder if there are others. In Grandville and Uptown. And maybe there have been weird bugs before. And look at this."

Professor Alban stared at the unfolded paper plane in Victoria's hand and the scrawled plea for help.

"I took this when I went to the Home yesterday," Victoria whispered. The air around them seemed suddenly quieter. "Someone wanted me to see this."

Professor Alban kept looking back at the door. He wiped the sweat from his face.

"We should keep looking," he said. "Put that away. Please."

Victoria did, and they kept searching, through one hundred issues of the *Belleville Bulletin*. Sometimes pieces of the film were blacked out with scribbly marks, burned away, or cut away.

The last issue they looked at was from so long ago that Belleville was little more than Town Square and farms.

Next to an advertisement for A. C. Sherman's Feed Store was another advertisement, so tiny that Victoria almost missed it.

"Wait," said Professor Alban, pointing at the reader. The hot yellow light made his tired face look gravely ill. "There."

A little square said, NEW RESIDENT BUILDS CHILDREN'S HOME and THE CAVENDISH HOME FOR BOYS AND GIRLS and CONSTRUCTION and other things, but black blobs smudged the print. The smears covered almost everything, including the photograph of the Home itself. Victoria could only see the chimneys.

"Is that . . . ?" she said, leaning closer.

At the front of the photograph stood two figures—a woman in a white dress, and a man in dark work clothes. The man carried a rake. The woman stood with hands clasped at her waist. Smudges blocked their faces and most of their bodies, but Victoria could see enough. One familiar bright eye stared back at her from the woman's face.

Cold ran down Victoria's arms, but it wasn't the strange coldness from before. It was the coldness of understanding something awful.

"It looks just like her," she said, pointing. "Like Mrs. Cavendish. And that's Mr. Alice. It has to be. But there . . . how is this *possible* . . . ?"

Victoria pointed at the faded date near the top of the page.

"That's over a hundred and fifty years ago," whispered Professor Alban.

"Well, those people in the picture have to be their—their ancestors or something," said Victoria, backing away from the table. "Maybe her great-great-grandmother. And Mr. Alice, his great-great grandfather. Right?"

"Maybe ownership of the Home got passed down through their families," said Professor Alban, but he didn't look like he believed that.

Victoria couldn't stop staring at the two smudged figures.

"If it is them," she said, not wanting to say it, but knowing she must, "if those people in the picture are *our* Mrs. Cavendish and *our* Mr. Alice . . . how could they still be alive?"

She and Professor Alban stared at each other, the horrible question floating between them.

Bang.

Something slammed into the door. It slammed again and again, louder and louder.

Bang.

Bang.

"They're coming for me," said Professor Alban. He grabbed Victoria and shoved her into the corner farthest from the door. "The shadows. The eyes in the wall. They're coming."

Victoria rubbed her arms. They hurt where Professor Alban had pinched them. She stared at him as he backed away from the door.

"What do you mean?" she said.

Professor Alban didn't answer. He backed into a table and fell into a chair that was suddenly too big for him. He looked like a child drowning in grown-up clothes, frightened and shaking.

Victoria moved toward him.

"No," he whispered. An outstretched hand stopped her. "Hide. *Hide.*"

The only sounds Victoria could hear were the slamming door and her own heartbeat. They began to match up. Her heart *was* the slamming door.

She shrank back into the corner and put her hands over her ears. The slams kept going, rattling the walls, making the white light around the door pop in and out, closer and closer . . .

Darkness shadowed the frosted glass.

Two dark streams of . . . *something* . . . slipped through the white light from outside into the Records Room. They disappeared into the shadows of the wall. More dark streams joined them from underneath tables and behind cabinets. The room crawled.

Scuttling sounded from everywhere. Cold seeped in through the white-ringed door, toward Victoria's toes.

The scuttling grew louder. Victoria peeked through her fingers at her arms. They were bare and whole, but she felt like something was there, scratching her, trying to wind her up into evil knots.

She heard the horrible sound of a very small boy whimpering in terror.

It was Professor Alban.

Victoria dared to look up and saw the dark streams converging on the chair where he sat, sliding around his legs, clicking and swarming and waving their feelers all over him.

The door slammed open at last, into the wall.

Victoria hid her face. She heard heavy, scratching, dragging sounds. Professor Alban started to scream. Victoria pressed her hands to her ears, squeezed her eyes shut, and recited French to occupy her brain.

Crier. To scream.

Je crie. I scream. *Tu cries*. You scream.

Il crie.

He screams.

Silence. Silence. That was the same.

The door closed, and after several minutes, Victoria forced herself to look up.

The cold dark of the Records Room returned. The microfilm reader buzzed its yellow light.

Professor Alban's chair was empty.

Victoria came out of her corner to investigate. The strange noises and dark, scuttling things were gone, the cabinets closed, the microfilm put away. Victoria tried to open the cabinets but couldn't.

She grabbed her things and snapped everything closed like she was getting ready for school, like it was any other day.

"I don't know what I saw," she said, over and over. "Nothing happened. It's fine."

But it wasn't fine. She had seen and heard something awful, and now Professor Alban was gone.

There was only one thing to do, Victoria realized as she stared at the now-quiet door.

Run.

She lunged for the door and yanked it open. Dashing out into the white, clean library, she realized she was alone.

All the people were gone. She almost began to cry at the thought of being forever locked in a library of black bugs and white lights, but she was running too fast to cry.

She made it to the exit. It wasn't locked. As she ran out onto the steps, Mr. Waxman, standing alone at the front desk, called out, "Come back soon, Victoria."

Town Square was just as busy as ever, like nothing at all had happened in the library. The people gleamed and twirled and smiled, everything silver, everything sharp.

Victoria pushed her way into the neighborhoods just beyond Town Square, through streets of grim black gates, hedges shining with rain, clean houses and clean shutters, and every now and then a red warning notice in a yard with grass an inch too tall. She ran all the way to Silldie Place. The cobbled walks were so slick with rain that she could see her reflection in the stone—a pale ghost flying in a raincoat.

She stopped at home only long enough to root through her father's impeccably ordered shelves in the garage. Someone was calling her name from the kitchen, but she ignored whoever it was, muttering, "Where is it, where *is* it?" until she found it—a can of bug spray.

"Victoria?" It was her mother from just inside, near the kitchen, and for the first time since she was very small, Victoria wanted her mother. She wanted to hide. She wanted to admit failure. The door leading into the house was so close. If she just reached out a little bit, she could grab the doorknob. . . .

But her grip on the cold metal can kept her from going inside. She could not hide; she had to find Lawrence. The image of her favorite street sign popped into her head: VICTORY. Victoria Wright did not admit failure.

Shoving the spray can under her raincoat, she slipped back outside into the damp afternoon, running past Five and Seven on one side and Four, Six, and Eight on the other. She was too frightened to stop, too desperate to understand what she had seen in the library. It wouldn't happen to Lawrence, *it won't, it won't*, she repeated to herself with each step.

Nine Silldie Place: the gray wall, the bright flowerbeds, the dark nameplate. The Home's gate stood open, and once Victoria ran inside, it closed with a heavy, metallic click.

She wanted to turn back, climb over it, and get away. But she couldn't forget Professor Alban and all the evil, dark things swarming on him. She couldn't forget the slamming door, the empty library, the smudged pictures of Mrs. Cavendish and Mr. Alice.

Maybe it wasn't them, though. Maybe Victoria had gotten a little silly with all this.

But if it *was* them . . .

She had to know. She had to see this place for herself.

Maybe, if she got a good look at the inside, and at Mrs. Cavendish, she would have a better idea of what to do next. It could help her figure out what happened to Professor Alban. She would have to be careful, she would have to sneak around and remain unseen, but if she could manage it, if she could find out more in person about the Home . . .

It could help her find Lawrence before he got snatched away for good too. She didn't want to imagine hearing Lawrence screaming, but it happened anyway. She imagined him crawling with roaches too and screaming and crying like Professor Alban had, and no matter how hard she tried, Victoria couldn't get to him.

At the front of the house, wide steps led up to the porch and the front door, but Victoria avoided that and slunk around the right-hand side of the Home, pressing close to the gray brick walls. She slipped a hand under her raincoat and withdrew the spray can.

"Just try and come at me, stupid bugs," she said. "See what happens if you do."

Every few steps, Victoria paused to listen for signs of life, but she heard nothing except the wind in the trees, rustling and snapping. Ahead, past the corner of the Home, flower bushes and shrubberies and stone paths stretched across the grounds. Gardens.

I can start there, Victoria thought. *Maybe someone's outside to spy on*.

She crept forward, paused, crept forward again, and took a step around the corner—

—right into Mr. Alice's stomach.

"Uh-oh," he said, smiling down at her. In one hand, he held an enormous shovel with dirt and rot clinging to it.

"I—I—" said Victoria, staggering back. She tried to say something, *anything*, but her throat was too tight for words. A dark movement across the ground caught her eye—a roach, scuttling out from behind Mr. Alice to squeeze into a hole in the brick.

Victoria didn't think twice. She lunged toward it and pressed down on the spray can's button. A poison cloud covered the roach—Victoria saw it with her own eyes—and yet the bug only paused and stared at her, clicking its beady black eyes. She sprayed again, and again, and it waved its feelers and did not die.

Victoria lowered her arm. "I don't understand."

Mr. Alice knocked the useless spray can away with his shovel. At the movement, the skin along his neck seemed to roll and bulge.

"I want to speak with Mrs. Cavendish," Victoria said, putting up her chin. She would not act afraid. She would act as though she had every right to be there, as if it were the most normal thing in the world. "*Now.*"

He smiled widely. "Come."

Mr. Alice put his naked white hand at Victoria's neck and led her back to the front of the house. Strangely, the door knocker looked different this time, like a pig with a great, gaping snout instead of a rose. Victoria frowned at the knocker hard enough to calm her racing heart and gather her courage. She smoothed her curls.

Remember, you're Victoria Wright, she reminded herself. Maybe in her imagination she couldn't get to Lawrence, but real life was quite another thing; in real life, Victoria Wright always got exactly what she wanted. She tugged her raincoat straight and put on her fiercest dazzle.

Mr. Alice pushed open the door. Something darker than shadows stretched away from him into the Home, forming a hallway with a tiny prick of light at the end. A rush of cold gusted out past Victoria.

"Go on," Mr. Alice said, gesturing with his shovel. "She has been waiting for you."

THE HALLWAY WENT ON FOR WHAT SEEMED LIKE days, between closed doors on either side. Victoria wondered if it would ever end.

Mr. Alice led the way. He used his shovel like a walking stick, tapping the end of it into the carpet. *Pat, pat, pat.* Shadows in the carpet clicked and whirred alongside them, too dark and quick for Victoria to see. She stared straight ahead, refusing to think about the roach outside, dripping with poison and very much alive.

Perhaps this was not such a good idea.

She considered making a run for it, but when she looked back over her shoulder toward the front door, she saw nothing but darkness. Surely the door was there, but Victoria had the feeling

The hallway went on for what seemed like days, between closed doors on either side.

that if she ran back and tried to find it, she would be lost forever. The hallway would keep twisting around and never let her out.

Ridiculous, she told herself. The hallway could not have been any longer than a regular hallway. After all, the Home was only so large. She had seen it from outside, plain as anything. It had only had three floors and a normal amount of windows. She was just frightened, that's all.

Very frightened.

The prick of light in front of them grew larger till it formed a doorway. Mr. Alice stopped and gestured toward it with his arm.

"After you, Victoria Wright," he said, smiling.

Victoria set her jaw and walked past him into a golden hallway lit with soft lamps in sconces. She was determined not to show any sort of fear at whatever lay on the other side.

But what lay on the other side was impossible.

She didn't see a kitchen or anything close to normal, like she had the first time.

Instead, a wide gallery stretched to Victoria's right and left, farther than she could see. The gallery's walls held balconies and windows. Everything past the first floor was darker, and there were six floors altogether, with shadowed railings and hallways, and curling columns that spilled over the walls like vines. Painted birds covered the ceiling, leering down at Victoria. There was something odd about them. It took Victoria a long time to figure out that instead of claws for feet, they had long, sharp hands.

On the second floor were rows of windows, and inside the windows hung paper heads, blackboards, screens—classrooms. On the third floor were paintings large as walls, paintings of balloons and kites and wolves and bones. On the fourth, fifth, and sixth floors, things moved in the archways between columns, dark shapes that slithered around the balconies.

In fact, *everything* was moving. When Victoria unfocused her eyes, the entire gallery, the six floors, the windows and balconies, the classrooms and hanging paper heads, shimmered and crawled.

"This doesn't make sense," Victoria said, crossing her arms. The ridiculousness of everything around her outweighed her fear. She grabbed on to that feeling and held tight. "This doesn't make sense at all."

Pat, pat, pat came Mr. Alice's shovel along the carpet. "Come along."

"But this—this is too big. The Home is only—"

"The Home is just what it needs to be," said Mr. Alice. He smiled, tracing the edge of his shovel with his bare hand. "She'll be angry if you're late."

"It's not like I have an appointment. She didn't know I was coming."

Mr. Alice only laughed.

Victoria followed him past a room of dark pianos. Their lids stood open, strings trailing into piles on the floor. It reminded Victoria of Professor Carroll's classroom in Building Five, but a wrong, turned inside-out version.

"Lawrence," Victoria whispered.

"What's that?" said Mr. Alice. "What's that now?"

"Nothing. I sneezed."

"Gesundheit."

They stopped at a tall, narrow door beneath a painting of a woman and a boy and a girl. At first the painting looked rather lovely. As they approached, however, the woman's face grew longer and thinner. Her bones looked ready to burst through her skin. And the children's smiles became frantic. The woman's fingers dug into their shoulders and disappeared into their flesh.

Victoria hid her shudder.

The door had etchings of scenes upon it, in rows from top to bottom. The one at Victoria's eye level looked like a fox hunt. The one above it, girls blowing fire out of their mouths. The one below it, a circus with a two-headed ringmaster. A small, knobby-headed ghoul dancing with a naked woman.

An orchestra conductor on an empty stage, waving his arms to musicians who weren't there. His hands had fallen off.

Mr. Alice knocked on the door, which had no handle. A pretty voice from beyond the door said, "Come in," and the door opened. Mr. Alice pushed Victoria through.

"Excuse me," Victoria said, yanking herself away. "I can walk by myself."

The pretty voice laughed. "Of course you can, Victoria. You're quite capable of many things, aren't you? Please, come in. Sit down, why don't you?"

Victoria marched into the room. As her eyes grew used to the soft light, she realized the walls were bare and of a deep crimson color. One wall held a giant window. Here Mrs. Cavendish stood, her hand on the curtains. She seemed to be looking at something, but beyond the window was solid black. Victoria couldn't see a thing.

"Well? What do you think?" said Mrs. Cavendish. She did not turn from the window.

"Of what?" said Victoria. It was a fine line, between being brave and being too brave. She got the feeling it wouldn't be wise to snip at Mrs. Cavendish like she could get away with snipping at everyone else.

"Of the Home, of course. Of my Home."

"Well, it's big. And it has lots of interesting rooms."

Mrs. Cavendish laughed. "What else?"

Victoria's sense of order being so completely offended, she wanted to shout out, "The Home makes no sense!" and demand an explanation, blueprints, schematics of the piping.

Instead, she shrugged. "It's very nice and fancy."

"Perhaps you'll want a tour someday?" Mrs. Cavendish said, stroking the tasseled drapes.

"Maybe."

Mrs. Cavendish sighed and turned. Once again, Victoria could not help but stare at Mrs. Cavendish's pretty face, and the quiet, calm way she held herself. The curling brown hair, the steady blue eyes, the folds of her dress falling neatly around Mrs. Cavendish's body made her seem like just the sort of person you'd like to burrow into after a nightmare.

"So, Victoria," said Mrs. Cavendish. "Why have you come to see me?"

Victoria paused. How could she say what she really wanted to say? She couldn't demand outright that Mrs. Cavendish give Jacqueline, Donovan, and Lawrence back, or any of the other missing children. First of all, she didn't really know that Mrs. Cavendish had them. Maybe the paper airplane had been an orphan's joke. Maybe Jacqueline really was sick, and maybe Lawrence really was just a good grandson, and maybe Donovan O'Flaherty had finally received punishment for the Mallow Cakes thing. Maybe he had been transferred to the Learning School in the city, where the bad kids went.

But then, what about the in-the-middle feeling that had been plaguing Victoria all week? And how strange everyone was acting? What about the bug dripping poison, and Professor Alban's screams?

"Well?" said Mrs. Cavendish, sitting in her fine chair, which had talons for feet. "Cat got your tongue?"

Near the door, Mr. Alice laughed. Mrs. Cavendish's mouth twitched. Victoria thought quickly, remembering pieces of things she had seen in the *Belleville Bulletin*. She needed to somehow investigate without seeming like she was investigating.

She thought of Lawrence screaming somewhere all alone, and gulped.

"I just—well, I wanted to see the Home for myself, that's all," said Victoria. She smoothed her coat and sat on the chair opposite Mrs. Cavendish. The next words were hard to say; she still wasn't used to this lying and being sneaky thing, after all. "People say bad things, you know, but I've never believed them."

"Bad things?" said Mrs. Cavendish. Her smile froze, sweetly. She tilted her head, politely. "What sorts of bad things?"

"Oh, like it's a dump and all the kids are mistreated and you hog their money and all that," Victoria said, waving her hand. She laughed the same high, breezy laugh her mother used around company. But of course Victoria had never heard anyone say anything about the Home, good or bad, and remembering this shamed her. How had she never *noticed* any of this before?

Mrs. Cavendish's eyes widened. "Mistreated, you say?"

"Oh, you know how people get silly with rumors sometimes. But I wanted to see for myself."

"And what do you see, Victoria?"

"I see lots of things." Victoria paused. "I saw your piano room."

Mrs. Cavendish smile flickered the tiniest bit. Her teeth flashed. "Oh?"

"That was interesting. All those open pianos."

Mr. Alice shifted his weight; in the silence, the sound seemed deafening. Mrs. Cavendish scratched the side of her mouth with one fingernail.

Victoria waited a couple of breaths before she spoke again. "My friend Lawrence. Lawrence Prewitt? He played the piano."

"Played?" said Mrs. Cavendish, her eyes sharp. "You mean, he no longer plays?"

"He's gone, I guess." It hurt Victoria to say the words out loud in this quiet, blood-colored room.

"Gone?"

"He's been gone for a few days," said Victoria, getting up to pace. She needed the slow, measured steps to keep from running away. "His parents say he's with his grandmother, but I don't believe them."

"Why wouldn't you believe them?" said Mrs. Cavendish.

"I just have a feeling."

Mrs. Cavendish laughed. "A feeling? I thought you were beyond such things, Victoria."

"You say that like you know me," said Victoria kindly. "We really only just met the other day."

"Oh," said Mrs. Cavendish, settling back into her cushions, "I know you quite well, actually."

Bang.

Victoria jumped.

The bang sounded like the slamming door in the library, just before those dark things—those *roaches*—snatched Professor Alban away.

Bang.

It came from the big, dark window. Something was slamming against it, so hard Victoria thought the glass might break. Small, pale blurs pounded on the glass.

Mrs. Cavendish was quick. "Handle this," she spat at Mr. Alice, who yanked the window's curtains closed before leaving through a door in the corner. Mrs. Cavendish grabbed Victoria's arm and pulled her through the tall, narrow door with the etched wooden rows. On her way out, Victoria caught sight of a row she hadn't seen the first time—a long table, empty chairs, and a feast piled high.

"I'm terribly sorry to cut your visit so short, Victoria," said Mrs. Cavendish, dragging Victoria down the gallery. Above them, the balconies writhed in lamplight as the banging behind them suddenly went quiet. *What will she do with me?* Victoria thought, with a sudden jolt of fear. *Will she lock me up?* Frantically, she looked around into the shadows for a door or window standing ajar. She could perhaps make a run for it.

"Stop pulling so hard," said Victoria. She tried to pry Mrs. Cavendish's fingers loose, but they wouldn't budge, even when Victoria pounded on them with her free fist. "Where are you taking me? Let me go, right now."

"But, you see, I'm a busy woman, and I only have so much time for visitors."

"What was that stuff hitting the windows?"

Mrs. Cavendish turned down the hallway of forever, back toward the front door, which Victoria couldn't see in the dark. She wondered if Mrs. Cavendish would throw her in the shadows, where she would get lost till she starved—or something worse.

"I don't know what you're talking about, Victoria," said Mrs. Cavendish, her smile stretching in the dark.

"The windows. Things were hitting them."

"Were they?" Mrs. Cavendish threw Victoria forward. Victoria hit the front door, turned, and shrank back against the handle.

"I like you, Victoria," said Mrs. Cavendish, watching Victoria's face carefully. "We're alike, you and I."

"Alike?" said Victoria. "I don't think so. I mean, you—"

"Yes? Me?"

"You—" Victoria swallowed down her fear and all the awful things she wanted to say. "You're so grown-up and smart, I mean."

"You should leave. Go home and be a good girl like you know you want to be."

Victoria decided to be bold. This could be her only chance to ask, after all. Mrs. Cavendish did not seem like she would want Victoria back here ever again. Her pretty blue eyes flashed. Victoria opened her mouth. *Where's Lawrence?* she almost said.

But Mrs. Cavendish cut her off before she could begin.

"Thank you for visiting the Cavendish Home for Boys

and Girls," said Mrs. Cavendish, as if reading off a script. Her smile was wide, her voice bright. "Normal visiting hours are from four o'clock to six o'clock on weekday afternoons and every other Saturday from ten till noon. . . ."

Mrs. Cavendish opened the front door, one hand on Victoria's neck as if Victoria were a kitten. Victoria wanted to kick and bite at her, but she let herself be led out as Mrs. Cavendish continued her speech about tours and upcoming activities. Who knew what would happen if she tried to fight back?

Behind Victoria, the house yawned and creaked. The floor shifted. The walls glistened with black wings.

". . . and of course," said Mrs. Cavendish, looking back down the hallway, her shoulders hunched, her pretty blue eyes darting to the ceiling and walls, "do let us know of any children who might benefit from education at the Home." She pushed Victoria onto the porch and licked her lips. "We are *always* looking for more children to help."

Victoria landed on her knees. By the time she turned back, the door was closed and Mrs. Cavendish was gone. A tiny ripple raced along the front side of the house, like the bricks were skin and the ripple was the blood underneath. Beneath Victoria's feet, the porch shuddered.

Victoria brushed her knees clean and straightened her

coat. Her knees shook, but she refused to let herself fall. It had begun to rain. The tiniest of drops pattered down through the thick trees overhead. Looking back at the Home, she took her time examining all the gables and eaves and windows.

It was not big enough for a gallery and six floors, a piano room, and towering balconies. It was not big enough for a hallway of forever. As she walked home, Victoria tried to make sense of it and failed. *She let me go*, she thought. *Why did she let me go? And why did she say I was like her?* The longer she walked, the fuzzier the memories of what just happened became, leaving a sour feeling in her throat and stomach, like from meat gone bad.

The Home's gate stood open at the end of the drive. After Victoria passed through, it quietly clicked shut behind her. Her head, full and heavy, swam with dark shadows, but through them all, she could still see Lawrence's face, if she thought about it hard enough. She could hear his happy humming as they walked together to the Academy and smell the dirt on his shoes. Clenching her fists, she focused on those things, and her head began to clear.

At home, everything was dark because of the storm. Victoria hung up her raincoat and flinched at the echo of each rain-soaked step.

"Hello?" she said. "Um, Father?"

It was one thing to go sneaking around the Home. It was quite another to face her parents after disappearing with nothing but a note left behind, after *lying* when she'd never lied before.

The only light was a dim, flickering one beneath her parents' bedroom door. Victoria raised her hand to knock, but a tiny noise from the kitchen made her stop.

Beatrice waved her hand at Victoria through a crack in the door. "Come here," she mouthed.

Victoria didn't show it, but inside, her heart was racing. The house had a bad feeling about it; *like the Prewitts' house*, Victoria realized—too dark and too quiet. She followed Beatrice into the kitchen.

And Beatrice closed the door and turned toward Victoria with a gleaming knife clutched in her fist.

VICTORIA'S MOUTH WENT DRY. TINGLES OF TERROR raced up her arms, gathering as a knot in her throat.

"Beatrice . . . ," she said, backing away slowly.

"I've been waiting for you," whispered Beatrice, stepping forward.

"Wh-wh—" Victoria tried to say, "What are you doing?" but the words would not come. Fear had seized her and would not let go.

I am going to die, her brain recited calmly. *I am going to be stabbed until I am dead. How infuriating. I have so much left to do*.

Beatrice frowned. "Why do you look so—? Oh." She noticed the knife and set it down on the countertop. "I'm sorry, Victoria. Did I frighten you? It's just that with things the way they are, I needed to be careful. I won't let anyone take me."

Victoria slumped against the oven. The terror inside her *fwoosh*ed away like a sigh. She glared at Beatrice.

"Maybe put the knife down first, next time," she hissed.

Beatrice put a finger to her lips. "Quiet," she whispered. "Quiet."

"What? Why?" Victoria said, crossing her arms. Then she noticed how strangely Beatrice was dressed. She wasn't wearing the uniform Mrs. Wright made her wear—the fine work dress and apron, the little cap, the shining shoes. Beatrice instead wore a long raincoat and a kerchief about her frazzled white head. The skin under her eyes was dark. At her feet sat a piece of luggage.

Victoria narrowed her eyes. "What are you doing?"

"Oh, I stayed up all night worrying and wondering, waiting, watching . . ." Beatrice murmured, her hands working furiously at her waist.

"Watching for what?"

"I won't watch it happen again, not *again*. Too many times, far too many." She frowned, rubbing her forehead. "But then, it's so hard to remember."

Victoria grabbed her arm. "Watch *what* happen?"

Outside, lightning flashed. Beatrice glanced down the hall toward the master suite. The light around the door froze, like someone had been moving around and then stopped.

"Quiet," said Beatrice, taking Victoria's shoulders and hunkering down with her beside the kitchen island. "Don't let them hear."

Victoria narrowed her eyes to inspect Beatrice's face. "What do you mean? You mean don't let Mother and Father hear? Does this have something to do with that note you left me? " 'Be careful' "?

Beatrice nodded, but when she looked up again, Victoria saw how her eyes had that strange fuzzy look she had seen there before. If Beatrice was tired or if it was something else, Victoria couldn't tell.

"And the roaches?" she said. "Professor Alban?"

Beatrice stared at her blankly. She shook her head and wiped her eyes.

"But what about the Home? The missing children?"

Beatrice's face crumpled. "The children."

Victoria thought about how happy and warm she had felt in Mrs. Cavendish's kitchen, how it had been hard to remember why she was there, how it had been hard to speak. She had stood and let Mrs. Cavendish pet her hair.

Beatrice's eyes looked like that sensation Victoria had felt—hazy, peaceful, quiet.

"It's Mrs. Cavendish," Victoria whispered, her skin prickling as she said the words out loud. "Isn't it? It's true. I'm not imagining things."

Beatrice nodded once, sadly. Then she put her hands to her temples. Tears glinted in her eyes.

"I went there today, I—"

"You what?" said Beatrice. "Oh, no. Oh, you didn't."

"I did. First I went to the library to investigate through the newspaper. I met Professor Alban there, and—" Victoria paused. "Well, I don't know what happened. I think he may be gone now too. And I've had just about enough of all these weird things happening everywhere, so I went to the Home to sneak around, but Mr. Alice caught me and took me inside, and—"

"How did you get out?" Beatrice whispered. "No one ever gets out unless *she* wants them to."

"She let me go. She likes me, she said."

Beatrice put a hand to her heart. "Maybe there's still time, then." She grabbed Victoria's shoulders, hard. "Listen. Are you listening?"

Victoria rolled her eyes to hide the fact that Beatrice was really scaring her. "Yes, I'm listening. Stop pinching."

"You may be all right, if she let you go, if she *likes* you, or maybe you're worse off than anyone, I don't know," said Beatrice, in a frantic rush. She kept peering around the island toward the closed door. "But if you know what's good for you—and I know that you do, Victoria—just do as you're told. Go to school, eat your supper, do your homework, attend your lessons. Don't ask questions. Do you understand?"

"How do you *know* all this?" Victoria demanded. "What's going on? And where are you going?"

"I'm leaving. I can't stay here anymore. I've been so scared but . . . no. I won't let her take me." Her eyes filled with tears. "I don't know if I *can* leave, but I'm going to try."

Victoria crouched lower, eyes wide. "*Take* you? So it's true. She takes people? And you've seen it happen before? How many times has it happened? Did you have friends who got taken? Did they ever come back?"

"Mr. Tibbalt," said Beatrice, the quietest yet. Victoria had to squint at her lips to make it out. "Ask him. He knows. He'll . . . remember."

"Remember what?"

"I can't, I can't. Too much." Beatrice tightened the kerchief about her head. "Just stay safe, Victoria. Don't go poking around. Behave. Pretend you haven't seen me. I'm sorry, I—I'll miss you." She kissed Victoria's head and left.

Victoria stood at the front door, watching her go. Mr. Tibbalt's dog yapped his way down the street, bouncing along after her.

So. Something *was* going on. It wasn't a dream, it wasn't imagination, or maybe Beatrice was crazy, or maybe they were all crazy. Victoria sat at the kitchen table, alone and thinking, till the enormous grandfather clock in the foyer chimed seven and her parents came to supper.

"Well, where's supper?" said Mrs. Wright, her copper hair gleaming, not one wrinkle in her fashionable clothes. "Where's my dear Beatrice gone off to?"

Victoria watched her mother circle the kitchen, peeking brightly behind pots and cabinets like she was looking for something. She trailed her fingers softly along the steak knives' handles.

Mr. Wright stood humming at the kitchen threshold, knotting his necktie. A sharp, wolfish look flashed across his face. Victoria convinced herself it was only a trick of the light.

Best to play it safe, she thought, remembering Mrs. Cavendish's words: "Be a good girl like you know you want to be."

"Mother, Father," Victoria said, going to each of them and planting kisses on their cheeks. Their skin felt hard and cold. "I'm so sorry about everything today, I really am. I researched all sorts of things for my History of the World class. We're studying the Aborigines in Australia."

"History of the World?" said Mr. Wright. "Who teaches that?"

"Oh. Professor Alban." Her parents turned to face her, their faces ravenous in the dim light. Victoria tried not to back away, wrinkled her nose, and sniffed with disdain. "I don't like him much," she lied. "He's—*nosy*."

Her parents relaxed. Mrs. Wright smiled brightly. "Yes. Nosy. That's it. That's it, exactly."

"He bugs me a lot of the time. Always asking questions. I want to tell him to mind his own business and let me do what I want, because I can be the best all by myself, right?"

Mr. and Mrs. Wright nodded.

"Nosy," Mr. Wright said.

"Own business," said Mrs. Wright.

"Well, so anyway. I made all As this quarter," said Victoria, forcing a smile. "Could you sign my academic report?"

Her parents relaxed even more.

Mr. Wright smiled widely. "Of course."

Mrs. Wright tightened Victoria's hair ribbon. "Such a good student."

And that was that. No one mentioned Beatrice's absence

or wondered if she would come back soon. Victoria didn't dare, and her parents seemed to have forgotten that Beatrice had ever existed. They ate leftover roast for supper. Victoria ate as quickly as possible before shutting herself in her room; the sight of her parents smiling brightly at her and chomping down meat with their mouths half-open left Victoria with very little appetite.

For the rest of the weekend, Victoria was a model child, studying and doing her homework, practicing her *-ir* and *-re* verbs. On Monday, she went to school with a signed academic report in hand. At Round Table, she turned it in. Jill Hennessey stared at Victoria's report from beneath her red hair, catching the new grade with horrified eyes.

Victoria smiled and waved at Jill, but inside, she wasn't even thinking about the report. Instead, thoughts of her parents' closed bedroom door filled her mind. They hadn't come out for breakfast or to say good morning. Victoria had woken to a silent, dark house.

In History of the World, Professor Alban was gone. Victoria hoped nothing showed on her face when she saw his empty chair. Inside, though, she felt like someone had kicked her in the stomach.

"Ahem," said Dr. Hardwick, the thin, white-headed headmaster, standing at the head of the class. "Miss Wright, is it?"

"Yes," said Victoria.

"If you'll please take your seat."

For the first time in her life, Victoria disobeyed an Academy employee. She did not take her seat. "But where's Professor Alban?"

Dr. Hardwick slid his fingers across Professor Alban's podium, back and forth, around the corners. "Professor Alban has been dismissed."

Jill laughed. "Thank goodness. Definitely the worst professor I've ever had."

"The worst," echoed the others, laughing.

"Dismissed?" said Victoria. "He was the best professor at this school. At least he isn't lazy, and at least he makes us work and *cares* about his students, and he even—he even—"

She stopped. She had been about to tell the whole story about the library and the awful things that had happened there. Dr. Hardwick's eyes brightened. His diamond-white smile gleamed.

"Yes? He even . . . what?" he said.

"Nothing," said Victoria, sitting down. Her cheeks flushed a bright red, but it wasn't because of Jill and everyone laughing about how crazy Victoria Wright had gotten.

Victoria's cheeks burned because she had finally had enough.

This time she wouldn't let her fear get the best of her. She wouldn't run straight into trouble armed with nothing but some stupid bug spray.

She would do what she did best—*homework.*

After school, she didn't go home. She didn't go to *the* Home, either. She walked to Six Silldie Place, through the yard of trash and clutter, and knocked on Mr. Tibbalt's door. The little red dog bounced at her heels, hardly able to contain himself, but Victoria didn't notice. Her thoughts were full of Lawrence, locked up in a buggy room with Professor Alban somewhere, wondering where Victoria was and if anyone would ever find them. She drew deep breaths to keep from pounding the door down. There was no more time to waste.

When Mr. Tibbalt opened the door, Victoria put up her chin.

"Hello, Mr. Tibbalt," she said. "Tell me everything you know about Mrs. Cavendish."

AT FIRST, MR. TIBBALT JUST STARED, HIS HAND shaking where it gripped the wall. Victoria wondered if he would slam the door shut in her face.

Then he said, rather croakily, "About—about who did you say?"

"You heard me." Victoria didn't want to say it out loud again. The wind had hushed. Things were too quiet.

"Hurry," said Mr. Tibbalt, waving her inside. Once the door was shut, he peered past the blinds for a long time. At Victoria's feet, the little red dog sat and panted, smiling up at her. Getting Mr. Tibbalt's permission to come inside seemed to have upped his opinion of her.

"What are you doing?" said Victoria.

Mr. Tibbalt took off his hat and backed into the corner. Dust clouds floated up around him.

"Why do you want to know about her?" said Mr. Tibbalt. Slumped against the wall, his voice heavy and slow, he seemed a completely different person than the neighbor Victoria had always known, feared, and despised.

"I'm curious about her," said Victoria carefully. "I'm writing an article for the Academy paper. About local businesses."

Mr. Tibbalt scoffed. "Of course you are."

"You don't believe me?"

"No, but I know why you're lying. I've lied, too. I've never stopped lying."

"What are you talking about?" said Victoria.

"Come, let's sit and have a talk," said Mr. Tibbalt. He led Victoria down the main hallway. More garbage lined the walls, which bore pictures so black with neglect that Victoria only caught snippets of things, much like the old photograph of Mrs. Cavendish at the library—a flower, a cabin, a road, dark hair, all faded with age.

Mr. Tibbalt kept an old, tall piano shoved in the corner of his living room.

Lawrence, Victoria thought, that pang pinching her throat again. She hurried to the piano and pressed one of the keys. It was so out of tune that the note hurt her ears. Mr. Tibbalt's dog howled.

"Quiet, Gallagher," said Mr. Tibbalt.

"Gallagher?" said Victoria, raising an eyebrow.

"Is that a problem?"

"No." Victoria sat on the edge of the piano bench, avoiding the questionable dark patches on the cushion. "It's a very proper name, that's all."

Mr. Tibbalt set a bowl of food at Gallagher's front paws. "A proper name for a proper gentleman."

Gallagher began eating, his tail wagging. Victoria watched Mr. Tibbalt settle on the sofa that bore the imprint of where he must sit all day, all night. It was the only clean spot in the room. She felt uncomfortable when she noticed how he sometimes stumbled on his feet, and how the act of sitting creased his gaunt face with pain.

"Well," said Mr. Tibbalt. "Been poking around where you shouldn't, have you?"

Victoria kept her voice cool. "I'm only writing my article."

Mr. Tibbalt leaned back. He didn't have much hair left, and what remained stuck up in halfhearted tangles.

"I wouldn't," he said. Then, quieter, "I wouldn't."

"Why not?"

"You'll get stuck, just like her, just like everyone."

"Stuck?" Victoria took out her notebook and began scribbling. It would help to look the part of a reporter. "Just like who?"

Mr. Tibbalt waved his hand at her. "Oh, put that garbage away."

"Funny you should say that," said Victoria, wrinkling her nose as she caught a rotten whiff of something from behind the piano.

"You don't fool me. I know about the little boy. The musical boy."

Victoria forced herself to keep breathing and scribbling. "What boy?"

"Lawrence," said Mr. Tibbalt, rolling his eyes. "Drop the act and talk to me, or leave. I don't have time for shenanigans."

Victoria snapped shut her notebook. "Fine."

"Well? You're looking for him, aren't you?" said Mr. Tibbalt.

"I am. And I think some other kids, too. Kids from school."

"What kids?"

Victoria sat up straighter. "What do you care about them?"

"Do you want my help or don't you?" Mr. Tibbalt said.

At his feet, Gallagher paused in his eating to growl at Victoria, his kibbled whiskers twitching.

"I don't know if I can trust you," said Victoria.

"Well, no, you don't," said Mr. Tibbalt. "But you can."

Victoria shot Mr. Tibbalt a demon dazzle, and Mr. Tibbalt shot one right back. Then and there, Victoria decided to trust him. Anyone who could muster up a dazzle of that quality had to be all right.

"Jacqueline Hennessey," said Victoria. "And Donovan O'Flaherty. No one knows about Donovan, and Jill says Jacqueline's sick, but—"

"But you don't believe them."

"That's right."

Mr. Tibbalt scratched his unshaven jaw. "Who's Jill?"

"Jacqueline's sister. They're twins."

"Yes, family." He nodded. "Isn't it awful when your own family gets involved in such a thing? You think you're safe at home, but so often, you're not."

"What are you *talking* about?" said Victoria.

"I'm sorry to tell you this, but they're gone, they're all gone. If you're lucky, they'll come back." Mr. Tibbalt wiped his face with a soiled handkerchief from his jacket. "But sometimes, you're not lucky."

Gallagher left his supper to climb the sofa and lay his head in Mr. Tibbalt's lap.

"Where did they go?" Victoria said, but Mr. Tibbalt just sat, staring into the room's dark, messy corners.

Thunder broke the silence. The lightning made the house look even worse and Mr. Tibbalt look even older and more tired. Gallagher raised his head to howl.

Victoria didn't have time for people being dramatic. After picking her way through all the filth, she wrinkled her nose and poked Mr. Tibbalt's shoulder.

"Where did they go?" she repeated. "Tell me, or *I'll* leave."

Mr. Tibbalt blinked sadly. "She took them."

"Mrs. Cavendish?"

"Yes."

"You're certain?"

"Yes," said Mr. Tibbalt. "They're with her. They're at the Home."

"I knew it," whispered Victoria.

"Why are you smiling?"

"Because I guessed right." Victoria began to pace. "Well, I'll just tell their parents, and they'll call the police, and they'll go get them out. I mean, you can't just steal kids and take them to your orphanage. I'm sure that's against the law. My father—"

"You don't understand," said Mr. Tibbalt. He put his cap back on and stumbled to his feet. "This way."

Victoria grabbed a poker from the hearth and followed him, Gallagher trotting at her heels.

"What's that for?" Mr. Tibbalt grumbled, pushing on a

door wedged shut with stacks of papers and books.

"In case you try to hurt me," said Victoria. "I exercise, you know, so just watch out."

Mr. Tibbalt nodded. "That could come in handy, if you're serious about this."

"About what?"

"Getting them out," said Mr. Tibbalt. "Parents, police, reporters, they won't help you. You'll be on your own. And it probably won't work. You'll get stuck too. She'll have you. And if you get out, you won't remember enough to tell anyone, and even if you do end up remembering, you won't want to, and you won't want to say anything. You'll be too afraid. Like me. And if you don't get out, you'll never, ever leave."

Mr. Tibbalt mumbled this as he tried to open the door. Victoria stared at him. His words sounded crazy, but he was the first person to take her seriously and actually talk to her. She relaxed her grip on the poker.

"It happens all the time, year after year, decade after decade," Mr. Tibbalt continued, pushing through old sofa cushions and a hat rack. The room had a lot of windows and a large chandelier. Shelves of trinkets covered most of the walls. "She's been here a long time, and Belleville has always been hungry for perfection. People don't care about much as long as everything looks as it should, as long as they can show off and feel good about themselves." Mr. Tibbalt paused and raised a bushy gray eyebrow. "You understand about that, Victoria."

Victoria put up her chin and said, "Yes, I do," refusing to look away.

"Sometimes, though," Mr. Tibbalt continued, "she gets overly ambitious. Takes groups of children at a time. That's when people wake up and start noticing. They can't help but notice. That's when things get bad." He sighed, wiping his brow. "Like when I was a boy."

"But where does she come from?" said Victoria. "She just appeared one day and started snatching kids?"

"As far as I can tell."

Victoria almost stamped her foot. "But what does she *want* them for?"

"Haven't you been listening?" said Mr. Tibbalt, his mouth going all twisty like a wrinkly fruit. "She wants to *fix* them. A place like Belleville doesn't think well of odd children or ugly children or children who don't quite do what's *normal.* That's where she comes in."

"But . . ." Victoria paused. If she wasn't careful, Mr. Tibbalt's mouth might twist around till it disappeared forever. "Why does everyone let her?"

Mr. Tibbalt's mouth twitched into a frown. "Sometimes

you get what you ask for, and sometimes . . . you get more than that. Much more."

Victoria's mind rebelled against this nonsense, and yet . . . the knot in her stomach wouldn't go away. "But how does she make her house so much bigger on the inside than on the outside?"

Mr. Tibbalt froze. "On the inside? How do you know about the inside?"

"I've been there," Victoria said. "I went there, just to see what I could see. There was something beating on the window in her parlor. And she let me go, but I don't know why. I thought she might lock me up, but she didn't. She said she liked me. She said I was like her."

"Ha. She *would* like you, yes."

Victoria bristled. "What is that supposed to mean?"

"You like things to be just so, no matter what the cost," said Mr. Tibbalt, pulling out a large photo album from underneath some moldy newspapers. "So does she. So does everyone around here. And as far as *how* she does what she does, I'd rather not know." Mr. Tibbalt glanced up at her. "There are magic tricks, like pick-a-card and white rabbits, and then there are other tricks. Nasty ones. I'd guess that's what Mrs. Cavendish is all about. But I surely don't want to find out."

Deep in her bones, in a place she'd never felt before,

Victoria shivered. She quickly changed the subject. "Beatrice said I may be all right, since Mrs. Cavendish likes me."

"Or maybe you're worse off than anyone."

"Yes, that's what Beatrice said."

"Poor Beatrice," said Mr. Tibbalt. "She's seen it happen before, several times, just like me. But it's hard for her to see awful things. Not strong enough. She never spoke up, just like I never did. It kept us safe, you see. We were so afraid. We *are* so afraid. You can't help being afraid, being a child and seeing your friends get taken away and not really remembering they were your friends at all—till they come back. Different. Changed. Or maybe they don't come back at all, and you never remember they were there, and you have mad dreams, wondering how many people you've known and forgotten." His voice was bitter. "But staying quiet, it kept us safe. *Safe*."

"Beatrice left," said Victoria.

"She'd almost left several times, over the years. But it's hard to leave a place when you're tied to it by fear, when it's broken you with fear, when it's all you've ever known. Even then, though, even then . . . there's only so much a person can take." He sighed. "I wasn't always like I am now, you know."

Victoria's eyes filled with tears as she stared at the floor. "My parents are being weird."

Mr. Tibbalt paused.

"They aren't acting like themselves," said Victoria. The tears grew, but she didn't let them fall. Everything looked like she was inside a bubble. They surprised her, these tears. Till this point, she had been so busy trying to figure things out that she hadn't had time to worry about her parents. Now the worry struck her right in her belly. "Will they be all right?"

"Hard to say," said Mr. Tibbalt. "Come here, look at this."

They sat on two wobbly stools, and Mr. Tibbalt opened the photo album and spread it out on his knees. Photographs, newspaper clippings, and sketches lined the pages. Mr. Tibbalt turned them slowly. His fingers, purple and gnarled with the cold, smoothed out wrinkles and cleared away dust.

"This is from when I was a boy. I lived here with my parents." Mr. Tibbalt pointed to two waving people with a boy in the middle. "I was sixteen when it happened."

"When what happened?" said Victoria.

"When Vivian disappeared."

Mr. Tibbalt turned another page and pointed to a photograph of a young girl. She had wild black curls and a crooked smile. She wore overalls rolled up to the knee and a wide hat, and she held a basket full to the brim with berries. Around her neck sat a cheap-looking heart-shaped locket.

Mr. Tibbalt pointed to it. "She kept my picture in there, you know."

"Who is she?" said Victoria.

"Vivian Goodfellow," said Mr. Tibbalt. He wilted a bit in his seat as he stared at the photograph. "She had such a lovely voice. She lived at Eight."

"The Bakers live there now."

Mr. Tibbalt continued over her softly. "Vivian was always saying things she shouldn't have, going where she shouldn't have been, poking her nose into places she shouldn't have poked. When Teddy Tibbalt disappeared, she was the only one who noticed, the only one who bothered to look for him."

In her surprise, Victoria almost stepped on Gallagher's paw. "Teddy Tibbalt? Was that you?"

"No. He was my brother." Mr. Tibbalt turned back to the photograph of the waving people. He pointed to the boy in the middle, and then to another boy Victoria had missed the first time—a smaller boy crouched in the background. "See? There he is. He never liked pictures. All he liked was burning things, and building things in the backyard and breaking them."

"Why would you want to build things only to break them?" asked Victoria, wrinkling her nose.

"That was just Teddy. He wasn't a bad boy. He was just

a strange, angry boy." Mr. Tibbalt breathed in and out, his throat rattling. "Till he disappeared. And when he came back, he wasn't Teddy. He was someone else, like someone had broken the old Teddy and built a new one."

"And your parents didn't do anything when he was just gone all of a sudden?" Victoria sniffed. "I find that hard to believe."

"Do you?" said Mr. Tibbalt, frowning.

Victoria thought of her missing schoolmates. Her shoulders felt suddenly heavy as she considered the thought that she and crazy old Mr. Tibbalt, who was too frightened and too old to do anything about it, might be the only ones who realized they were gone. "Well . . . no. I guess not. After all, nobody seems to care about"—she took a deep breath—"about Lawrence being gone. I believe you."

"Quite so. I can't even explain to you how it happened, Victoria. One day he was there, and the next he wasn't, but I didn't care. Neither did our parents. There was a cold fog over us. The days were blank but peaceful. I went to school, did my homework, went to bed, just like normal."

Something crashed outside. Victoria darted over to the window, but it was impossible to tell anything, what with the storm picking up and the wind blowing Mr. Tibbalt's garbage around.

Mr. Tibbalt wiped his sweating brow again. "Vivian tried to figure it out. She was the only one to keep her head. I'd always thought she was swell. She was a real beaut, you know. Inside and out. She tried to tell us something was wrong, she came over every day to search the house, all of that. My parents threw her out over and over. She got so angry with me that one afternoon . . ."

Victoria waited at the window for Mr. Tibbalt to continue. When he didn't, his hands covering his face, she started feeling extremely uncomfortable. She hated soothing people.

"There, there," she said, gritting her teeth and patting his shoulder. "Keep going."

"She said she thought I was different, that I could see people's value. But then she said, 'You're just like everyone else, Bernie.' And she cried, she was so angry. She left. She went to the Home—I saw her march straight through that gate."

Mr. Tibbalt raised a finger and pointed through the walls of his house toward Nine Silldie Place.

"Teddy came back one day," he whispered. "I remember. I hardly recognized him, but I didn't say anything. Life went on. But Vivian never came back."

"But how did you figure out that it was Mrs. Cavendish?"

said Victoria. Talking seemed really impolite, what with Mr. Tibbalt's tremendous old-man tears pooling at his eyes, but she had to stay focused. *Just like at school,* Victoria, she reminded herself. *Just like at school with all those idiots trying to distract you.*

"I never forgot Vivian," said Mr. Tibbalt, but he wasn't speaking to Victoria anymore. He was speaking to himself, or maybe to the photos in his lap. "How could I? But everyone else could. And it kept happening, year after year, and no one noticed. I would have been one of them, I think—happy to let children come and go, happy to ignore the fact that they were coming back different or not coming back at all. But Vivian was always there in the back of my mind, not letting me forget.

"And one day I went to the Home, just to see. I went inside. I thought I would find some house of horrors. But all I found was an orphanage, a nice lady, happy children playing games. I saw what she wanted me to see."

"But it's not normal like that, it's awful, it's much bigger than it looks, and there's something really creepy about it," said Victoria.

"Yes," Mr. Tibbalt said, wiping his eyes. "Mrs. Cavendish sends me nightmares about it, I think. She knew I wouldn't let go of my questions—let go of Vivian—unless I thought

I was crazy. And I did, and I do. And here I am, caught forever. I know what really happened, and yet . . . and yet it's so hard to think about it. It's like there's something weaving around in there, confusing my memories into knots." Mr. Tibbalt tapped his temple and waved his arm at the filthy house. "And I won't ever be able to clean all of this—never."

"Well," said Victoria after several moments during which she seriously questioned her sanity because of what she was about to do, "Mrs. Cavendish doesn't know *everything*."

"She doesn't?" Mr. Tibbalt said, stroking Vivian's picture with one trembling finger.

"No. For example, she doesn't know that I'm not afraid of her, that I'm still thinking quite clearly, thank you, and that I won't let her do this to people." Victoria set down the fireplace poker and headed toward the front door. "It's completely illegal."

Mr. Tibbalt's hand stopped her from grabbing the front door latch.

"You don't understand, Victoria," he said. "No one will help you."

"But my father's a very important lawyer—"

"That doesn't matter. He won't help you. Neither of them will." Mr. Tibbalt's eyelids lowered a bit, like he was too tired to keep them open much longer. "She goes for the parents, those closest to you. She *does* things to them, gets them all wrapped up, makes them forget and ignore what's happening. They can't help it. And no one else will want to step in and help them. They'll be too afraid to get involved. They'll be too afraid it might happen to them next. Just like me."

"Professor Alban was helping," Victoria said, her shoulders squaring with Academy pride. "He was at the library with me. He knew something was wrong, and *he* wasn't afraid."

"Oh, yes? And where is Professor Alban now?"

Victoria paused. "He's . . . gone."

Mr. Tibbalt's eyes narrowed. He nodded in grim triumph. "There you have it."

"But why didn't she take me? And, really, why doesn't she take *you*? Why only *some* people and not others?"

"She takes whoever is useful to her, and of what use am I to her?" Mr. Tibbalt laughed. "I'm old, I'm frightened, I don't even step outside my gate. She's gutted me, this *town* has gutted me. I'm a shell. I'm not dangerous. You, though . . ." Mr. Tibbalt rubbed his stubbly mouth. "She said you were like her. She said she liked you, which I very much doubt. She doesn't like many people, I wouldn't think. But she did *say* it, and that could be something, couldn't it? That could be something, indeed."

"Something . . . like what?" Victoria frowned. "I'm not like her. I don't steal people."

Mr. Tibbalt watched her, saying nothing.

The silence made Victoria bristle. "Well, I *don't*."

"Let me ask you something, Victoria." Mr. Tibbalt leaned forward. "What scares you the most?"

"Failure," Victoria said. She did not even have to think about it. "I'm the best. I'm *always* the best. I have to be."

"And what could keep you from being the best?"

Victoria paused. "Jill. Jill Hennessey, at the Academy."

"And why is that?"

"Because she gets good grades too. She's smart and studies a lot, and—" A chill raced up Victoria's arms. "She's like me. Other people aren't smart enough, don't study hard enough, I can beat them, easy, but not Jill. She's too . . . like me. But I don't like Jill. I pretend to, but I really don't. I want her to fail all her classes, I want her to fall on her stupid face, I want her to . . . stay out of my way. . . ."

"You might say this Jill is dangerous, then," Mr. Tibbalt said. "She could keep you from accomplishing your goals."

Could I be dangerous to Mrs. Cavendish*?* Victoria thought. "Mrs. Cavendish said she liked me," she said slowly, "but maybe it's the opposite. Maybe she's only pretending?"

Mr. Tibbalt settled back into his chair and made a *hmm* sound in his throat.

"Well, I'm not going to just sit around like you did," said Victoria, stalking outside. She did not want to think about Jill or if she, Victoria, was like or not like Mrs. Cavendish. It was late; she had wasted enough time here, and Lawrence could be screaming and crawling with bugs somewhere, right this very minute. The thought made her slam the front door open in fury. "I *hate* when things don't make sense or get all mixed up. I'll *make* them make sense."

Mr. Tibbalt hobbled after her, using the poker to hobble down the steps. "This isn't school, Victoria."

"Oh, don't act like you know me."

"I suppose I don't, do I? Not like Lawrence, anyhow, eh?"

Victoria stopped at the gate.

"If you know what's good for him, you'll just go home and do as you're told," said Mr. Tibbalt. Gallagher paced in nervous circles in front of him. "Maybe it's not too late for Lawrence. Vivian went after Teddy, and he came back wrong, and she was gone forever. Is that what you want?"

"Well, no offense, Mr. Tibbalt," said Victoria, opening the gate, "but Vivian wasn't top of her class, was she?"

"What does that have to do with anything?"

"Thank you for your time," Victoria said briskly, slamming the gate shut behind her. Once it was closed, the wind wailed and snapped at her skin. It tried to push her down the street, toward the Home, but Victoria put her head down and fought it. Getting through her own gate and up the walk toward her front porch was the hardest of all.

"Stop it," Victoria scolded the wind, although she could hardly speak past it. The storm was so cold that Victoria's skin pricked into painful chills. She kept hearing things in the flower gardens and whirled around, ready to fling her book bag at whatever roaches or gardeners lurked in the shrubberies—but she saw only wet black branches and bright autumn flowers coming apart in the storm.

"Oh, they're all going to jail, every last one of them, once Father gets ahold of them," Victoria growled, tugging at the door latch. It wouldn't budge. She put in her house key, and it wouldn't turn. She pounded on the door—

—and something pounded back.

Victoria jumped away.

Bang.

That one almost knocked Victoria's teeth loose. She turned and ran, hoping that maybe the back door would be unlocked and she could get in and grab her parents before it was too late.

Surely Mrs. Cavendish hadn't gotten them. Surely they wouldn't be all roachy and weird like Mr. Waxman and Professor Carroll and the Prewitts and—and *everyone*, except for Mr. Tibbalt, who didn't have anything left for Mrs. Cavendish to snatch. No, they wouldn't let anything happen to their daughter.

Would they?

She had to climb over the stone wall into the backyard because the gate wouldn't open. The fall skinned her knees and tore her stockings, but she kept going because *something* was right at her heels, something cold and dark and clicking, scratching at her ankles.

The back door didn't budge, not when Victoria tugged and kicked at the latch, not when she threw her whole body against it.

She turned and pressed herself back against the stained glass. As she tried to catch her breath, her eyes darting around into her mother's rose gardens, she felt hot pinches on her arms, hands, and legs.

Victoria had felt those pinches before. Before she even decided to look down, she knew what she would see—gleaming wings, black beetle eyes, sharp feelers, ten little feet digging into her skin.

"Mother?" she whispered. She squinched her eyes shut,

imagining the door swinging open to reveal her parents, and her father would pat her on the back for being brave, and her mother would call the police, and everything would be fine. "Father? Where are you?"

She gulped and looked down.

The roaches were everywhere.

She tried to count all of them, glinting on the porch and on her shoes and hands, clicking their tiny black eyes, waving their feelers and wings.

Pretend it's a test, Victoria, she told herself. *You need an A. Count.*

One, two, three, seven? She managed only that much before all those hundreds of legs tugged at her stomach and hands and feet, like they were trying to smash her into a little ball. Black wings flitted over her eyes, sucking away the sounds of the storm. They swarmed over her, covering her head to toe, until she almost couldn't breathe. She was falling, down, down . . .

She was flying, or no—she was being dragged, past wet rocks—or was it a black ocean?—or was it a starless sky? The roaches roiled all around her, between her fingers and legs and across her face, tugging her on with their stinging pincers. They were underground, Victoria realized, perhaps in a tunnel. She smelled mud and rock and stink, and the air was cold. She wanted to cover her ears to block out the buggy clicks and hisses coming from everywhere, but she couldn't move her arms. Tiny legs crawled all over her and beneath her, sweeping her along, pinching and pulling her skin like hundreds of burrowing hooks. Mud and grime got in her mouth, filled up her nose and ears. She coughed and choked and tried to claw for air, but she was too covered in bugs to move her arms.

Everything stopped.

Victoria blinked and blinked again, and nothing changed. When she closed her eyes, darkness; when she opened them, darkness. When she allowed herself to breathe past the buggy pinches she realized the roaches were gone. There was no more pain, and her arms and legs were normal again.

But she was alone, and the floor was cold. She wouldn't let herself cry, not yet.

"Pull yourself together," she said, but her voice sounded so shaky and unlike herself that it scared her. Mud clung to her lips, and her throat tasted like dirt.

"Hello?" she said, wiping her mouth. The floor beneath her was damp stone. She crawled around to get her bearings, patting the floor as she went. Before she could move much, she bumped into a wall, and then another one at the other side. When she tried to stand up, she hit her head. There wasn't even room to push herself fully up onto her hands and knees. She had to crawl around like one of the bugs that had brought her here.

Victoria shrank into a corner. Scuttling noises sounded from somewhere—*everywhere*—or was she imagining things? Was she dead? Was this a coffin? A nightmare?

She hoped it was a nightmare. She pulled her legs up to her chest and squeezed her eyes shut, which made her tears fall, but she was too afraid to be angry with herself.

Over and over, she whispered, "Wake up, Victoria. Wake up."

FOR A FEW SECONDS—OR WAS IT WEEKS?— Victoria lay in the corner of this low, damp room. It was too dark, and she was too frightened, to measure time. She couldn't sleep or move.

She started to think that the walls, which she couldn't see in the dark, were moving.

Wild thoughts began forming in her head. Was she floating, or was she in fact lying on a cold floor? Was the dark really dark, or was it roaches mashed into a film covering her eyes? Was she upside down? Inside out?

Things itched and scratched her. She swatted bugs that weren't there and realized the things scratching her were her own fingernails raking her skin raw.

She heard a dripping noise and began tapping her tongue against her teeth in time with the drips.

Drip.

Drip.

Her mouth felt drier with each tiny splash.

She recited things to keep the silence from becoming any louder:

Penser. To think.

Je pense. I think.

Je pense beaucoup de choses. I think many things.

Dans le noir. In the dark.

Le noir. The dark.

After a while, Victoria's mind raced with too many words, and they were all screaming. She began to hum a little made-up tune to drown out the silence, scratching the floor with her thumb because that kept her from flying away.

She hummed and hummed and thought about Lawrence. If Lawrence were there, he would turn being trapped here into some sort of game, and Victoria would say out loud that it was stupid, but inside she wouldn't be so scared anymore.

The floor beneath her shifted.

Victoria cried out and buried her head in her arms. Now she was imagining that the floor was moving. It would drop away, and she would fall and fall forever. The bugs would get her again and chew off all her hair, and then her skin, until they found her black, glossy bug skin underneath, and then she would be one of them.

She hummed louder. *Lawrence. Think about Lawrence. Lawrence hums when he's happy.*

From somewhere outside, footsteps approached, cutting her off. She heard the turn of a key and the slide of something heavy. White light filled the seams around the opposite wall. Victoria scooted back. This was *her* little dark room. She stared distrustfully at the seams of light. Would they start popping closer and closer with loud *bangs* like right before Professor Alban disappeared?

The opposite wall slid away with a clang, locking in place somewhere Victoria couldn't see. The light seams became a bright rectangle that burned Victoria's eyes. She hid her face from the glare.

"Had enough of the parlor, have you?" said a voice.

Victoria blinked for several seconds. The dark shape in front of the white light became what it really was—Mr. Alice, rake in his gloved hand, the bare hand reaching toward Victoria with curling white fingers.

It was so strange to see another person after all this time—months had it been?—that Victoria didn't shy away. She let him grab her by the collar and pull her out of wherever she was. As Mr. Alice led her away, Victoria managed to look back over her shoulder.

She saw the empty space of her tiny room, which was really like a cabinet set in a tremendous black wall. She saw the open metal door Mr. Alice had unlocked. The empty cabinet was the only thing in a wall that never seemed to end, stretching from the floor to a ceiling that didn't exist, going on forever from left to right. A forever wall, like the forever hallway. One lonely cabinet.

"The parlor?" Victoria said, as Mr. Alice dragged her out of that room into another one—a smaller room with nothing but a red cushioned bench against the wall.

Mr. Alice didn't answer. Instead, he gestured at the bench and said, "This is the lobby."

After they passed through that room, Mr. Alice shoved Victoria free. She stumbled to stay on her feet. Mr. Alice gestured with his rake.

"No funny business," he said, "or it's back you go."

Back in the parlor? Victoria shuddered but tried to hide it.

"I don't know, it was nice to have a bit of peace and quiet," she said, tossing her curls. That didn't quite work, because her hair was matted and dirty from the bugs, and her voice was a little shaky.

"She said you'd say that," said Mr. Alice. "She's so clever. She's been watching you. She liked you, but then you started getting too nosy, didn't you? And now it's time to learn your lesson. She's so clever."

"Who's she?" said Victoria, although she already knew.

"Mrs. Cavendish, of course." Mr. Alice's tongue lingered on the words, drawing them out into something slimy.

Victoria jerked her chin up. "My parents will be here any minute now, you just wait. They won't let you do anything to me. Father will sue you and take all your money."

Mr. Alice laughed. The sound scratched its way into Victoria's brain and wouldn't let go.

They emerged onto a balcony. It was familiar, with swirling rails made of dark iron and wood. Victoria looked over the edge and saw, far below, the polished wooden floor of the gallery she had walked through the other day. She looked up and saw the ceiling with those strange birds, so close now that she could see how real their feathers looked.

"Strange," she said, reaching up to touch the nearest one.

Mr. Alice snatched her hand away. "I wouldn't. She doesn't like her children deformed, and the birdies get hungry." He chomped perfect white teeth at her. "*Snap*."

Victoria jumped back, although a part of her brain thought of how eager her father would be to discuss teeth-cleaning regimens with Mr. Alice.

"The . . . birdies . . . get hungry?" she said, and as Mr. Alice pushed her toward the stairs, Victoria saw the birds shifting on the ceiling. They ruffled their feathers and blinked beady eyes at her.

Victoria and Mr. Alice walked down five flights of dark, narrow wooden stairs. Victoria went first. Whenever she hesitated, Mr. Alice jabbed her shoulder with the rake's prongs.

"Where are we going?" said Victoria at last. They had reached the bottom, and now Mr. Alice was leading her through the gallery. Victoria looked around as much as Mr. Alice allowed her. Sometimes he got impatient and jabbed her shoulder. Just as the first time Victoria had been there, the balconies and rooms above her shimmered and crawled. Unlike the first time, she heard faint sounds of life—running footsteps, echoing whispers, people calling out to one another.

But these sounds weren't comforting. They felt like nightmare sounds, only this wasn't a nightmare; it was real.

"Just keep walking," said Mr. Alice.

"I'd really like to get some more information."

"Of course you would," a new voice said. "You like figuring things out, don't you, Victoria?"

"Mrs. Cavendish," said Victoria, trying to remain collected despite all the muck covering her. "How nice to see you."

"That's what I like about you, Victoria," said Mrs. Cavendish. She stood in a doorway ahead of them, her hands clasped at her waist. "You may not know when to mind your own business, but you're certainly polite."

Victoria just barely kept from spewing all sorts of decidedly impolite things at Mrs. Cavendish.

"Thank you," she said instead, but Mrs. Cavendish seemed to know what Victoria was really thinking. That smug look on Mrs. Cavendish's face, the kind smile, the pretty dress and hair and eyes—all of it seemed to say, "That's right, Victoria. Keep quiet like you're supposed to."

Mrs. Cavendish thought she had won, at least this round. Victoria imagined a blackboard with tally marks. Mrs. Cavendish already had several; Victoria, none. Her mind reeled in disgust. She simply *must* start doing better.

"Let's walk this way, shall we?" said Mrs. Cavendish. She gestured behind her, into the part of the gallery Victoria hadn't yet seen. "I'd like to give you a tour before lights-out."

Victoria followed Mrs. Cavendish past many closed doors and oil lamps in the walls. As they walked, Victoria noticed that with each passing moment, the lamplight grew dimmer.

"What's lights-out?" said Victoria.

"When all the lights go out, of course."

Mr. Alice, bringing up the rear, laughed.

"It's important for the Home's structure," said Mrs. Cavendish.

The word "structure" had never sounded so sinister before.

"Mrs. Cavendish does her best work at night, she does," said

Mr. Alice, bobbing his head as though he were quite pleased with himself. "With her knives and her strings and her—"

Mrs. Cavendish snapped her head around at him. "That's quite enough, Mr. Alice."

He ducked away to hide his face, staring at the ground.

Victoria froze. *What was that all about?*

"Now, you saw the parlor and the lobby, of course," said Mrs. Cavendish, her voice sweet and soft once more, although she gave Mr. Alice one last glare. He shrank away, cuddling his rake. "That's where I keep new arrivals till I'm ready for them. It's also where I put children who misbehave."

Victoria's mind instinctively latched onto the idea of rules. "What counts as misbehavior?"

Mrs. Cavendish only smiled. They passed into a long room with a long table in the center. At either end of the table sat two grand black chairs that looked like thrones. The chairs along the sides of the table were smaller versions.

"This is the dining room," said Mrs. Cavendish. "We eat meals here. It's important that we eat as a family. Also, I like to watch how those I love enjoy my cooking."

Deciding to ignore the disturbing way Mrs. Cavendish said "love," Victoria made quick work of counting the dining room chairs. Twenty-eight, twenty-nine . . .

"I wouldn't bother counting the chairs, Victoria," said

Mrs. Cavendish. "It all depends on how many we have at each meal. Children . . . come and go."

All the same, Victoria held the number thirty (not counting the two big chairs) in her head. Perhaps it would be useful later. *But useful for what?* Victoria asked herself. She did not have an answer.

"This is the library, the Classroom of Manners, the Classroom of Beauty, the hanger," Mrs. Cavendish said, leading Victoria through room after room after room, Mr. Alice a lean, hulking shadow behind them. Even with all her memorization skills, Victoria had trouble keeping track of everything.

"What's the hanger?" she said.

"Oh, you'll find out soon enough," said Mr. Alice, laughing again.

Mrs. Cavendish started walking faster, glancing around her into the shadows, and Victoria had to jog to keep up. Every time they passed a room, the lighting faded a bit more. When they came back to the gallery, the walls, polished floors, and balconies overhead were practically roiling. Victoria rubbed her eyes to make sure she wasn't seeing things.

"The gardens," said Mrs. Cavendish. Her eyes flicked here and there, obviously looking for something, and she kept licking her lips. A piece of her hair fell out of place, and she pulled it back around her ear, irritably. Victoria didn't know what to make of that. Perhaps it was nothing.

They came out onto a flat terrace at the rear of the Home. Tall lamps lit the terrace and also the gardens, which stretched away beneath the trees in swirling aisles and patches like a grand maze. Near the back of the gardens were two small cottages, lit up with soft amber light.

On the left side of the gardens loomed a sprawling, crooked tree.

In fact, everything seemed crooked, like the reflections in funhouse mirrors. And everything . . . *moved.*

Victoria rubbed her eyes again, trying to wake up.

"I'm afraid a more thorough tour will have to wait till morning," said Mrs. Cavendish, sliding her fingers back and forth along the terrace railing. In the growing darkness, she seemed much twitchier than she ever had before. "But they're my pride and joy, you see, these gardens."

"That patch looks kind of messy," said Victoria, pointing to the sprawling tree. It was much bigger than the others, fat and deformed, and dark.

Mrs. Cavendish's hands tightened on the railing. She looked at Victoria with a sweet smile and quiet eyes.

"It's a stubborn bit of the gardens," said Mrs. Cavendish. She hooked her arm through Mr. Alice's and petted his hand.

"Mr. Alice works hard at it, though. Don't you, my darling?"

Mr. Alice smiled, not taking his eyes from Victoria. "I'm an excellent gardener."

"He's been with me for a long time," Mrs. Cavendish murmured, stroking his arm. "After all, it's such a big house to keep in order." She smoothed a lock of Mr. Alice's dark hair back into place behind his ear. "He's my special project, Mr. Alice. My special helper."

"I'm an excellent gardener," repeated Mr. Alice. His eyes never stopped moving—*like a roach's eyes*, Victoria realized, taking a tiny step back. For a horrible instant, the image of Mrs. Cavendish and Mr. Alice reminded her of herself and Lawrence. "Special project," Mrs. Cavendish called Mr. Alice. And Lawrence was Victoria's project. Or at least, he had once been.

The comparison made her stomach turn. She was no Mrs. Cavendish. . . .

Was she?

But even Mrs. Cavendish had said it: *You're like me, Victoria*. And Mr. Tibbalt hadn't said it aloud, but he had seemed to think it too.

From behind them, within the Home, something groaned. Victoria jumped. Mr. Alice did, too, muttering to himself, his eyes darting about so fast they seemed likely to pop out.

Mrs. Cavendish, however, stared coldly at the Home, scanning the roof.

"What was that noise?" asked Victoria, her heart pounding.

Mrs. Cavendish's head snapped around to her. "I don't believe I gave you permission to ask questions, Victoria," she said. Then she smiled and took Victoria in hand to reenter the Home. "We've got to get you to bed. Cleaned, scrubbed, dressed, and in bed. All that nasty dirt."

"But I—"

"Please be quiet, Victoria," said Mrs. Cavendish, her hand pinching Victoria's. "It's almost lights-out."

The lamps in the gallery were now so dim that the floor was a shimmering black ocean and the walls of balconies were cresting waves. Every now and then, Victoria caught swooping motions overhead out of the corner of her eye.

"Don't mind the birdies," said Mr. Alice, grinning. "They won't snatch you when you're with us."

"But you should remember, Victoria, that after lights-out, we mustn't wander, hmm?" said Mrs. Cavendish. "Sometimes . . . the Home has a mind of its own."

Victoria wondered if this was really the case, or if Mrs. Cavendish was the Home's mind, and why Mrs. Cavendish's voice had sounded so strange just then. She didn't have a lot of time to think about this, though, because soon they were in a low hallway of doors with a mirror at each end like in a hotel.

"Get cleaned and dressed," said Mrs. Cavendish, pushing Victoria into a bathroom with a tiny tub and sink. Little patters of feet following Victoria made her turn to see two tiny squashed people with fat bellies and toothpick arms.

She gasped and jumped away. The people were horribly ugly and reminded her of those dogs with squashed, wrinkled faces. Their backs bent weirdly. They had knobs here and there instead of hands or feet, and patches missing from their skin. They had only one wide, watery yellow eye each, and neither of them spoke. They just made little grunting noises as they moved, like it hurt them.

"Who are you?" Victoria said.

"They're my gofers," said Mrs. Cavendish, watching from the doorway. "It's such a task, taking care of so many children. Sometimes Mr. Alice and I need assistance." Her voice turned hard. "Gofers aren't good for much else."

The gofers put a towel and a set of pressed clothes beside the tub. They grunted at Victoria, stared up at her from beneath the sagging skin over their eyes, and hobbled out to hide behind Mrs. Cavendish's skirt. Mr. Alice hit the gofers with his rake, and they scrambled away.

"Why did you hit them?" said Victoria. Even though the gofers were disgusting, something about their ugly, wide-eyed

They had knobs here and there instead of hands or feet, and patches missing from their skin.

faces reminded Victoria of how she felt at the moment—small, and confused.

"Hurry up" was all Mrs. Cavendish said before she shut the door.

Victoria did not want to bathe in this tub. She did not want to take off her clothes or put on the new ones, but disobeying Mrs. Cavendish was surely a horrible idea.

"I've got to be careful," Victoria whispered. *For now*, she added silently. She had only just arrived, after all. It was better to do exactly as Mrs. Cavendish instructed, pay close attention to everything that happened, and figure out what, exactly, was going on here.

The more Victoria thought about this, the better she felt. It was easy to settle into her lifelong habits of being good, paying attention, and staying silent. This method had never failed her before, and it wouldn't fail her now.

She bathed in the hottest water she could stand because even the soap felt scratchy. She dressed in the clothes the gofers had left—a collared pajama shirt and matching pajama pants.

"Oh, Victoria?" said Mrs. Cavendish from outside. "The lights are almost out."

Mrs. Cavendish's voice crawled with impatience. Victoria opened the door and smiled politely.

"Sorry," she said. "I just wanted to make extra sure I got all the dirt off."

Mrs. Cavendish wasn't fooled, Victoria could tell. But Mrs. Cavendish pretended. She smiled and dragged her warm fingers through Victoria's hair. Victoria watched Mrs. Cavendish's face carefully, and Mrs. Cavendish watched Victoria's face just as carefully.

"Much better," said Mrs. Cavendish. "You look like a proper girl now, fresh and ready."

Victoria stepped out into the hallway and froze.

"But I thought . . . ," she began.

Mrs. Cavendish folded Victoria's hand into hers. Her grip pinched Victoria's skin. "Yes? You thought what?"

The hallway from before had vanished. In its place was a narrow staircase Victoria had never seen before, wedged between polished stone walls. A lamp at the top was the only light. The ceiling flickered in waves, and then silence fell.

"You'll find an empty bed," said Mrs. Cavendish. "Go to sleep. Breakfast is at eight o'clock. I'll expect you to be punctual."

"But—"

Mrs. Cavendish grabbed Victoria's face with her free hand. At first it hurt, but then Mrs. Cavendish's fingers loosened and stroked Victoria's cheek. Victoria stared at her, refusing to blink; this close, she could see the tight gray color of Mrs. Cavendish's skin, and beneath the pretty blue of her eyes, an angry red. Victoria thought, *She's exhausted.* Last time she had seen Mrs. Cavendish, she had looked bright and happy, but now her hair was not quite as shiny, her skin not quite as smooth. Perhaps she was simply having a bad day.

It was like Mrs. Cavendish could hear her thoughts. "Go to bed," she said, shoving Victoria toward the stairs.

Turning her back on Mrs. Cavendish—and on Mr. Alice, who was picking bits of filth off his rake—was the last thing Victoria wanted to do. But the light at the top of the stairs was almost out, and in the growing darkness, Mrs. Cavendish's image twitched with shadows.

Victoria hurried up the stairs. At the top, she put her hand on the doorknob and turned back.

"Pleasant dreams, Victoria," said Mrs. Cavendish from the dark. The only things Victoria could see were the glinting prongs of Mr. Alice's rake and the shine of four watching eyes.

Victoria turned the knob and cracked open the door.

The light went out.

10

BEHIND VICTORIA, IN THE DARKNESS, THE ENTIRE Home stretched and sighed. The ground felt suddenly wet and shifty. Grunts and wing beats whispered at Victoria's heels.

She hurried past the door and closed it.

Past the door lay a long, high-ceilinged room lined with clean white cots, a more conventional setup than Victoria had expected. An empty fireplace stood at the far end. Each cot also had a tiny lamp overhead, but they of course were not lit.

"Lights-out," Victoria whispered.

The only reason Victoria could see anything was that moonlight was coming through the only window in the room, high in the corner near the ceiling, far too high to ever reach.

The cold stone hurt Victoria's feet, so she hurried to each cot, checking for the empty one. She saw girl after girl after girl lying in the cots, all in the same pajamas as her own. Some of their faces were very thin, and some were very pretty. A girl in the corner lay completely unmoving and awake with her eyes wide open. She didn't move even when Victoria waved her hand over the girl's face.

"Hello?" Victoria whispered.

The girl didn't move. Victoria turned away with a shiver, folding her arms over her chest.

Victoria tried to count the number of cots but kept losing her numbers. She blinked a few times and tried again, but her brain kept turning to mush. Finally she gave up and found an empty cot near the fireplace. A dark nameplate on the wall above it said VICTORIA. She climbed into the soft white sheets and realized that she had lost her book bag somewhere. Alone and cold, she lay down and tried to sleep. In her dreams, her parents held her and said, "We love you, Victoria," over and over. It felt wonderful and warm and safe. But then they said, "Time for bed, Victoria," and it wasn't them anymore; it was Mrs. Cavendish, and she shoved Victoria into a box and locked it.

Two hands grabbed Victoria's arm and shook her awake.

"You're the new girl, right?" said a voice.

Victoria awoke with a start and sat straight up. She was not in a box. She was in her cot, in the girls' dorm, in the Home.

Sunlight from the window in the high corner made a white square in the middle of the room. Several girls were lining up at the door. Some of the girls were Victoria's age, some younger, and some a little older. Some of them seemed to be avoiding Victoria, looking anywhere but at her. Some of them whispered and glanced at her with mean or frightened faces. Some seemed sad for her. A couple of them tried to smile.

"You—what?" Victoria said to the girl who had shaken her awake, trying to notice everything in case she needed it later. A dozen girls. Twenty girls? She couldn't be sure.

The girl repeated, "You're the new girl," but then she saw the nameplate on the wall. Her jaw dropped. She moved closer. "Victoria?"

Victoria narrowed her eyes at this girl. "Yes?"

"It's me," the girl said. She smiled, and it was too bright, too perfect. "Don't you recognize me? It's Jacqueline."

"Jacqueline Hennessey?" said Victoria. She tried not to show how horrified she was, but something was definitely wrong here. The girl in front of her was not strange, freakish Jacqueline, with her ratty hair, hunched shoulders, and splotchy face. This girl had glossy red waves to rival Jill Hennessey's, and even her pajamas seemed pretty.

"Don't be ridiculous," said Victoria. She put on a version of the dazzle she reserved for when Lawrence did something exceptionally stupid. "I've gone to school with Jacqueline my whole life. You're not her."

"Oh, I promise I am," said Jacqueline, flashing a beautiful smile that Victoria knew would send her father into jealous fits.

Her father.

She had worked so hard to impress him, to be the best so he could show her off to everyone, to make him smile (which didn't happen very often). And now she was here, because he had forgotten her. They both had forgotten her. Or worse, they had let her go.

A twinge of loss and anger in her chest pricked tears from Victoria's eyes.

"No, don't cry," said Jacqueline quietly, in a more normal, less cheerful voice. "Crying singles you out. You've got to stay calm, or some of the others will make things bad for you. Really bad. And then there's the Home." Jacqueline looked around at the sunshine-coated walls. "If you knew some of the things that've happened . . ."

"*What* is going on?" Victoria said. "What do you mean,

bad things? And who are all these girls? And where is everyone going? And—"

"Shh. Later. Right now, it's breakfast time. Come on, we can't be late."

Someone started opening the door with a metal *click-click-click.*

"Hurry," said Jacqueline, yanking Victoria forward. They reached the end of the line just as the door opened to reveal a gray-and-brown gofer with a droopy mouth and one leaking yellow eye. The girls began to file out, and Victoria clenched her teeth together to stay calm. *Just pretend this is how all your days start,* Victoria told herself.

As she and Jacqueline crossed the threshold, the gofer began shutting the door, but before it could, a voice shrieked from near the fireplace, "Wait! Wait, I'm coming!"

"Oh, no," whispered Jacqueline, tightening her grip on Victoria's hand. "Gabby."

Running toward them, tripping over the ends of her sheets, was the girl Victoria had seen the night before, the girl who had lain wide awake instead of sleeping.

"What's happening?" said Victoria.

"Just watch," Jacqueline said. Her eyes hardened as she watched Gabby run for the door. "Pay attention, or it could be you."

The gofer shut and locked the door before Gabby could reach it, even though she screamed for it to wait. Victoria heard Gabby's sobs as she pounded on the door from the other side. All the girls on the stairs watched, some of them smirking, some of them crying.

"Let me out, let me out," Gabby screamed, but the gofer hobbled down the stairs, grunting. The girls followed it out as Gabby's cries grew louder. Her pounding fists became nails scratching the door. Her sobs and screams became higher and louder. Then silence fell.

"What happened to her?" Victoria dared to whisper as she followed Jacqueline into a new hallway, a stone one with paintings of meadows on the walls.

"She was late," said Jacqueline. "When you're late, you get locked in and left behind, to teach you a lesson. And you're there alone till we come back for lights-out."

"That doesn't sound so—"

"You don't want to be alone in the Home. Not in the dorm, not anywhere." Jacqueline stared straight ahead at the backs of the girls in front of them. "Trust me."

In the dining room, gofers served breakfast—egg casserole with big chunks of meat in it. The girls lined up at one door, and Victoria peered past people's heads to see a line of boys waiting at another door across the room.

Mrs. Cavendish sat down, followed by Mr. Alice, both looking fresher than they had the night before. The girls filed in and took their seats on one side of the table. Then the boys came in, and Victoria saw him—a boy with a silver streak in his dark hair.

Her heart and stomach did a strange joint somersault.

Lawrence.

Before she could even think if it was a good idea, and before she even took a bite of her casserole, even though she was starving, she shoved her chair back and ran around the dining room to throw her arms around him. She laughed into his collar. She didn't even stop to think how stupid she looked.

"Lawrence," she cried. Only when Lawrence pried her loose, his eyes wide, whispering, "No, no, no," did Victoria pause long enough to see everyone staring at her, including a sharp-eyed Mrs. Cavendish.

Victoria had just made her first mistake.

11

"SUCH BEHAVIOR, VICTORIA," SAID MRS. CAVENDISH, the poisonous, honeyed words dripping from her mouth. She held her face very tight and still. Her long, pretty fingers drummed the polished tabletop.

Victoria backed away from Lawrence and forced her face blank, trying to ignore Jacqueline's little head shake of *no*. All right, so she maybe shouldn't have yelled quite so loudly, and maybe Mrs. Cavendish was picky about people running indoors, but that didn't explain why everyone was looking at her with such horrified expressions.

Lawrence averted his eyes and shoved his hands in his pajama pockets.

"I'm sorry, but I only—" Victoria started to say.

"Don't be sorry, Victoria, just be quiet," said Mrs. Cavendish. "Pockets, Lawrence."

Lawrence slid his hands quickly to his sides.

"Sit down, everyone. Eat your breakfast."

The children obeyed, pulling out their small, dark chairs, unfolding their napkins, and picking up their cutlery. Victoria noticed that some of them looked green in the face as they dug into their plates of steaming eggs and meat. Others looked grim and determined.

Victoria and Lawrence made to join them, but Mrs. Cavendish said, "Oh. Not you two."

They froze in place.

Mrs. Cavendish rose from her seat. She glided toward them and clucked her tongue. She circled them slowly, smoothly. Victoria felt like a piece of meat being inspected for quality. She caught a whiff of Mrs. Cavendish's light, floral perfume. Mixed with the eggs and meat, it was rather stinky.

"You must understand that there are rules here, Victoria," said Mrs. Cavendish. She stopped in front of them, and even in her fright, Victoria couldn't help looking over Mrs. Cavendish approvingly. She looked much better today than she had the night before—glossy hair, clear skin, impeccable (if somewhat old-fashioned) clothing. Mrs. Wright would call it *vintage* and ask Mrs. Cavendish for shopping tips.

Victoria's throat tightened as she thought of her mother, but Mrs. Cavendish kept on.

". . . of course, I understand that you're new to our Home, Victoria. It can be difficult to adjust."

Some of the other children had stopped eating to watch. Mrs. Cavendish noticed and slid her eyes sideways.

Mr. Alice whispered, "Eat, eat," and the children resumed, some of them with such vigor that they smeared egg on their faces.

Victoria kept trying to catch Lawrence's gaze, but he wouldn't look at her. He stared at the floor, his gray eyes sharper than they had ever been, and the skin of his cheeks saggy, like he'd had something sucked out of him.

"Mrs. Cavendish," Victoria began, putting on her most effective polite voice, the one she used on her professors, her parents, everyone. It was the voice that bent people to her will. They couldn't help themselves because the voice had a curve to it that said, "Oh of *course* you know *best*, *forgive* me for asking, but *please*, if you wouldn't *mind* . . ."

"I'm really, really sorry for—" Victoria said, but Mrs. Cavendish put two warm fingers over Victoria's mouth.

"Shh, shh, shh," whispered Mrs. Cavendish. "Listen to me carefully, Victoria."

Victoria couldn't decide whether to be offended or scared out of her mind, but she did not look away and forced herself not to blink.

Mrs. Cavendish knelt and dragged her fingers from Victoria's lips to her hair, twirling her curls. She examined Victoria's face.

"I've decided to go easy on you this once," said Mrs. Cavendish. Her voice was so soft and sweet that Victoria suddenly wanted to fall asleep in her arms. "You're new, and I can be lenient. But only to a point. We don't misbehave around here, do you understand?"

Victoria's cheeks flushed at being treated like such a child. "But it's not like I meant—"

Something sharp dug into Victoria's skin—Mrs. Cavendish's polished fingernails, cradling her neck.

"Now, now," said Mrs. Cavendish.

Mr. Alice chuckled and wiped his mouth with his napkin to clean away meat flecks.

"We don't run indoors. We don't disobey our elders. We don't speak too loudly. Sometimes we don't even speak at all, hmm? Sometimes children shouldn't say a word."

With an elegant flourish of her free hand, Mrs. Cavendish made a zipping motion over Victoria's mouth. Those polished fingernails scraped so close that Victoria thought

Mrs. Cavendish might rip her face open.

"Do you understand?"

"Yes, Mrs. Cavendish," said Victoria. She sounded braver than she felt.

"Unfortunately, I can't let misbehavior go unpunished. Someone has to face consequences."

Mrs. Cavendish turned to Lawrence and pet his drooping cheek. He didn't move, but his eyes flinched.

"It's too bad that you have to suffer for your friend's poor judgment, isn't it, Lawrence?" Mrs. Cavendish smoothed Lawrence's hair and slowly gathered up his collar in her hand. "It's not your fault Victoria behaved so poorly, but you want to help me teach the others, don't you?"

Rising to her feet, Mrs. Cavendish came to horrid life. "Breakfast is over," she said, and everyone dropped their forks and knives onto their plates, and as she yanked Lawrence out of the room, everyone else followed, like this was routine. The gofers began cleaning up, shoving whatever they could into their misshapen mouths. Some of them fought over the biggest meat scraps, slobbering over one another's scabbed, knobby hands.

"Quickly," said Mr. Alice, his gloved hand on Victoria's neck, pushing her forward.

"But I haven't eaten yet," said Victoria.

"Oh, you'll get your chance."

Mrs. Cavendish led them down a hallway. The columns on either side were snakes with long, sculpted hands that clutched the carpet. As she stumbled alongside Mr. Alice, Victoria felt those sculpted fingertips inching toward her feet.

"This is yet another example of what we've talked about, children," Mrs. Cavendish called out. "Rule fifteen. Do you remember?"

Some of the children recited brightly, others choked back tears:

Be careful of what friends you pick.
You'll catch their faults, they'll make you sick.

"This morning, Victoria demonstrated to us some of her faults," said Mrs. Cavendish. She opened a door in the wall and pulled Lawrence down a staircase with pictures of swings and trees and ship planks hanging from banister to ceiling. "Can anyone tell me what they are?"

"Being impetuous," said one of the boys.

"Yelling indoors," said one of the girls. Another said, "Speaking out of turn."

"Associating with *degenerates*," said the tallest boy. They all came out at the bottom of the stairs into a low, deep room of damp stone. The tallest boy kept his hands folded at his waist and a cruel smile on his face. His sharp face also looked like something had been sucked out of him, but instead of looking tired and gray-faced about it, like Lawrence, this boy had glittering eyes and a hard smile. *I know him*, Victoria realized, startled. *He goes to the Academy*. Remembering him was like trying to remember a dream.

Some of the children snickered in Lawrence's direction. The word "degenerates" lingered in the air.

"Very good, Peter," Mrs. Cavendish said to the tallest boy. She smoothed his collar lovingly. "Maybe—just maybe—it's near time for you to leave us."

Some of the children huddled as close together as they dared. Victoria couldn't tell if it was because they were afraid or excited. Peter kept his eyes on Mrs. Cavendish, smiling. He didn't look quite right; the smile was too automatic. Victoria remembered how Mr. Tibbalt had talked about when his little brother, Teddy, came home: "He was someone else, like someone had broken the old Teddy and built a new one."

That was exactly it. Although Victoria's memories of this boy Peter—yes, she had to have known him; the longer she stared at him, the more flashes of Academy memories came back to her—were a bit fuzzy, she could tell he looked . . .

different. He looked not-quite-right, false, *new*. The tight smile on his face stretched his cheeks like rubber.

"But, first things first. Lawrence, do you have anything you'd like to say to Victoria before we begin?" said Mrs. Cavendish, curling one finger around Lawrence's jaw. "It's her fault, after all, that you're about to spend a day in the hanger."

"The hanger?" Victoria opened her mouth to say, but Jacqueline shook her head again.

Lawrence said nothing, his skunk's hair falling over his forehead. For once, it didn't annoy Victoria.

Mrs. Cavendish slapped Lawrence's face. Victoria felt like *she* had been slapped. She couldn't contain her gasp. Fury turned her skin hot, but she clenched her fists till her nails pricked her palms. Speaking up might make things even worse.

"Do you have anything you'd like to say?" Mrs. Cavendish said again.

"No, Mrs. Cavendish," said Lawrence, and that was the most terrible part, because there was very little Lawrence in his voice. All his Lawrence-ness—his mischievousness, his laziness, the things that made him annoying (like his humming and singing and waving his fingers in the air like he was playing an invisible piano), the things that made people avoid him in the Academy hallways and made Victoria force her friendship upon him for his *own* sake—all that was gone.

"Hang him," said Mrs. Cavendish. She turned, and the other children started following her out.

Victoria stared at Lawrence in horror.

A tiny lightbulb switched on, dingy and buzzing. It illuminated a device of thin, unfriendly straps, attached to the ceiling and hanging low to the floor.

"Hang him?" Victoria whispered. Her skin froze.

The *hanger*.

"No . . ."

Someone grabbed Victoria's wrist—Jacqueline, pulling her out.

"No!" Victoria shouted, digging her heels into the cold, hard ground. She reached out toward Lawrence and hit Jacqueline and grabbed for the wall, but Jacqueline wouldn't stop dragging her away. Just before a gofer slammed the hanger door shut, Victoria caught sight of Mr. Alice strapping Lawrence into the hanger. The walls surrounding him began to *move*.

The door slammed shut, separating them.

Lawrence was gone. Again.

"WHAT JUST HAPPENED?" SAID VICTORIA AS THE gofers herded them upstairs. Speaking out loud made it harder not to cry. She stamped her bare feet on every step to distract herself. Her cheeks burned. She wanted to curl up and hide with Lawrence, somewhere far away from that awful, dirty room. "What's the hanger? What are they doing to him?"

"The hanger's for punishing degenerates," Jacqueline said, hiding her mouth behind her shining red hair. "It's for when she wants to make an example of someone. I'll bet she's hanging him because she doesn't want anyone to like you or trust you. The hanger's not as bad as the parlor, though. You remember that?"

Victoria nodded. That cramped, dark room, the *drip-drip* of water, the feeling of not knowing who or where or *when* she was—oh, she remembered the parlor, all right.

"The parlor's for when you do something really bad, something so bad that she just wants you out of the way," said Jacqueline. "Most people who go to the parlor don't come back. Gabby did. She was in there for a week straight. She's never been the same. She doesn't sleep, she barely talks. Mrs. Cavendish just lets her get left behind everywhere, lets her get scared and go crazy. It's to keep the rest of us in line, I think."

"But will he be okay?" Victoria said, not caring about Gabby or parlors or anything but Lawrence. Well, and herself. And maybe Jacqueline, a little. Maybe, for now.

"I don't know," said Jacqueline. She wouldn't meet Victoria's eyes. "We'll just have to wait and see."

Life at the Home was like life in other places, but not *quite*. For one thing, they went to school, which was normal. But on the second floor, classrooms lined the hallways in a grand circle. Each classroom had one wall of windows that faced the main gallery, and two walls of dark murals and books, and one wall that consisted entirely of a giant picture window facing a dark space, like in Mrs. Cavendish's parlor. Along the windows overlooking the gallery hung rows upon rows of those paper heads Victoria had seen before.

Beneath each head hung a sign, and each sign showed a different word. FEAR. JOY. ANGER. DESPAIR. Each head wore the matching expression. The JOY head was little more than a giant, toothy smile. The FEAR head's skin hung in long folds like pulled taffy. Victoria couldn't look away from that one's sagging eyes and screaming mouth. The longer she looked, the more it felt like only her and this FEAR head, all alone in the dark, quiet Home.

"We have classes every day," said Jacqueline through her teeth, careful to speak only a few words at a time. "They're always different. Very confusing. No patterns. She teaches us things. How to be good. How to be better."

A pretty iron nameplate topped each classroom doorway. The first one they entered said CLASSROOM OF MANNERS. They took their seats in desks much more old-fashioned and much less ergonomic than the modern desks at the Academy.

"See?" whispered Jacqueline.

Victoria looked out the picture window—and down into the hanger.

There, in something that looked sort of like a sad playground swing and sort of like monstrous marionette strings, hung Lawrence. He was a fly wrapped up in spider silk.

All around him, the floor and walls writhed.

For the first time in her life, Victoria thought she understood the word "heartbreak."

"Is he—?" Victoria whispered.

"No," said Jacqueline, "he's not dead."

Victoria gulped. "What will happen to him?"

"He'll just be—well, people are always different after a hanging."

"Enjoying the view?"

Victoria and Jacqueline whirled to face Mrs. Cavendish, who seemed somehow taller, sharper, and hungrier than before Lawrence's hanging. Victoria clenched her fists.

"You—you—" she said, but she couldn't think of words that wouldn't get anyone in trouble.

Mrs. Cavendish smiled. "You learn quickly. Sit down."

Manners class was about manners, and the books in each desk were *Fitzgerald Flannagan's Guide for Youngsters*, 616 pages of tiny text about how to be good boys and girls.

"Open to page one," said Mrs. Cavendish. She flipped a switch at the front of the room, and a projector whirred to life. Page one appeared on a screen at the front of the room, on all the walls, shimmering across the picture window, and across everyone's skin in wiggly, lit-up tattoos.

The children began to read the first paragraph in unison. It was about how important this book was, and how it would serve as a guide for young people who wanted to be respectable, and how Fitzgerald Flannagan had studied this thing and that thing, which showed just how much he knew about manners.

Victoria opened her own copy and stared at the first page, hardly able to breathe. She had never before been so angry. The hot rushes through her chest and up her arms shook her whole body.

It's fortunate, she thought, *that I'm so disciplined.* One could not lose one's cool and be the best year after year.

She started to read along with the others, even though doing something so stupid while Lawrence dangled in the hanger made each word hurt:

> Children, whether they are boys or girls, educated or ignorant, must be as silent as possible as much as possible. Children are neither clever nor experienced enough to judge for themselves what is and what is not to be said. They must therefore and at all times defer to the wisdom of their elders. They must never speak out of turn. They must never be contrary. They must be extraordinary without being out of the ordinary.

At each paragraph break, the children stopped. The first time, Victoria watched in astonishment as they opened notebooks from their desks and began scribbling the first paragraph as quickly as they could onto lined paper. They wrote so fast and finished so close together that it seemed synchronized, some kind of frantic, scribbly dance.

Then they started reading again, paragraph two. Read, write, read, write. After the first read-write, Victoria joined in, too. She didn't want to; it was an outrageous waste of time. But she couldn't ignore Mrs. Cavendish, who was circling the room with leisurely clicks of her fine heels. She held a thin black switch, its leather braid coming apart at the end. The switch gleamed like a serpent in her hands, and whenever someone stumbled over words, or whenever someone's handwriting got messy, Mrs. Cavendish would flick the switch. It whistled through the air, leaving behind little red marks on sweating cheeks and shaking hands.

After an hour of this, Mrs. Cavendish flipped the lights off, and everyone hurried to the door and down the hall for the next class, and so on, all day long, to and from classes about how to dress just so and talk just so, what was appropriate to learn in school and what was not, and what they should think about science and presidents and art and yard trimming, and everything was repetitive and pointless. Worst of all, Victoria felt, was the indignity of being herded around in her pajamas.

"Don't we ever get real clothes?" she whispered to Jacqueline at lunch.

"No. It's to make us like prisoners, I think," said Jacqueline over a mouthful of cold meat slices and toast. Mrs. Cavendish and Mr. Alice weren't there. They never ate lunch, according to Jacqueline. No one knew where they went at lunchtime. But gofers slunk around in the shadows, and even if Victoria had wanted to try anything risky—like escape or help Lawrence, even though she didn't know how to do either of those things—she thought the Home might tell on her. Each of its lamps and curving rafters seemed like an eye, or an arm ready to snatch.

"To make us like prisoners?" Victoria repeated.

The boy across the table nodded. "It's to keep us feeling like animals, like we're nobodies."

"Well, she'll have to try a bit harder than that," said Victoria. "I don't know about the rest of you, but I'm definitely not a nobody."

"Just because you're Miss Goody-Goody doesn't make you safe," said the boy. "I'm Harold, by the way."

Victoria shook his hand. Some of the other children

glared at them and whispered behind their sandwiches.

"I don't know, though," Harold said. "Being such a rude snob all the time might actually help you here. Might keep you from letting things get to you, you know."

Victoria recognized him at last. "Harold? Hyena Harold?"

"Yeah," Harold said. He laughed, but it sounded weird. "That's me."

Taking a bite of her sandwich, Victoria thought about this. She could only vaguely remember Hyena Harold. Harold . . . Norbett? Noble? Something like that. He had been a troublemaker at the Academy, a class clown. He had loved pranks and tricks, and when he laughed, he would shriek and howl, winding up all the students into a frenzy, so he was Hyena Harold.

But that had been years ago. In another city, maybe. Or was it a dream? Were these memories even memories, or was she imagining things?

Victoria narrowed her eyes at Harold.

"Can't remember me all the way, huh?" he said. "It's okay. That's part of it. You come here and people forget about you. People don't like to notice. They turn the other way."

"*She* turns them the other way," said Jacqueline. "Pushes them around, confuses them. But they let her. It's easier than fighting."

"How long have you *been* here?" said Victoria. She put down her sandwich. The meat was rubbery and rank with a strange spice.

"Me? Oh, a few months," said Harold. He squinted at the ceiling. "I think."

"I've been here eight weeks," said Jacqueline.

A tiny girl with two black braids squeaked, "For me it's been five days."

"How long will she keep you here?" said Victoria.

"Depends on how well we do what she wants," said Harold.

The girl with black braids choked on her food. Jacqueline thumped her shoulder and said, "Pull it together, Caroline."

"So we don't really know how long anyone's going to stay," Harold continued.

"But we *do* know," said Jacqueline, leaning closer, "that nobody stays past their thirteenth birthday."

The children nearest them nodded solemnly as they ate.

"Mine's next week, you know," said Harold, grinning. "I'll be out soon."

"What happens on your thirteenth birthday?" said Victoria.

"Either you get out before then or . . . she takes you," said Harold.

"Everyone?" said Caroline tearfully.

"Everyone," said Jacqueline.

"But where does she take you?" said Victoria. "What does she do with you?"

"Nobody really knows," said Jacqueline.

"I wouldn't think about it, if I were you," said Harold through a mouthful of meat and toast. "Don't worry, though. As long as you do what she says, you'll get out fine."

Victoria slammed down her lunch without taking a bite. "But Mr. Tibbalt told me—"

A cold breeze hissed up the table, like Victoria had felt at the Academy. She glanced around, but Mrs. Cavendish was nowhere to be found.

"He told me," she continued, lowering her voice, "that his brother got taken here, and when he came back, he was really different. He wasn't himself."

"It happens," said Harold, licking his fingers. It was only then that Victoria noticed how false everything about Harold appeared, from the movements of his eyebrows to the way he chewed his food. His skin was waxen. Like that boy Peter, Harold seemed new and different from what he should have been, and false, like a doll or a toy.

"Best thing you can do is try to get along with her and keep quiet, and then you can go home." Harold wiped his mouth. His eyes shone a little too brightly. When he smiled at Victoria, it stretched his face into an ugly shape. "Easy as pie. Oh, I hope she makes her pies tonight. They're the best."

That night, Victoria lay on her cot after lights-out, staring at the ceiling. She would have liked to go to sleep, but she couldn't erase Harold's fake, grinning face from her vision.

Nobody stays past their thirteenth birthday.

Victoria's birthday was in August. That was easy enough. There was a lot of time between then and now. And surely her parents would start looking for her soon, no matter what Mr. Tibbalt or Harold said. They were Wrights. They wouldn't fall for Mrs. Cavendish's tricks for long.

But Lawrence's birthday was November 1. Two weeks away.

She remembered this because his were the only birthday parties she had ever gone to—the two of them, Mr. and Mrs. Prewitt, and sometimes Mr. and Mrs. Wright all in party hats (Victoria hated party hats; they messed up her curls). Once at the Prewitts' dining room table, once at a table at the city park (which had offended Victoria's sense of hygiene), once at a fancy Uptown bistro. Victoria would tell Lawrence that he wasn't blowing out his candles correctly and then tell him *how* to blow his candles out, and Lawrence would joke about all the fancy gifts he didn't like and ask if his parents would ever get him music like he asked. The parties were really quite sober affairs.

Only now did Victoria realize how much she had enjoyed herself.

Victoria's fists clenched in her blankets. *How dare Mrs.*

Cavendish take him so near his birthday, she thought. *He doesn't have a chance.*

But then she remembered how small and shriveled and beaten Lawrence had looked when Mr. Alice took him out of the hanger after supper. Mrs. Cavendish made everyone watch. There were red marks on Lawrence's wrists and ankles where the straps had bound him. His head hung low, like his neck had gone rubbery. Mr. Alice had had to half drag him by his collar.

Maybe Lawrence had more of a chance than she thought. Maybe he was already on his way to being changed.

Victoria got out of bed, ignoring the quiet sobs she could hear from various cots—and the utter silence from Gabby's cot—and tapped on Jacqueline's shoulder.

"Too scared to sleep?" said Jacqueline.

"I need to talk to Lawrence," said Victoria. "How can I do that?"

Jacqueline sat up. "You can't. He's in the boys' dorm."

"And how do I get there?"

Jacqueline stared in horror. "You can't walk around after lights-out, remember? It's not safe."

"But is the door locked?"

"Well, of course it is." Jacqueline paused. "People have tried, you know. To sneak around before bed. They slipped out past the gofers when they shut us in for the night and ran down the hall. But then it was lights-out, and they never came back."

Victoria ignored the quiver of fear in her throat. "There has to be a way. I won't just sit here like a dog or something, all tied up. I need to talk to Lawrence."

"But there's no way to—"

"Of course there is." Victoria started at the corner nearest her and started working her way around the room, patting the walls. "I always find ways to."

Jacqueline followed. "People are watching, Victoria."

And they were; as she crept close to the walls, kicking around in the shadows and peeking behind furniture, Victoria felt the eyes of the other girls upon her. Some were sleepy and some were sharp and hard, and some of them whispered things to each other. Victoria was glad she could not hear what they said.

"I don't care, let them look," she said. "There has to be another way out, and I'll find it."

"But there *isn't*. Let's go back to bed, Victoria."

At the door, Victoria jiggled the doorknob and hinges. She shoved hard against it. She poked her fingers beneath the door, into the hallway beyond.

Something rustled past her fingertips, stinging them.

She yanked her hand back, glaring at the red marks on her skin.

"Victoria, *please*," Jacqueline whispered. "I don't like this."

Victoria scoffed. *No wonder Jacqueline isn't top of the class*, she thought. *She whines too much.* She turned and looked back down the aisle of beds, trying to ignore the other girls' stares. At the bottom of the opposite wall stood a tiny black spot.

The fireplace.

"I wonder," said Victoria, and she headed for it with her chin in the air. All these girls with their staring and whispering and hiding in bedcovers were annoying her. What did they care what she did? If she had the time, she would dazzle every last one of them under their beds.

The fireplace was small, and when Victoria knelt before it, her hands scraped against ash and grubby bits, like old food or crumbly fingernails. Trying not to think about how disgusting that was, Victoria gritted her teeth, crawled a few inches forward, and waved her hand around in the dark. It was silly, it was stupid, but she had to try. She *had* to talk to Lawrence. Every minute that passed was a minute closer to his birthday, a minute closer to him either disappearing or changing, forever. She couldn't decide which would be worse.

My name is Victoria Wright, she recited to herself, *and I'm going to make this work*.

Jacqueline tugged on Victoria's pant leg. "What are you doing? Have you lost your mind?"

Victoria shrugged her off and crawled a bit farther, then farther still. She reached out into the dark, and her fingers brushed a dirty brick wall.

She sighed and sat back on her heels. It was a dead end.

"Like I said," began Jacqueline, but then cold air rushed out at Victoria and hit her face, and the dirty floor just ahead of her . . . *trembled.*

Jacqueline backed away, eyes wide. "What's happening?"

"I don't know," Victoria said. It felt strange to admit such a thing out loud. She crawled forward, one hand out in front of her. Where she expected to brush against the dead-end wall, she met only more cold air, and more and more. This new cold, dark space swallowed her away until she could not see her own fingers right in front of her.

"You'll get in so much trouble for this," came Jacqueline's voice from somewhere far behind her.

Although Victoria wanted to see Lawrence more than almost anything and warn him not to be an idiot and ensure that he knew about the thirteenth-birthday thing, because he probably hadn't paid attention—the phrase "get in so much trouble" sent chills down her spine.

She gulped but didn't turn around. "Don't worry. I never get in trouble."

"I could get in trouble, just for talking to you while you're doing this. Someone could be watching, someone could tell."

"Sorry about that."

"You're acting like a *degenerate*."

"Nonsense," Victoria said. "I just want to talk to Lawrence."

After a moment, Jacqueline said quietly, "This place isn't like home, Victoria."

"I'd figured out that much, thanks," Victoria snapped.

"Getting in trouble here isn't like getting in trouble at home."

At the fear in Jacqueline's voice, Victoria almost turned around and went back to bed, but her pride wouldn't let her stop now. And besides, Lawrence was hopeless without her; he needed her.

She crawled back into the fireplace, sneezing on soot—she *hoped* it was soot—and kept crawling. The floor turned slicker, slippery with a thin coat of slime. Victoria wiped her face with her sleeve and caught a sour whiff off her fingers. When she looked back over her shoulder, she saw no fireplace, no Jacqueline—nothing but more darkness.

Then the walls began to change.

IT BEGAN FROM BEHIND VICTORIA, BACK NEAR THE opening of the fireplace—a soft rumble and rustle, like something enormous and slow turning in its sleep.

Then the slimy, gritty floor beneath Victoria began to ripple.

The walls on either side of her expanded and contracted.

If she didn't know better, she would have thought this little tunnel was *breathing*. All around her, the walls heaved. A low buzzing sound began, from all around her. She tried to scramble away, first to one side, then the other, but the damp stone walls moved too quickly. Soon they surrounded her on all sides, and the buzzing grew into a whir and then a drone of wet, flapping wings. Darkness pressed in close, mere inches from her face, closer, closer . . .

Victoria curled into a ball, breathing fast. "No, no," she murmured, but the walls did not listen. They would crush her, they would smash her to bloody bits between them, they would devour her with buggy teeth. Curling into a knot on the floor, Victoria buried her head in her arms, as she had done in the parlor. "Getting in trouble here isn't like getting in trouble at home," Jacqueline had warned her, and Victoria had not listened, and now she was in the parlor again. It had to be. Somehow, Mrs. Cavendish had trapped her here, and she would never let her out this time.

"No, no," Victoria wanted to say again, but she could not find her voice, so she had to settle for saying it in her mind: *No, no, no, no . . .*

She began to hum.

At first, she didn't even realize it. All she knew was the cold, heavy dark pressing in on her and the wings swarming over her as though trying to burrow beneath her skin. But soon the never-ending buzzing quieted, and then it was only a few lonely wing flaps as the walls around her fell away, and then there was silence.

Victoria opened her eyes and stared. Of course, she couldn't see anything, but the darkness seemed somehow quieter than it had been a moment before. It seemed, in fact, to be holding its breath.

Rachmaninoff's Piano Concerto no. 3. Victoria recognized the melody now as she drew herself up onto unsteady feet. She could almost picture Lawrence's hands banging and flying across the keys. As she stood there, shaking, waiting, the sounds of bugs and wings returned—quietly, from a distance. The walls around her began shifting again, creaking a little this time, as if straining against something that was trying to hold them back.

"No, wait," Victoria whispered, sinking to the floor, hiding her head once more. It was all a trick; they were coming back. Mrs. Cavendish was toying with her, drawing her into this dark place only to trap her and release her and trap her again, between stone and bugs and blackness. Victoria hid her face in her knees, folding up as tightly as she could, and forced herself to start humming again. At least if she thought of Lawrence and his stupid, wonderful piano and imagined that she was sitting in his living room watching him play, caught between jealousy and awe, she would be distracted when the bugs came back and started peeling back layers of her skin with their pincers.

The buzzing stopped. The walls stopped. Silence returned. The only sound there in the darkness with Victoria was her own trembling voice humming the opening bars of Rachmaninoff's concerto over and over again. She did not lift her head. There was safety in this, in the thought of Lawrence's smiling face bent over his piano, in the shaky, ugly notes of Victoria's voice. She had never been a good singer.

Finally, after what could have been hours, Victoria did not have the breath to continue. She looked up, slowly, taking long, shuddering breaths to steady herself.

Immediately, a whisper of wind rushed past her from a corridor in the dark. It breathed, "*Don't stop.*"

Victoria shrank away into the nearest wall. "What?"

"*Lonely, so lonely,*" the whisper came again, but it was more like a thousand whispers all blended into one. Their words didn't all quite line up, echoing off one another into gibberish, but "lonely, so lonely" remained clear.

I'm hearing things, Victoria thought. *That can't be good.*

"*Don't stop,*" the echoes whispered again. Victoria felt the shadow of a breath behind her, in front of her, the trace of a finger, the brush of a foot against her own.

"This is insane," she said, and started crawling. Her heart would surely burst from her chest, it pounded with such fear.

"I can't be afraid." Her words shrank in the dark, but she would not think about to where. "I have to find Lawrence." Lawrence, who hummed when he was happy. Well, Victoria was the farthest thing from happy, but it would have to do. She began humming once more, and the walls sighed and shifted around her, catching her off guard.

She froze and fell silent. So did the walls.

Odd, she thought. She crawled a few hesitant steps forward, humming again. The walls moved again, pushing her gently to the right, in a different direction from before.

Ridiculous, she thought, but all the same, a tiny thrill raced up her chest. The floor fell away, and steps formed beneath her, causing her to stumble, but she climbed up and up. The faster she crawled, the more she hummed, the faster everything shifted. The ceiling shrank so low, she had to slither up the stairs on her belly. She did not like the closeness of the ceiling; it reminded her of the parlor.

Then, in rolls of movement like waves, the floor dropped away.

She was falling.

Through cold air and blackness, Victoria tumbled, banging her knees and heels against stone. She reached out for something to grab hold of, but her fingers only scraped slimy stone, and then dry stone, and then rubbery, fluttery things that felt suspiciously like wings.

Victoria finally caught enough breath to scream, and yanked her hands back. She hit something, belly first—*oof*—and was still. Something had caught her. Cautiously, she felt around for it and felt a long, spongy thing with rough edges. She tried to use it to push herself up, but it disappeared, *fwooping* away like a spring, and she fell again—

—but only a few inches or so, onto a carpeted floor.

Victoria's heart drummed so loud she could hardly hear herself think.

Once she realized nothing was moving anymore, Victoria climbed to her feet using the nearby wall, which wasn't slimy anymore; it was smooth, with polished wood panels. Victoria flexed her toes to feel the plush carpet underfoot. She was in a hallway lit by a pale light from a window at the far end. It cast just enough light for her to see that what had caught her was a long, finger-shaped tangle of tree roots, now creeping away from her and . . . sinking into a wall?

"Wait," she whispered, and rushed for them, but they seemed to be in rather a hurry. By the time she reached their corner, they had disappeared into the crack between the floor and the wall. Victoria poked around and pulled at the carpet and, rolling her eyes at herself, said, "Come back. Please?" They didn't. Everything was silent.

Victoria backed away and turned around. She looked up to see the fireplace tunnel she had fallen from, but it was only a ceiling, with molding along the edges painted with pictures of pigs gnawing on the feet of sleeping children.

"Where am I?" Victoria whispered.

A faint laugh answered her, a whispering echo of a girl's laugh.

Victoria pressed herself against the wall, clapping a hand over her mouth to silence her breathing. For what felt like hours, she waited for the laughing girl to show herself, but nothing happened.

She crept forward, inching along the wall toward the dark wooden railing to her left. She sank to the floor and crawled till she could peek out between the railing posts and look down . . .

. . . and down and down, to the gleaming wooden gallery floor below her.

Her head reeled. Already dizzy from trying not to breathe too loudly, she imagined slipping through the railing and falling forever. Or worse, splatting her head open.

"*Don't go, don't go,*" someone said behind her. It was a boy this time.

Victoria scrambled to her feet and whirled around. "Lawrence?"

Again, she saw nothing—only the hallway with the window at the end. She turned left: a steep staircase. She turned right: another hallway, with the railing on one side and paintings on the other, framed in heavy golden swirls of fishes and curlicues of water.

"What is going on here?" Victoria said, backing up into the railing. Overhead, something fluttered. Wet wings zipped past her ear, followed by a distant, frustrated scream. Victoria almost shrieked, and her elbow bumped the railing, and then the railing wasn't there.

The floor rippled, throwing Victoria up in the air. The staircase flattened—she watched it happen below her as if in slow motion, not believing it—and when she fell, she slid down it, and it was flipping over, twisting around and around in a knot of angry wings and scrabbling pincers . . .

She tumbled out into a dark room. The air stank of onion, and something worse, a heavy tang of rot. It was so awful, Victoria almost threw up. She blinked several times to see better and caught the shapes of a table and countertops and a pair of pots. Piles of something scattered across the floor. Shining tools.

A cloud of flies swarming over the stovetop.

It's the kitchen, Victoria realized, recognizing the room from that first night she'd met Mrs. Cavendish. *And if this is the kitchen, the door must be . . . there!*

She ran blindly to the left and found a rattly doorknob, but it wouldn't turn, and the door wouldn't budge.

Voices called out from what sounded like very far away. From the other side of the room came a sharp snap—a

Through cold air and blackness, Victoria tumbled . . .

cacophony of hissing wings. The walls shook. Someone was *inside* the walls, slamming to get out. The kitchen floor jumped, and something snaked toward Victoria beneath the floor, cracking the tile. But this did not carry with it the sound of buggy wings; it carried the echo of voices.

The voices grew louder, spiraling closer and closer, till one of them whispered her name. It came up from the cracking floor:

"Don't stop, Victoria," they whispered sadly.

A wild thought came to Victoria. She remembered humming and not humming in the darkness past the fireplace; how the noises of the bugs had faded while she sang and come back when she didn't; how the voices asked her sadly not to stop and said they were lonely, and how those narrow, winding steps had appeared out of nowhere, more and more the longer she hummed, until she fell safely out of darkness, caught by that tangle of fingerlike tree roots.

She closed her eyes and started to hum. The angry noises in the walls fell away as though they'd been slapped, and that frustrated scream rang out again. Blindly, Victoria ran for the hallway, hoping she wouldn't trip and fall, hoping that whatever was about to burst up from the floor would just leave her alone.

But it did not leave her alone; something long and twisty

and covered with brambles burst up from the floor and shoved her forward, and she tumbled headlong through the hallway, safely out of the kitchen. Darkness reached up and grabbed her as the buzzing and frustrated scream faded into nothing, and she was falling and falling just as she had the first time. Then she landed hard on her hands and knees with a smack and a *crack!*

She whispered, "Ow."

Unseen in the shadows, someone said, "That must have hurt."

14

VICTORIA SNAPPED HER HEAD UP TO GLARE INTO the darkness. "Who's there?"

"Hello?" said a voice. "Did you just fall through the fireplace? Am I dreaming?"

Victoria blinked and shook her head from side to side. A dim light in front of her illuminated a small, dark figure.

Victoria caught her breath and crawled toward this figure. The ground beneath her had that same gritty, filthy feel from the fireplace in her dorm. In fact, this *was* another fireplace, Victoria realized, seeing the outline of a hearth appear within the light in front of her—or maybe it was the same one? Had she found her way back to the dorm? Victoria crawled out cautiously and found two long rows of beds, but these held boys instead of girls. A small, wide-eyed boy stood bent over near the fireplace, staring at her.

"I heard a big crash," he murmured. It was the same voice from a moment ago. "Are you the new girl?"

"That's me," said Victoria, climbing out of the fireplace and to her feet.

Yes, it was the boys' dorm. There was just as much soft crying from here and there as in the girls' dorm, but it smelled different, and there, a few cots down from the fireplace, sat Lawrence. The moonlight coming in from the boys' own high window made his skunk streak shine.

Victoria brushed off her pajamas and walked over to him, like it was the most normal thing in the world to walk through a fireplace and get thrown around a bug-filled house that moved like it was alive. The tall boy, Peter, sat up as Victoria passed him.

"You'd better be careful, Victoria," he whispered. The angles of his face glowed sharply in the moonlight. "I'm going home soon. I won't have you getting us in trouble."

"No one's getting in trouble," said Victoria, although she wasn't sure if she believed that. She sat down beside Lawrence, just as she had that first lunch in fourth grade, and said, "Lawrence, you'll never believe what just happened. I wanted to come talk to you, so I snuck out through the fireplace in the girls' dorm, and I crawled and crawled. It kept going, not like a regular fireplace, but like a secret passage or something. At first it trapped me and I thought it was Mrs. Cavendish getting me stuck there, and maybe it was, but then—you'll *really* never believe this—I started humming, and I think that did something, because suddenly I wasn't trapped anymore. Steps came out of nowhere, and I climbed up them, and then I was falling, and I came out on the . . . fourth floor, I think it was? I was in the stinky kitchen next. Everything kept moving around and spitting me out in a different place. There were voices and buzzing—that was the bugs, those roaches, they're *everywhere*—and someone screaming, and it was almost like the bugs and the voices were fighting each other. The voices kept saying they were lonely, and . . . and"—she forced herself to stop and breathe deep—"and I'm sorry. About the hanger, I mean. She put you in there because of me, and I'm sorry."

It took Lawrence a minute to look at her. When he did, his expression was so foggy, his eyes so strange, that he didn't look like himself. Suddenly, Victoria felt stupid for having blurted everything at him like that.

"Oh, Lawrence, you can't give up," she said. "Don't you know your birthday is coming up? You'll be thirteen. Don't you know what happens when children here turn thirteen?"

Lawrence nodded slowly. "You either leave or you . . . don't."

"Do you know what happens to the kids who don't leave?" Victoria whispered. "Jacqueline didn't know."

"I have my guesses."

Victoria paused at the sudden darkness of his expression. Deciding to try something different, she put her hand on his arm and spoke to him like she would have to a tiny child, pronouncing each word clearly.

"Lawrence Prewitt. Do you know who I am?"

Lawrence sighed. "Vicky, I'm not dumb. I'm just tired."

Victoria's heart leapt to hear that awful nickname. "Oh, you're *not* gone, after all."

"No, I'm not gone. I might as well be, though."

"What do you mean?"

"They're trying to make me give up my music, Vicky," he said, and at the mention of music, a bit of light came back to his eyes. "That's why I'm here. Mother and Father got sick of it. They *let* her take me."

"Well, what in the world's wrong with music?"

"Everything, to them. You know that. It's not what they want. It's not respectable."

"But you're *supposed* to play music, obviously," said Victoria.

Lawrence looked at her in surprise. "You mean it? I thought you hated it."

"I do mean it," said Victoria. She felt pretty shocked herself. "It's annoying sometimes—well, a lot of the time, really—but it's obviously the thing you're best at, so why shouldn't you do it?" Embarrassed at how happy Lawrence looked, she tried to smooth the wrinkles out of her dirty pajamas. "I mean, it's only logical, isn't it?"

"If you weren't, well, *you*—I'd want to kiss you right now."

It was fortunate that the room was so dark. Victoria's cheeks turned bright red.

"Well," she said. "Well."

Lawrence grinned. "So, you came here to warn me, huh?"

"Yes. I thought—well, after the hanging . . ."

"Don't worry about that. I've been in there before. And anyway, I was so happy to see you, I didn't care."

Victoria's cheeks turned even redder. "You didn't seem happy to see me."

"Well, at first I was just scared because you were here. I didn't want you to get trapped here because of me." Lawrence paused, fiddling with his pajamas. "That's why you came, right? Because of me?"

"I came because *she* brought me here," said Victoria. "I mean, yes, I was trying to figure out where you'd gone. I think I got too nosy, and she didn't like that, and—"

"You were looking for me?"

Victoria wondered if she would be red for the rest of her life. "Yes."

"Isn't that something. Perfect ice queen Victoria looking for skunkish old me."

Victoria flinched. "I'm not an ice queen." She couldn't even get angry properly. It felt strange sitting there, with all those crying boys sniveling in their beds and tall Peter at the side of the room, staring at her, and Lawrence being broken one minute and mean the next.

Lawrence put a hand on her arm. "I'm sorry. I didn't mean that. You know I don't think that, Vicky. Not me."

Victoria shook off his hand.

"Wait," Lawrence said slowly, "you were saying something about . . . going through the fireplace to get here?"

"Yes," Victoria said, flushing. The truth sounded silly when Lawrence said it.

"I don't understand."

"Well, I don't either, but it happened. How else do you think I got here?"

Lawrence scratched his head. "I guess I can understand a passage between the fireplaces. I mean, old houses have weird things about them, right? But how did you fall into a hallway? And then into the kitchen? And . . . you said something about humming?"

"And voices," Victoria said, and the more she thought about it, the fuzzier the memory of all that falling and tumbling became. *Had* it happened? she wondered, peering back at the fireplace. "I don't know. It happened, though. I think."

Lawrence frowned. "Maybe you were imagining things?"

"My imagination's not *that* good. Or . . . I don't know, maybe . . . well, now I can't remember."

"It's all right, Vicky," Lawrence said, patting her arm. "This place does things to people. Believe me, the dreams I've had . . ." He shuddered.

Victoria swallowed down her protests. It *had* happened, she knew—or, she thought it had. But the harder she tried to remember the hallway, those voices, the stinky kitchen, and the sound of her voice struggling through Rachmaninoff, the faster the images slipped away, just like in a dream. Maybe it had been a dream. Maybe she had been crawling through the fireplaces for so long that she fell asleep and dreamed it all. But she had to have gotten to the boys' dorm *somehow*. Was it really just a simple passage between the fireplaces, like any old house might have?

A soft sound echoed around at the edges of her mind. It sounded like a woman's laughter.

"You all right?" said Lawrence, scooting closer to her.

Victoria hurried to her feet, straightening her shirt. She

did not like feeling crazy. "Well, so, what are we going to do about this?"

"This?"

"Yes, this!" Victoria waved her hand about the room. "How we're all here, and why, and how we can leave. And what's going on with this house, anyway? Even without the fireplace thing, it's strange."

"Don't talk so loud," said Lawrence.

"Loudly."

"Whatever. Look, you can't just talk about those things where everyone can hear." Lawrence turned to block his face from Peter's view, Victoria could tell. She smiled. She had managed to hammer *something* of common sense into his music-addled brain after all.

"How we got here was those beetles," said Lawrence. "Don't ask me how—I don't know. But they do whatever she says. Sometimes I wonder—"

Lawrence paused.

"What?" said Victoria.

"Well, sometimes I wonder if those beetles *are* her. If you know what I mean. Like, they're a part of her, so she can control where they go and what they do?"

Victoria raised an eyebrow. "Now that's just ridiculous."

"And crawling through fireplaces isn't?"

Never in her life had Victoria thought she would discuss whether or not a woman was made of beetles. However, Lawrence had a point.

"All right, fine, we'll go with that for now," she said. "It's not like I've got any better ideas."

"Right. So, *why* we're here, from what everyone says, is because there's something wrong with everybody here. Mrs. Cavendish finds the kids who are wrong, brings them here, and tries to fix them. Degenerates, she calls us."

"Yes, I've figured out that much, and if she fixes you, you can leave," whispered Victoria, remembering lunch with Jacqueline and Hyena Harold. "But if she can't . . ."

Lawrence said nothing.

"Well? What does she do?" said Victoria.

"I don't know," said Lawrence, but he obviously had an idea. You learn things about a person when that person is your only friend, and Victoria could see it on his face—he knew something, but he didn't want to know it, and he was afraid to say it aloud.

Victoria clenched her fists. She really felt like hitting something. "But how can she do that? Doesn't anyone realize we're gone? Surely our parents won't let . . ."

But even as she spoke, Victoria knew it wasn't true. She wanted to believe someone in Belleville would realize they were gone and try to come find them, but whenever that had happened before—with Vivian, for example, and Professor Alban—whoever had tried it hadn't come back. And Jacqueline had been here for eight weeks, and Harold for months . . .

Lawrence shook his head. Someone nearby began to cry harder. Victoria remembered Mr. Tibbalt, his brother Teddy, and Vivian Goodfellow. Mr. Tibbalt said he hadn't really missed his brother when Teddy disappeared. He said it felt like living in a blank, cold fog. It was peaceful. It made you forget things and not care about the people you were supposed to care about most.

Victoria gulped, hard. People were forgetting them. And if they ever got out of here, everyone at home, at school, in town, would forget they had forgotten their children, and things would go on like before. Mrs. Cavendish would go on snatching kids. No one would say a word. It wasn't the Belleville way to talk about unpleasant things.

Victoria gritted her teeth till the tears and images of her parents faded. There were things to figure out first. *We mustn't go soft, Victoria*, she told herself.

"And the Home?" she said. She thought about how the floor had rippled beneath her feet and the kitchen floor had cracked like in an earthquake. "Do you think it could be . . ." She swallowed hard. She did not want to say it. "Could it be alive?"

Lawrence frowned. "I don't know."

"I think so," whispered a small voice from the next cot over. "It does whatever she wants. Just like those roaches and Mr. Alice. She makes rooms pop up out of nowhere, and the hallways are different every day. You'll see."

"Go back to sleep, Donovan," said Lawrence.

"I should know, though, shouldn't I? All those nights in the parlor . . ."

Victoria recognized the flabby sack of boy on the next cot and gasped. "Donovan? Donovan O'Flab—I mean, er, O'Flaherty?"

Lawrence jabbed her side with his elbow.

"That's me," said Donovan. He turned over, so Victoria could see the flaps of skin hanging off his cheeks, like the FEAR head hanging in the classrooms. "Hi, Victoria."

Ignoring the urge to kick the ugly version of Donovan away like Mrs. Cavendish might kick a gofer, Victoria said, "What's *happened* to you?"

"Coaching," said Donovan. He sighed. His face drooped even more. "You'll see. It happens to everybody, one way or the other."

"But what is it? What's coaching?"

"It's when Mrs. Cavendish tries to make you stop doing whatever's wrong with you," said Lawrence quietly.

"But how can she change a person like that?" said Victoria.

"She just can. I'd never have thought before, ever, that I could hate music and want to leave it behind, but now—"

"Lawrence Prewitt," said Victoria. Her voice was shaking, but she stood up and put on such a fierce dazzle that even Donovan seemed to wake up. "Don't you dare ever start talking like that again, or when I get out of here, I'll leave you behind with the gofers."

Lawrence smiled. "I've missed your threats, Vicky."

"Did I hear someone mention leaving?" said Peter, strolling over. He sat down at Donovan's feet and stared at Victoria. His mouth and fingers twitched in a sharp, wolflike way.

Victoria narrowed her eyes. She recognized that look. The Academy professors had had it. So had Jill and the Prewitts, when they weren't all bright and smiling. Victoria had the feeling that when people looked like that, Mrs. Cavendish was somewhere very close.

"Yes, you did hear someone mention leaving, Peter," said Victoria, smoothing her pajamas. "*I'm* leaving. I'm going back to bed."

With that, Victoria got up and headed for the fireplace. She wished she were wearing her nice Academy shoes with the buckles and heels. Stalking away barefoot did not have quite the same effect.

"Careful of the dark, Victoria," said Peter, suddenly at her side, leaning on the fireplace wall, staring at her. "Sometimes it . . . changes things. You never know."

Victoria rolled her eyes. "Oh, be quiet. You can't scare me."

Peter grabbed her arm.

"I won't let you get me in trouble, Victoria," he whispered, his eyes hard and afraid. "Just remember that. I've done enough, I'm a new Peter now. It's my turn to leave. I won't let you ruin it."

"Thank you for the information," said Victoria. She pulled her arm free and crawled till she was in the dark again and the soot turned to slime.

"I won't let you get me in trouble, Victoria," she said, making fun of Peter's shaky voice. "I'm a new Peter now, blahbity blah."

But her own voice sounded teensy in the shifting, twisting passage, and the floor crunched and bulged beneath her hands. *Don't throw me around again*, she thought. *Please?*

She concentrated on crawling, moving forward bit by bit, clenching her teeth till her jaw hurt. This time, she did not have to hum or do anything at all; a dank passage awaited her, heading straight forward into darkness. Victoria paused. She did not like that one bit. She even thought about turning back and hiding in the boys' dorm, but she didn't think that would go over well with the gofers when they came to unlock the door in the morning.

"Hello?" she whispered. Nothing answered her—no buzzing wings, no ghostly voices. The passage remained steady and solid. Victoria looked back over her shoulder; Peter remained at the fireplace, a black figure hunched over and watching her.

Victoria gulped. "I'm not afraid." She put up her chin and set her jaw. "I'm not, I'm not. I'm Victoria Wright." She started crawling again, humming just in case, and kept waiting for the floor to fall out from under her again, or a staircase to shift out of the walls—but before she could think about that too long, her hands hit the fireplace grate, and she was back in the girls' dorm. Her nameplate glinted on the wall. Jacqueline had gone to bed. Everyone was asleep. Victoria felt so relieved to be back that she sat in the soot for several minutes before she could stand up. She looked behind her to find a dirty brick wall. The passage had disappeared.

What does it mean? she wondered, frowning. Did *I imagine the Home moving like that, and spitting me out in all those different rooms?*

"I must have imagined it," she told herself, slipping into her bed and shutting her eyes tight. "I imagined it, I imagined it. Houses don't move like that. Houses aren't alive."

"WELL?" SAID JACQUELINE THE NEXT MORNING as they gathered at the door to go down to breakfast. "What happened last night?"

"Our fireplace goes to the boys' fireplace," Victoria said. "There's a passage that connects them. So, I went over there, and I talked to Lawrence." She shrugged, trying to seem casual about it. Falling forever and ever and coming out in that hallway; the strange voices, the stinky kitchen, how she had hummed and what that had done, or what it *hadn't* done—no, she wouldn't tell Jacqueline anything about that. Besides, it hadn't actually happened.

Houses aren't alive. She had to believe that; she would not let Mrs. Cavendish turn her crazy. *Houses aren't alive*. *Houses aren't alive*.

"I just can't believe it," said Jacqueline. "I watched you go through, and I *still* didn't believe it. People have tried to mess with the fireplace before. Even I've tried. But there's always just been a brick wall. No one's ever gone through it like that."

So, Victoria thought, *was that especially for me, Mrs. Cavendish? Did you let me through on purpose? Were you trying to scare me?*

That must have been it. Of course. It made perfect sense: Mrs. Cavendish pulled some nasty trick and sent Victoria on that wild ride to frighten her into not making any trouble. Victoria smiled and gave herself a couple of tally points on the blackboard in her head. Obviously, Mrs. Cavendish thought she was a worthy opponent. And after all, why wouldn't she? She was Victoria Wright.

But then . . .

A certain pesky thought wouldn't go away.

"Or maybe . . . ," Victoria began. She frowned and stared at the fireplace.

"What is it?" asked Jacqueline. "You look strange. Is everything all right?"

Maybe Mrs. Cavendish had nothing to do with the passage moving, Victoria thought. She remembered how, in the gardens two nights earlier, Mrs. Cavendish had kept looking around the Home like she was searching for something.

Victoria herself had seen the front of the Home move when she came to question Mrs. Cavendish, just the other day.

Letting Victoria get through the fireplaces and throwing her around to scare her was one thing; but why would Mrs. Cavendish have made the Home move that day, when she was shoving Victoria out onto the porch, trying to make her leave?

"I wonder why I could get through," Victoria said slowly. "Why me?"

Jacqueline tilted her head. "Maybe it was a trap or something. Maybe she's spying on us."

"Maybe," said Victoria, but then a gofer came to get them, and Victoria changed the subject. That awful *between* feeling was back, where Victoria didn't know what to think.

In scattered whispers, on the way down to the dining room, Victoria and Jacqueline discussed what they thought Mrs. Cavendish did to the children who failed coaching, and why Jacqueline was here. She had been ugly, with hunched shoulders and ratty hair and a splotchy face, and she had insisted on painting that freakish, ugly art of hers. Victoria studied Jacqueline's face. Her coaching was making her into something different, prettier, more normal—better, supposedly. Victoria wasn't sure she agreed. It would be one thing for Victoria to help Jacqueline be prettier and more normal while they were both safe at home. Why, it would be just like helping Lawrence keep his hair combed and reminding him to please not hum to himself in public.

But what Mrs. Cavendish does is different, Victoria thought. *Isn't it?*

An uncomfortable feeling unwound in her belly, all the way down a new hallway made of shiny gray stone with jeweled eyeballs for doorknobs. In the gallery, gofers scurried between chores, and the shadow-eyed birds settled back into the ceiling.

At breakfast, Victoria picked at her eggs and avoided the meat bits. They looked funny and tasted even funnier, and she couldn't stop thinking about that awful, rotten-smelling kitchen. When she caught Mrs. Cavendish staring at her from the head of the table, Victoria stared right back, but she didn't pay attention to her fork and ended up eating a chunk of rubbery, spicy, stinking meat. Mrs. Cavendish smiled, and on the way to the first class of the day, she petted Victoria's hair.

Victoria tried to distract herself as they walked single-file down the second-floor corridor of classrooms by planning her and Lawrence's escape—but she didn't really know where to start.

Walking out the front door was no good. Surely before they got there, the Home would wind around and trap them somewhere till Mrs. Cavendish found them.

They couldn't persuade Mrs. Cavendish to let them go,

either, although Victoria thought it might be either funny or horrifying to try. Maybe Mrs. Cavendish would laugh.

Victoria shuddered. No, that wasn't an option. She would rather see Mrs. Cavendish angry than laughing.

Maybe if they looked hard enough, they could find a secret way out of the Home. If it was always changing, if that fireplace opened up for Victoria, maybe a door would open up somewhere, too, and let them out onto the grounds.

Maybe it was possible to . . . *ask* the Home to let them out? Would it take a trade?

But if the Home *was* Mrs. Cavendish or whatever, then it would just report to her, or Mrs. Cavendish would know herself, and then they'd probably be in big trouble.

Or would it? *Was* the Home a part of Mrs. Cavendish? Could she control it and turn it this way and that way as easily as she would walk or wave her arms? Or was the Home something separate? And if it wasn't part of *Mrs. Cavendish*, what was it?

And what was making it ripple and groan? What made it shift around? What made it look different every day? If Mrs. Cavendish didn't make the Home move, what did?

Victoria was so wrapped up in these thoughts that she entered the classroom of manners, sat down at her desk, and pulled out her notebook before she realized what was going on.

Donovan O'Flaherty sat at the front of the classroom on a

high stool, and on a high table next to him sat a pyramid of Mallow Cakes. Victoria recognized their white and yellow icing at once. After all, she had seen Donovan stuffing his face with them for years in the Academy lunchroom.

Now that he was up in front for everyone to see, Victoria realized how sad and misshapen Donovan looked. His skin was pasty and sweaty, and it didn't seem to know what to do with itself. It hung limply off arms and legs that weren't quite fat or skinny.

Beside Donovan stood Mrs. Cavendish, right at eye level. For some reason, she had never looked prettier. Victoria found herself entranced, like Mrs. Cavendish had put a spell on her. Mrs. Cavendish's blue eyes sparkled and shone. Her smiling mouth stretched wide.

Victoria's stomach turned. All around her, the other children also looked entranced and queasy.

"It's been a while since you've eaten, hasn't it, Donovan?" said Mrs. Cavendish.

Donovan nodded silently. Mrs. Cavendish's hand tightened around Donovan's arm.

"Hasn't it?" she repeated.

"Yes, ma'am," said Donovan. His eyes filled with tears. He kept looking at the pile of Mallow Cakes like they were the only thing he loved in the world.

Victoria thought back to breakfast and realized with a horrible lurch that on Donovan's plate had been—nothing. He had sat in silence while everyone else worked through their steaming piles of eggs and meat.

"Well, lucky for you, it's eating day again," said Mrs. Cavendish. She tied a napkin around Donovan's neck and put a spoon in his hand. "And remember, we must be tidy."

For several minutes, Donovan just stared back and forth between the Mallow Cakes and his spoon. Finally, Mrs. Cavendish lost her patience. She slammed her hand down on the teacher's desk. Everyone jumped. Then, just like that, she was smiling, sweet Mrs. Cavendish once more.

"Eat, Donovan," she said. "You won't get the chance for another week. Come, come, you know this by now, don't you?"

"Yes, ma'am," said Donovan, beginning to cry.

As he carved out a piece of the nearest Mallow Cake with his spoon, his arms and lips trembled, and his eyes got the empty, wild look Victoria felt deep in her belly whenever she got hungry.

Donovan brought the crumbling cake to his lips. It was a long way, and bits of it fell into his lap or onto the floor. He began to chew, and at first it seemed all right. His eyes lit up, and Victoria didn't think she had ever been happier in her entire life, but then his face went green and mushy, his stomach heaved, and he got sick all over the floor.

Mrs. Cavendish watched him, cold eyed, till he recovered.

"Keep going," she said, and he did, as Victoria watched in horror and the other children watched with less horror, because they had seen it all before. Donovan kept carving out cake chunks and making himself eat them. Sometimes he managed to swallow, and sometimes he got sick again or had to stop and catch his breath. His skin shone with sweat.

After he had forced down ten Mallow Cakes, Donovan put down his spoon and slumped over in his seat. He sagged till his cheek rested in the remnants of cake, and he held his stomach and groaned over and over. It seemed like his skin had turned into Mallow Cakes, all white and yellow and soft.

"And what rule has Donovan reminded us of, everyone?" sang Mrs. Cavendish.

The children recited, tearfully, stone cold, and a bit nauseated themselves:

Don't eat too much, or you'll get fat—
No better than a sewer rat

"Congratulations," Lawrence whispered to Victoria as they left Donovan behind on the way to their next class. He patted her arm. "You survived your first coaching. Well, someone else's coaching, anyway."

Victoria didn't know what to say. She couldn't erase the image of poor, sick Donovan from her mind. Her stomach roiled like it had been her up there, caught between wanting to eat and being too sick to eat.

She wondered what her coaching would be.

"It gets better," Lawrence said. "Don't worry."

"How could it possibly get better?" Victoria said. She heard the little angry quiver in her voice but couldn't stop it. "Did you see what she did to—is all coaching like—how can you *stand*—it's just not *polite*." She found Donovan, ahead of them in line, struggling to keep up with everyone and occasionally retching onto the floor. The sight made her stomach turn. Such rudeness. Such brazen disregard for social etiquette. Such disorder, with his sick everywhere. Such poor nutrition.

"Donovan." Victoria marched up to him and grabbed his arm. She was too furious at Mrs. Cavendish to think better of whispering it under her breath: "Don't you worry. You can have some of my supper, all right? I'll sneak it under the table if I have to."

Donovan gazed up at her with bleary eyes and clammy green skin. But despite all of that, he smiled tiredly. "Really?"

"Really. I mean, honestly, she can't get away with—it's completely illegal, I'm sure—"

"I'm glad to hear you have so many opinions, Victoria,"

said Mrs. Cavendish, coming up behind her and crooning as though to someone she loved very much (if it was possible for Mrs. Cavendish to love anyone, which Victoria seriously doubted). She put a hand around the back of Victoria's neck and steered her away from the other children. Victoria saw the terrified faces of Lawrence, Jacqueline, and Donovan, and then she saw mirrors.

Mrs. Cavendish led her through a hallway of them, only the mirrors didn't reflect Victoria and Mrs. Cavendish. They were more like windows into some other place, with swings, trees, and parks, and people dancing, except the parks were made of tar, the trees of red glass, and the people dancing had hard eyes and tusks coming out of their mouths.

"Where are you taking me?" said Victoria calmly, even though she wasn't calm at all. She held herself erect to keep from screaming and tried to dazzle all the horrifying images in the mirrors.

"As I told you before, I like you, Victoria," said Mrs. Cavendish. "And I'm interested in seeing how you . . . progress here. You have potential. But there are the other children to think of, aren't there? I can't have you stirring up trouble."

"I'm not a troublemaker."

Mrs. Cavendish laughed and pulled Victoria into the plum-colored parlor from that first day, but quickly they were through that, down a set of stairs, and into a horribly familiar room.

The hanger.

"But I haven't done anything wrong," said Victoria. Her throat jumped at the sight of the empty hanger and the dingy lightbulb, but she swallowed it down because while she might be forced to wear ugly pajamas, she certainly wasn't going to embarrass herself by vomiting.

"Honestly, I only went through the passage between the dorms," Victoria blurted. She didn't say anything about the other things, the falling and the voices. "That's all. And really, if you don't want people doing that, you should block the fireplaces."

Mrs. Cavendish stared at her, frozen except for her eyes, which widened just the tiniest bit. A lock of her hair fell over her forehead. She brushed it away irritably. "The passage between the dorms."

Victoria felt herself shrinking. *How could you have been so stupid, Victoria?* She thought quickly. "Oh, or actually, that might have been a dream. Yes, it was a dream. This place gives me nightmares. You should do something about that." *Stop talking, Victoria.* She had begun to sweat. "So, you see? I really *haven't* done anything wrong."

The lie sounded awful even to Victoria's ears. She tried to look wide-eyed and innocent, but it must not have worked.

Mrs. Cavendish smiled, and her teeth were like fangs.

"I'm so disappointed in you, Victoria. How could you misbehave so?"

"But I only wanted to see Lawrence!"

"Associating with degenerates again, tsk tsk." Mrs. Cavendish led Victoria to the center of the room, but she didn't put her in the hanger. Instead, she leaned down and cupped Victoria's cheek.

"You may think you can leave me, and that you matter, and that anyone out there will miss anyone in here," said Mrs. Cavendish. She paused. She twined a finger through one of Victoria's limp, golden curls. "But you're wrong."

Mrs. Cavendish flashed a bright smile. "I just want you to understand that right here and now. We wouldn't want anyone else getting in trouble on your behalf, would we, Victoria?"

Then she left.

Victoria kicked the hanger. It creaked of old leather and chains, a rickety thing. Investigation seemed the best thing to do, instead of just standing here and trying to figure out what Mrs. Cavendish meant by leaving her in the hanger but not *in* the hanger.

But the closer Victoria got to the walls, the more the shadows moved, and the more things began to scuttle and click and shine. She stepped carefully around the room, afraid that too-loud movements would awaken something awful—or *many* somethings awful. *Click*, *scuttle*, *whirr*, things kept softly sliding around the air above her.

After finding nothing helpful, Victoria saw some blurred colors at the far end of the room. She squinted and tiptoed closer to a piece of dirty glass set into the wall. It was so dirty that Victoria had almost missed it in the shadows. She tried to ignore the smudged handprints and finger tracks in the window's muck.

Closer now, she saw that the blurred colors were shapes—people, furniture. The furniture and walls were familiar. Plum colored. Small, tidy. Mrs. Cavendish's little parlor.

The people were also familiar. Victoria squinted harder. There in her chair sat Mrs. Cavendish. Mr. Alice, a tall, bulgy shape in the corner. Sitting on the sofa were two heads, one balding, one bright as a penny.

"Mother," Victoria whispered, her nose and forehead pressing into all the fingerprint grime. "Father."

Through the grime she saw mild concern on their smiling faces, but nothing more. She pressed her ear to the dark window and heard her name in a question.

Mrs. Cavendish smiled. She shook her head.

"But I'm here," whispered Victoria. Then she yelled it: "I'm here!" She beat her fists against the window and realized that what she had seen that first day in Mrs. Cavendish's parlor was someone in the hanger pounding on the glass for her attention.

Now *she* was that pounding, but neither of her parents seemed to notice or care. They stood jerkily, then thanked Mrs. Cavendish for their tea.

"Mother?" Victoria said. "Father?" She kept pounding till she bruised her hands.

Her parents left, smiling. Mrs. Wright waved her hand: "Oh, just a misunderstanding, I'm sure." Mr. Wright blinked dully at his wife: "Dear, why are we here again? Can't we go home?"

For many minutes after they'd gone, Victoria whispered, "But I'm *here*." She scooted back to the hanger because the floor wasn't as creepy there. She huddled up in the dingy light and cried into her sleeve.

MRS. CAVENDISH LET VICTORIA OUT OF THE HANGER in time for supper.

"And how was our day?" she asked Victoria, petting her hair.

Normally, Victoria would have looked Mrs. Cavendish straight in the eye and said, "It was excellent." She wouldn't have in any way let Mrs. Cavendish see that really the day had been the worst day ever.

But this wasn't normally. Victoria stared at the roach-covered wall. They weren't moving now or flicking their wings or anything; the wall stood shining, silent, and still. Victoria shrugged.

"It was fine."

Mrs. Cavendish jerked Victoria's chin up. "You must look me in the eye when you speak to me."

Victoria did. "It was fine," she said again.

A smile unfurled across Mrs. Cavendish's red lips. "That's a good girl."

Victoria followed her out of the hanger. She dutifully tidied herself up in a jeweled powder room that Mrs. Cavendish opened from the wall with a brass key. The jewels were golden hands and pearled teeth and bright ruby hearts.

Victoria went to supper. She ate every single one of the meat bits in her stew and cleaned her bowl. Mrs. Cavendish watched gleefully from the head of the table. So did Mr. Alice.

She followed the other girls upstairs. She sat on her cot. At lights-out, she got under the covers and stared at the ceiling.

Jacqueline crept over and whispered, "What happened? Where were you all day? What's wrong?"

Victoria said nothing. She hardly heard Jacqueline. She hardly heard anything at all.

"Did she put you in the parlor?" asked Jacqueline.

Still, Victoria said nothing. Jacqueline gave up.

Victoria didn't sleep much that night. Every time she closed her eyes, the dark place behind her eyelids became the dirty window in the hanger. The floating red and yellow light spots became her parents, leaving her, not caring about her.

They were forgetting her. Everyone was forgetting her. Everyone was forgetting all of them.

Victoria had never really given much thought to people caring about her or not. Her parents treated her well, she had Lawrence to boss around, she had the respect and fear of her professors and schoolmates. That had been enough.

But now the thought of her parents going on without her, and not even realizing they were going on without her, shriveled her up inside. Even seeing them through the hanger's dirty window had been wonderful. She missed seeing them, being proud of how beautiful they were, and hearing them brag about her.

She wanted to curl into the scratchy white sheets and hide, but she couldn't find the will to move that much. Instead, she turned her cheek into the pillow and stared at the wall.

The next day, Victoria went to breakfast. She ate her egg casserole and all the meat bits, leaving only some grease behind. When she started following everyone to the classrooms, Mrs. Cavendish grabbed her arm and pulled her away.

"Oh no, Victoria," Mrs. Cavendish said, tucking Victoria into a hug. "No class for you today."

Victoria found Lawrence's worried eyes and halfheartedly reached for him, but Mrs. Cavendish yanked her away. Then she kissed Victoria's hair. "Don't make me punish you any more than I already have to, Victoria."

"Where are we going?" Victoria managed to say, her

throat dry. She tried to be brave, but they were going toward the hanger now, and every step made her want to throw up.

"Don't be stupid. You know where we're going."

Tears formed. Victoria held them back. She might be afraid, but she wouldn't let Mrs. Cavendish see her cry. "Again? But *why?*"

"Because I've seen your kind before," said Mrs. Cavendish. She threw the hanger door open and shoved Victoria down the steps. "Nosy. Intrusive. Stubborn. You think you're so special. Oh, Victoria. " Mrs. Cavendish crouched down and pet her hair. "You're finally going to learn some manners. You're going to learn how to be quiet and *mind your own business.*"

Mrs. Cavendish shut the door. Victoria crawled to huddle beneath the hanger in the lightbulb's glow. Silence filled the room, except for the sounds of all the roaches in the shadows, clicking and scuttling and waiting for the lights to go out.

"*Une bestiole,*" Victoria whispered, plugging her ears. "A bug is *une bestiole.*"

A light came on in the far wall. Victoria squinted and saw shapes.

"Mother," she gasped, jumping to her feet. "Father."

She stumbled over to the wall with the window in it. Through the glass, she once again saw the blurred shapes of her parents—bald head, bright head. She saw Mrs. Cavendish. She heard the muffled sounds of conversation.

"Let me out of here," Victoria said. She started pounding on the window. Roaches scattered everywhere, dropping off the wall and plopping at her feet, waving their legs in the air. "Let me out! Mother! *Father!* I'm right here! Me, Victoria! *Let me out!*"

Once again, they didn't hear her. She pounded and screamed till it hurt too much to keep going, crawled back to the lightbulb, and half slept through a few nightmares. Later, she woke up to dozens of buggy black eyes staring at her from inches away.

Once again, Mrs. Cavendish fetched her for supper. "And how was our day, Victoria?"

"It was fine," Victoria mumbled. She tried to raise her head high, but for some reason that made her want to cry more, so she tucked her chin down, went to supper, and went to bed.

The next few days passed just the same—in the hanger, surrounded by piles of bugs, pressing her face to a dirty window, and calling for her parents. On the fourth day, she couldn't scream anymore. She could barely drag herself to the window.

She heard voices.

"These interviews have gone well," Mrs. Cavendish was saying. Victoria could hear her through the window—muffled, but easy to understand. "I'm *so* glad."

"Us, too," said Mrs. Wright.

Mr. Wright said, "*So* glad."

Mrs. Cavendish held up a blur of papers. "I'll send these home with you, then. Adoption is a complicated process, I'm afraid, but I'm sure you'll manage." She smiled. Even through the smeared window, Victoria could see her flashing white teeth. "Before you know it, you'll have one of my dear, precious children for your own."

Victoria sagged against the window. "What?"

Mr. Wright put his hand on Mrs. Wright's shoulder. "We've always wanted a child."

"A little girl, I think," said Mrs. Wright, dreamily. "I've always wanted a little girl."

"Of course," said Mrs. Cavendish, and then they were saying other things as Mrs. Cavendish ushered them out. Before she left, she turned to the window and smiled just for Victoria to see.

"But they *love* me," Victoria whispered. "Don't they?" She could not remember if they did or not.

She sank to the ground. It took her an hour to crawl back to the lightbulb because she kept stopping to cry and fall half asleep and wake back up with burning eyes.

"They've forgotten me," she said dully, and fell asleep in the hanger's shadow.

At supper, as always, Mrs. Cavendish fetched her. "And how was our day, Victoria?"

Victoria couldn't say anything. It was too hard. Mrs. Cavendish laughed prettily, her smile stretching back into her shiny brown hair.

"Excellent!" Mrs. Cavendish said.

Victoria went to supper. She went to the girls' dorm. She crawled into bed, stared at the ceiling, ignored Jacqueline trying to get her attention, and fell asleep. In her dreams, Mrs. Cavendish ate her parents for supper and made a piano out of their bones.

The next morning, she waited for Mrs. Cavendish to take her to the hanger again, but instead, Mr. Alice shoved Victoria toward the classrooms with the other children.

Victoria blinked in confusion but didn't say anything. What was the point in saying anything? No one cared what she had to say. All her efforts toward perfection meant nothing. Her parents didn't care about her and her trophies and honor rolls and awards. No one did. And without that, who was Victoria? Nothing. She was nothing.

She followed everyone to the classrooms, the birds in the gallery swooping and fluttering in the darkness overhead. Being nothing felt quite the same as being something. Maybe she had never been *something* at all.

When the birds' wings flap, it makes the air stink, Victoria thought. But she wasn't disgusted or scared or angry. She just . . . was. She noticed things without caring.

Victoria looked up dully at the nameplate over the door of the first classroom they came to. THE CLASSROOM OF ART, it read.

Art, Victoria thought. She took her seat. *Art is paintings and drawings and sculptures,* she thought. She took out the notebook and pencil from her desk and waited.

"Vicky," Lawrence whispered from behind her. A hand nudged her shoulder. "Vicky, what's wrong? What happened? Where have you been?"

There didn't seem to be any point to answering Lawrence, and even if she had wanted to, Victoria couldn't find the energy to do anything but wait with her pencil poised over her notebook.

"Vicky, *please,*" Lawrence said. "What is it?"

"Nothing," Victoria mumbled.

"Take your seat, Jacqueline," Mrs. Cavendish said, standing at the front of the room, the black switch gleaming and curling in her hand. Jacqueline climbed up onto a high stool beside Mrs. Cavendish and sat facing a blank easel and an array of brushes and paints. Mr. Alice, smiling, stood on Jacqueline's other side, his gloved hand at her neck. Grime covered him, like he'd just been out in the gardens.

Through her numb haze of thoughts about her parents and her desire to just go back to the dorm to hide, Victoria saw how pale Jacqueline was and how she held her mouth in a tight line.

"Whenever you're ready, Jacqueline dear," purred Mrs. Cavendish. She squeezed Jacqueline's hand.

Jacqueline took a deep breath, picked up the widest paintbrush, and dabbed it in blue.

Victoria waited and stared at her blank piece of paper, her pencil ready for whatever notes Mrs. Cavendish instructed them to copy.

Smack!

Looking up without much interest, Victoria saw a reddening mark on Jacqueline's painting hand. Mrs. Cavendish's sharp eyes watched Jacqueline's face.

"Careful, Jacqueline dear," whispered Mrs. Cavendish, curling her fingers around the black switch in her hand. "That was a bit off, wasn't it?"

"Yes, ma'am," said Jacqueline. Smooth, pretty blue streaks covered the top part of the canvas. A tiny bump in the paint showed where Mrs. Cavendish had slapped Jacqueline's hand. Jacqueline took another deep breath and started again, but not before Mrs. Cavendish clucked her tongue.

"Quite a sigh there, Jacqueline. I hope you're not annoyed?"

"No, ma'am," said Jacqueline. Her voice shone as prettily and inoffensively as her newly pretty hair.

Mrs. Cavendish drew two long, shining fingernails around her mouth, thinking. "Continue."

Jacqueline did, painting quietly and carefully—except for when Mrs. Cavendish caught a brushstroke that was too bold, a color that called too much attention to itself. Whenever that happened, Mrs. Cavendish would flick out the switch to whip Jacqueline's hand. After a few times, Jacqueline whimpered each time this happened. Her hand and wrist were turning red.

Victoria heard Lawrence growing restless behind her.

"She's hurting her," he whispered.

Well, yes, it does seem so, Victoria thought. She shrugged. *That's what happens in coaching*, Victoria supposed.

Lawrence made a small sound of disgust and pushed his desk as far back from Victoria's as possible.

As Jacqueline continued to paint, Victoria let her eyes unfocus and watched the colors on the canvas grow. In her blurry vision, she noticed the exact same colors all around her. She blinked and focused her eyes again.

On the walls, covering the classroom windows (except for the window looking down into the hanger), on the ceiling, everywhere—were paintings. In fact, it was the same painting that Jacqueline was working on now, over and over and over again. They all looked exactly the same, like they'd been run through a copier—a pretty gray house with smiling children in the windows, green trees, a blue sky, sunshine, flowers. It was a brighter, sunshinier version of the Home.

It was also perfectly boring—pretty, but boring. Victoria remembered the pictures Jacqueline used to draw all over her books and notes, and sometimes even on her own skin, while she sat hunched over in the back of class—monsters and dead people and dying things. They made Victoria uncomfortable if she looked at them for too long. These paintings of the Home were the exact opposite. They were very respectable. Victoria could imagine her father hanging a copy alongside all the other boring, respectable paintings hanging in the stairwell at home.

Victoria knew it must be difficult for Jacqueline to make herself do this over and over. But she couldn't really bring herself to care that much. Thinking of her mother's parlor made her feel even more dead inside. She slumped over in her seat and watched Mrs. Cavendish beat Jacqueline every time she moved her brush wrong or tried to add a bit of yellow to the trees this time, or a bird to the sky.

"Don't you dare," Mrs. Cavendish hissed. "Don't you *dare* deviate from how I've told you to paint this picture,

Jacqueline. You must do exactly as I say." Her lip curled. "There is no place for your ugliness here—not on your face, not on this canvas."

Jacqueline began to cry. "I'm trying," she was saying to Mrs. Cavendish. Mr. Alice tightened his hand on her neck. His giant, dirty hands left marks on Jacqueline's pajamas. Jacqueline started to sweat and shake.

"I won't have you ruining my pretty pictures," said Mrs. Cavendish, slapping Jacqueline again. "Now finish. Correctly. Or would you like to go pay my little darlings a visit?"

Mrs. Cavendish glanced delicately over at the hanger window, where her "little darlings" swarmed in the shadows. A few of them traced sinister images on the glass with their feelers and jagged, pinching legs.

"No." Jacqueline began sobbing.

"Well, then," said Mrs. Cavendish, dragging her fingers through Jacqueline's silky red hair. She found a frizzed knot and pulled till the hair ripped free. Jacqueline yelped, and Mrs. Cavendish's lip curled. "I see you'll need to be made over again soon."

Jacqueline shook her head. "No, I—please, not that."

"But isn't it better to be beautiful?"

"I—"

"Careful, careful," Mr. Alice said, laughing.

Little Caroline in her black braids, who shadowed Jacqueline everywhere, began to cry too.

"Yes," Jacqueline said quietly. "It's better to be beautiful." Then she returned to her painting.

Mrs. Cavendish smiled. By the end of the coaching, Jacqueline's hand was red and bleeding with welts from Mrs. Cavendish's switch. They left her finished painting to dry at the front of the classroom. The last thing Victoria saw as they filed out into the hallway was one of the smiling girls in the windows of the painted Home. The girl had golden curls, just like Victoria's.

This went on for days, weeks, hours. Victoria didn't really keep track of the time. *But it can't have been two weeks yet*, her brain reminded her every now and then, *because Lawrence is still here, isn't he?* And at some point soon, he would be thirteen years old.

And then he would either leave or be . . . gone.

Sometimes when Victoria thought about this, fear jolted her awake for a second or two. But then something would remind her of how big the Home was, and how strange, and how her parents were replacing her, and how all of Belleville didn't care about her or any of the other children, and how she was nothing and no one, and she would shrug and go quiet again. If she was nothing and no one, that meant the other children here were nothing and no one, too, and it shouldn't matter what happened to any of them. And it wouldn't.

Every day, there was a new coaching, and everyone attended and watched.

Peter had been an embarrassment to his father because tall, pale, skinny Peter preferred his computer games to the outdoors, and Peter's father had once been a football star. Mrs. Cavendish made him run lap after lap through the gardens till he lost all his color and passed out, time after time.

"Thank you for your patience, Mrs. Cavendish," he said after Mr. Alice threw a bucket of ice-cold well water over him to wake him up. Peter was shivering and could barely stand up, and later that night, he lay awake with horrible cramps and cried into his pillow with the pain—but he didn't show that to Mrs. Cavendish. He smiled adoringly at her and let her hug him close and kiss his forehead.

Little Caroline made really awful grades, so awful the Academy professors had started calling her "a lost cause" and were considering things like "academic probation" and "relocation." So Mrs. Cavendish breathed down her neck while Caroline worked through her multiplication tables at a high stool in the Classroom of Mathematics. As the other children watched, Caroline tried to solve the problems on the blackboard, and whenever she made a mistake, Mrs.

Cavendish would slap her hand with the switch. Lawrence, Jacqueline, and some of the other children looked away and turned green when little red spots spurted onto the board by Caroline's hand, but Victoria just watched quietly. So it was blood. So Mrs. Cavendish was hurting Caroline, who was only eight years old and would be here for years, maybe.

Oh well, Victoria thought. She shrugged. *There's really nothing anyone can do about it. We are nothing and no one. We* should *be here.*

Lawrence's coaching was the hardest to watch. It took place in the room with all the ruined pianos, their cut strings trailing the floor in spools of wire.

Mrs. Cavendish sat him down at the biggest piano, in the center of the room. Lawrence put his hands on the keys, and for a moment, hope skipped through the line of children watching him, because Lawrence smiled and seemed like a real person again. Even Victoria perked up a bit.

Then Mrs. Cavendish put her hands in the piano's open lid. Her sleeves bulged. They *crawled.* Mrs. Cavendish stepped back and shook a few last things from the ends of her sleeves. She took a shining pin from her pocket and picked between her teeth. A last little crawling thing popped out from her collar and fluttered down into the piano.

"Go ahead, Lawrence," said Mrs. Cavendish, trailing her

fingers up Lawrence's arm to tousle his hair. She sneered at the sight of the silver streak. "Play."

With the strings cut, the piano made no noise. The mallets hit only air, and sometimes the bottom of the piano's insides, with soft, broken thuds.

The piano began to crawl, just like Mrs. Cavendish's sleeves. Black things streamed out of the open lid and onto the dirty keyboard. Some of the children recoiled, and so did Lawrence, but Mr. Alice put the end of his rake at Lawrence's neck, the rusted prongs digging into his skin. Lawrence kept playing his invisible song. The roaches swarmed in confusion. They ran over Lawrence's flying fingers. Some of them stuck their pincers into him and bit, hard. Lawrence started to cry, although he screwed up his face to try to look brave.

Fury stirred deep within Victoria, turned over, and went back to sleep. She continued to watch Lawrence get bitten and cry. She cried too. She felt very tired.

But then something happened. Lawrence played and played, and something about the way his fingers hit the silent, buggy keys sparked a memory deep in Victoria's mind. The keys he was hitting, the rhythm, the way his back and arms moved—it was familiar.

Staring at Lawrence, only half seeing him, Victoria started to hum.

The piano began to crawl, just like Mrs. Cavendish's sleeves.

At first, she didn't realize it. Then Jacqueline jabbed her in the ribs. Victoria blinked but kept humming along. *How extraordinary*, she thought, blinking awake. *I appear to be humming*. Her voice matched the strikes of Lawrence's swollen, bitten fingers, singing whatever silent song Lawrence was trying to play. The tune was so familiar, but Victoria couldn't remember how she knew it.

Lawrence smiled through his sniffles and pounded the silent keys harder. His pounding started to sound like heavy drums.

Mrs. Cavendish stared at Victoria in shock. Mr. Alice almost dropped his rake, looking for once not evil but merely stupid. The gofers waiting at the doors in case Mrs. Cavendish should need them made awful, excited noises.

The roaches scattered, racing into the next rooms and up into Mrs. Cavendish's clothes, out of sight, flapping their wings in furious confusion.

The Home *moved.*

IT WASN'T MUCH. IT WAS LIKE WHEN A TRAIN PASSES nearby and the ground rumbles. It moved with a distant sigh.

Victoria paused in her humming, her skin warm with shock. This time, she wasn't the only one who had heard it; this was no imagined passage in the dark, no imagined wild ride through the Home that she could convince herself was a nightmare. This was in the middle of the day; everyone was around her, and everyone heard the same, groaning thing and felt the same, shifting floor. She had hummed, and Lawrence had pounded hard on those silent keys, and the Home had moved. But why, and how? And what did this mean?

The others looked around in confusion. Little Caroline blurted out, "What was that?"

From somewhere in all the dark twists of rooms around them, something groaned, creaked, whined. At the doors, the gofers muttered excited gibberish and stomped their feet on the ground. The window closest to them cracked. The ceiling rained down bits of dust and paint.

Mrs. Cavendish snapped out of her frozen, wide-eyed trance. "Silence!"

The gofers fell to the ground and hid behind their hands if they had them, whimpering.

Stalking forward, Mrs. Cavendish whipped the switch across Lawrence's face so hard that it flew out of her grip. Her face had bright red splotches. Her eyes gleamed. She glared at Victoria, snatched up the switch, and whipped Lawrence again, terribly beautiful in her rage. Her eyes were blue fire, sharp like dagger points.

"What," she snapped, "have we discussed about singing, children?"

No one said anything; they were too busy looking around curiously for whatever those strange noises had been.

Mrs. Cavendish cracked her switch through the air. Even Mr. Alice jumped.

"I *said*, *what* have we discussed about singing? Or talking too loudly, or making any unnecessary noise *whatsoever*?"

Immediately, a chorus of frightened voices said:

No one wants to hear you sing,

Or talk or scream or anything.

To Victoria's surprise, she found herself reciting the rhyme along with everyone else. She didn't really know the words, but there she was, saying them. It was like someone else was moving her mouth and making her voice sound.

That was just it, Victoria realized, with only a little surprise: she had started to feel like she wasn't Victoria at all, these days. She had become a nobody and a nothing, tugged here and there, made to do things, like a toy. The only time she hadn't felt that way was just now, humming a piece of music she was too tired to remember the name of. But the more she thought about this, the heavier she felt; all that was too much for one stupid nobody to think about.

"Oh, well," she said, sighing later, lying down in her cot. "There's nothing to do about it."

That night, Victoria's dreams were full of strange rumblings that came in waves, and the waves were made up of antennae, pincers, and fluttering wings. She awoke after the fifth one of these dreams and sat straight up in bed.

The rumblings weren't just in her dreams. They were real. The Home was shifting like it was built on water. It happened only every now and then, and subtly, but Victoria saw little ash clouds puff up from the hearth. Yes, it was moving all right.

But *why* was the Home moving so much, and all of a sudden? Questions began forming in Victoria's mind. Like a rusted old clock struggling to turn its gears again, Victoria began to think. She folded her sheet down and sat cross-legged as she listened for the next rumble.

When it happened, she got out of bed. It took every last bit of her effort. She felt as though she were waking from a long, heavy sleep. She went to Jacqueline's bed. It was easy to find her, even though there was only a sliver of moon that night, because Jacqueline had the shiniest hair and was crying over her hurt hand.

"Jacqueline," Victoria said slowly. It was so hard to move her lips, she had to feel them to make sure there weren't stitches there sewing them shut. She put a hand out to pat Jacqueline's shoulder; moving her arm was nearly impossible, the air around her heavy and sticky. She shook her head. *Wake up, Victoria,* she thought. *There's no time to feel sorry for yourself anymore.*

"What do you want?" said Jacqueline. "Leave me alone.

I'm a *degenerate*, don't you know? You don't want to be seen around people like me, Victoria. Not you, not Mrs. Cavendish's favorite."

Victoria bristled. "I'm *not* her favorite."

"Yes, you are. Shut up. Go to bed."

"But . . . do you feel that?"

"Feel *what?*"

"Listen." Victoria sat on the bed. It took so long for it to happen, Victoria thought Jacqueline would kick her off the bed with impatience, but finally—

A faint rumble sounded deep beneath them, from within the walls. At the far end of the room, Gabby rocked back and forth in her pillows with her hands over her ears. "Not again," she moaned. "Go away, go *away*."

"What is that?" said Jacqueline.

They waited for a long time, but it didn't happen again. The Home had gone silent.

It was still so hard to *think*. Victoria kept shaking her head to clear it, which made her dizzy. She looked around the room at all the lost, frightened girls tossing in their nightmares, and at the ones who slept peacefully because they would be going home soon. Mrs. Cavendish had taught them how to be different, had frightened them into being exactly what a Belleville girl should be.

"No one's coming for us," said Victoria.

"You're just now figuring that out?" said Jacqueline, sniffling.

"We're all alone," Victoria continued, slowly. It helped, to say it aloud, to accept it.

"You know, that really isn't making me feel any better."

"So, we can't depend on our parents or the police or anyone," said Victoria, "but maybe we can do it ourselves."

It felt like putting together the last pieces of a fuzzy riddle. Victoria caught the moonlight glinting off the nameplate over her bed: VICTORIA. It reminded her of her favorite street sign near the Academy: VICTORY. Her heart raced as though she had just laid her hands on the freshly copied pages of a new exam. She grinned. Jacqueline stared at her.

"You really *have* lost it," said Jacqueline. "Just like Lawrence said."

"Never mind," said Victoria. "I'll be right back."

"Where are you going?" whispered Jacqueline, but Victoria had already marched to the fireplace and begun to crawl. When she reached the dead end, the brick wall at the back of the fireplace, she put her fingertips to the wall and only felt a little bit silly when she started to hum. Her voice sounded loud in the dark, and she wondered for a moment if she would wake Mrs. Cavendish and bring her to the dorm in a fury, whipping and hitting with her switch.

But Victoria kept humming anyway, the Rachmaninoff again, and she whispered, "Hello? Are you there?" although she didn't know to whom she was whispering. *Those voices*, she thought, *whoever they are*.

Finally, the wall gave way, slowly, creaking awfully like a rusted hinge. The same dark passage appeared, shifting and tilting into place amid a wave of black walls and black ceiling and black, cold, dank air.

Victoria smiled and began to crawl. *I don't quite know what I'm doing*, she thought, *but I'm starting to figure it out*. Angry clicks and hisses roiled at the edges of her ears, as though things were trying to burrow into her through the walls, but the passage remained empty.

"*Hurry*," the ghostly, echo-y voices whispered. "*Hurry now*."

Victoria was afraid but pushed that aside. The heavy sleepiness that had covered her mind for the past few days fell away more and more. She was beginning to formulate a plan, and there were few things she liked better than formulating plans. After crawling for a few long minutes, the angry buzzing growing angrier and louder, little feathery things biting and brushing at her ankles, Victoria came out into the boys' dorm. She went straight for Lawrence's cot and shook him awake.

"Go away, Vicky," he said.

"No. Did you hear those rumbles?"

"I *said*—"

"I know what you said, and I'm not going anywhere," said Victoria. The words came easier now. "Look, the Home was rumbling just now. I heard it, and so did Jacqueline. It was just like at your coaching, when I started humming. And I've heard it before, too. The first night, when Mrs. Cavendish showed me around, we were out in the gardens, and there was this weird groaning noise, like a monster, and it came from the Home, and Mrs. Cavendish didn't seem to like it. But I don't know what that means. And I *did* fall down the fireplace that night. The Home moved me around to all these rooms. I know it sounds stupid, but it *did* happen. It happened just now; it happened earlier today, in the piano room. Remember? You were drumming away on the keyboard, and I was humming, and the Home moved, and then Mrs. Cavendish told us to be quiet. Well, so I did the same thing just now; I sang, I hummed, and the passage reappeared, and that's how I got here."

Lawrence sat up. "I don't hear anything."

"It'll happen again. Just wait. Sometimes it takes a few minutes."

"You're trying to tell me," Lawrence said, frowning, "that the Home likes music?"

Victoria frowned. "Maybe. It certainly seems to. But maybe it's not just music. All that pounding you did on the piano wasn't really music. Maybe it just likes noise. It *is* really quiet in this place most of the time."

"You make it sound like the Home is alive, like Donovan said. I thought you didn't believe that. I'm not sure *I* believe that."

"Look," said Victoria. She was growing impatient. The whispering, echo-y voices had said, "Hurry. Hurry now." This was not hurrying. "I don't understand it either, but I'm going to find out, and you can either come with me, which is why I came to get you, or you can sit here and not believe me, and then what if I find a way out? What if I can't come back and get you?"

Lawrence shook his head, his face pale, dark circles beneath his eyes. "I don't understand any of this."

"Well, I don't either. Just come with me—we'll figure it out. Trust me."

"Why should I? You're just like Mr. Alice. You sit back and watch her hurt people, and you don't even care."

Victoria felt like Lawrence had slapped her. "I've just been upset."

"It's not like you're the only one who's upset."

Victoria drew herself up into as grand a dazzle as she could muster. "For your information, she had me in the hanger for days, and I saw my parents. I yelled for them, but they didn't hear me. Or maybe they did, but they didn't listen, and then they left." She paused. "They're planning to adopt one of the children here. They're planning to replace me. And whoever it is won't remember me, and neither will they. I'll just . . ." She paused. "I'll be an orphan."

Lawrence said, "Oh," and fiddled with his sleeves.

"Yes, well." Victoria sniffed.

"I'm sorry, Vicky."

"It's fine."

"Really, I am." He patted her hand.

"All right, well, thanks."

"That was me that day, beating on the window to get your attention," said Lawrence. "When you came the second time? And the first time, in the kitchen, the paper airplane—that was me, too."

"I'm sorry it took me so long," said Victoria quietly.

Lawrence smiled. "But you're here. I knew you would come. I knew it." He rubbed his hands together and winced from the sting of all the bug bites. "So, what's the plan, then?"

"I want to investigate this place," said Victoria, "and figure out what's behind all this—the bugs, the Home, why it moves like there's an earthquake and shifts and pops hallways out of nowhere, all of it."

"I wonder why I've never noticed it doing things like this before," Lawrence said, wrinkling his forehead to think.

"I don't know. Maybe you're not paying good enough attention."

Lawrence glared at her. "Maybe I've been really scared."

"Maybe. But it *is* moving, and I want to find out why."

"Easy enough," said Lawrence, jumping to the floor. It was like old times—Victoria coming up with some grand studying plan for end-of-term exams, and Lawrence going along with it because that's what friends do, and he hadn't any others. "What's the plan?"

Victoria wanted to hug him but restrained herself. "Well, I don't know. We'll just start exploring, I guess. Maybe if you're with me, you'll be able to get through the fireplace too."

"And then what? If we figure everything out, then what do we do?"

"We get out," Victoria said firmly. "We escape."

"And the other kids?"

Victoria's chest twisted a little. "If there's time, we'll come back and get them. But *only* if there's time." Victoria gave Lawrence a stern look before he could say anything. "Look, this is my plan, all right?"

"But we'll try our very best to come back and get them, won't we?"

"Yes, we'll try. Our very, absolute best. I swear on my academic report."

Lawrence snorted. "I should be surprised you said that, but I'm really, really not."

"I'm *serious*."

"I know. That's what's so funny."

Victoria flashed a dazzle at him, and he coughed and cleared his throat and choked back his laughter. "All right, so what about Mrs. Cavendish?"

"What *about* her?"

"We'll just escape and leave her here to keep doing what she's doing? For all we know, she could snatch us right back the moment we step through the gate."

Victoria frowned. The truth was, she had no idea what to do about Mrs. Cavendish. She got the feeling that getting rid of her would not be easy. "I really don't know. But maybe if we explore long enough, we'll find something to help us."

Lawrence looked at her skeptically.

Victoria raised one imperious eyebrow. "Unless you've got a better idea?"

"No, not really."

"Well, then."

"But where do we start looking?" Lawrence asked.

"I'm not sure. . . ," said Victoria, but then she saw a lingering bit of dirt on Lawrence's neck, where Mr. Alice had pressed his rake earlier that day. "Actually, I do know. Let's go to the gardens."

"Outside?" Lawrence whistled. "You're crazier than I thought. Those gardens give me the creeps."

Frowning and thinking furiously, Victoria led him to the fireplace. "When she showed me the gardens, she called them her pride and joy. But what's the point of them? We never go outside except for coaching. And Mr. Alice is always working in the gardens, right? Why does he spend so much time there? It doesn't make sense, unless it's something important. Yes. We start there."

"I wouldn't do that," said a voice from behind them. They whirled to see Peter standing at the ends of the beds, straight and tall, leaning to the side because he was still stiff from his coaching the other day. He managed a small smile, though. But it wasn't his. "Not a good idea."

"Thanks very much for the advice," said Victoria, feeling quite herself again by this point and in no mood for creepy boys. She pushed Lawrence toward the hearth, ignoring Peter and the uncomfortable feeling the look in his eyes had left in her belly, and started to crawl into the shadows of the fireplace.

After a few crawl-steps, she took a deep breath and looked back at Lawrence. "Well?"

"But it's after lights-out," said Lawrence, eyeing the fireplace uneasily. "People have—"

"Yes, yes, they've snuck out before bed and never come back. I know. But I did it the other night, and I'm just fine, aren't I?"

"But . . . *outside*?"

"It could be our only chance to find out what's really going on and how to get out, don't you think?"

Lawrence sighed, crouched down, and crawled in beside her. Together, they peeked down the passage, which had remained in place since Victoria crawled through. It was too dark to see much beyond the first few feet.

"Um. Hello?" Victoria whispered. "I'm, er, I'm back. And Lawrence is with me."

Lawrence stared at her as though she had sprouted a second head.

Victoria ignored him and began to hum, trying not to

burn up of embarrassment. Her scratchy, wobbly voice bounced down the passage and was swallowed up in a sudden rolling wave of clicks and wings. Lawrence hid his face, but Victoria gritted her teeth and dazzled the darkness till her eyes felt like they would pop out of her skull.

"*Hurry*," the voices whispered. When Lawrence heard them, he yelped. Victoria clapped a hand over his mouth.

"Hello? We're, er . . . we're trying to get outside." Victoria paused. Any moment now, they would be swarmed upon and eaten alive. She fought not to scream. "To the gardens?"

The walls expanded and contracted, twisting and shifting. Steps formed in front of them, leading down and down. A few tiny black shapes tumbled down them, popping out of the walls, their legs waving uselessly through the air. The ceiling rumbled with wings and black eyes.

"*Hurry*," the voices repeated. "*Angry. So angry.*"

Lawrence shrank closer to Victoria, grabbing her hand.

"Vicky, I've got an awful feeling about this," he whispered.

"Me too," said Victoria, but she pulled on his hand anyway, to help him to his feet, held her head high, and, holding tight to Lawrence's sweating fingers, started downstairs into the dark.

"I DON'T LIKE THIS," LAWRENCE SAID AS THEY FELT their way down the winding staircase. The floor was slippery, and they had to hold on to the walls to keep from sliding all the way down. "What's *in* here with us?"

"You know what it is," Victoria whispered. Wings brushed past her neck, getting tangled in her hair. She batted them away, her throat twisting into a tight, sick feeling. There weren't too many of them—yet.

Lawrence groaned. "Those *bugs*."

"I hope they don't tell her what we're doing. If they're part of her, like you think they are . . ."

"Oh, great, I didn't even think about that."

Victoria brushed out some roach wings from her hair. She

wanted to scream and run, and her skin crawled, but she made herself go slowly. If they fell and hurt themselves, this would all be for nothing.

"*Hurry, please,*" the voices urged, sliding down the stairs alongside them, girls' voices and boys' voices and grown-up voices, but Victoria couldn't even be too sure of that. The voices were all tangled up in one another, scratchy and sad.

"What *is* that?" Lawrence asked. His teeth were chattering.

"I don't know," said Victoria. She wasn't entirely sure she wanted to, either.

When they reached the bottom of the stairs, the last step shoved them forward, and a wall whooshed up behind them. A pair of angry beetles plopped out onto their backs, wiggled their legs around to plop right side up, and scurried away. The staircase was gone.

"That's not good," Lawrence whispered. He felt around the wall to find the opening, but it had disappeared completely. "Where are we?"

"I'm not sure," said Victoria.

The floor beneath them moved, rippling down a long hallway that stretched from left to right on either side of them. In the darkness, the red walls and carpet were black as mud. Ten skittering legs, a million times over, raced away from them into the shadows. Through the high, narrow windows overhead, a little bit of moonlight glowed, illuminating smiling, golden metal faces on the walls—garish lips, wagging tongues, long hands beckoning them closer.

Victoria and Lawrence froze.

"Do you want to go back?" whispered Lawrence.

Yes, Victoria wanted to say. But she swallowed hard and said, "Absolutely not. Do you?"

Lawrence glanced at her. "Er. No. Not like I'd know how to go back anyway. We're stuck."

They slipped through a gap in those smiling, slobbering faces, down a narrow staircase they'd never seen before. Long, skinny emerald snakes formed the banisters. It was just wide enough that they could go down together, hand in hand. Victoria squeezed Lawrence's fingers so hard, she thought she might break them. He squeezed them right back.

They followed the steps down for ages. At the bottom, they passed through a curtain of beads that looked suspiciously like teeth, into the gallery on the first floor.

"*Finally*," said Lawrence, sighing with relief. "The gallery. We know where that is, at least. Now where do we go?"

Victoria didn't have time to say she didn't know, because a sudden stink washed over them from above. Gray feathers fell to their feet and dissolved into thin air.

"Get down!" Victoria fell to the floor and pulled Lawrence

along with her. One of the huge painted birds from the ceiling just missed them, swooping down with its sharp, ivory hands outstretched.

"It's coming back!" said Lawrence, yanking Victoria to her feet. They ran for the center of the Home, but the gallery was suddenly much larger than it had been before. The faster they ran, the larger it became. More birds dropped from the ceiling like bats. Beaks snapped at the hems of their pajamas. A clawed finger scraped Victoria's hair. She looked back to see a black tongue and razor-sharp feathers swiping at her.

"In here!"

They had reached the room with the broken pianos, and Lawrence dragged Victoria after him through the door, which was shrinking. Victoria had barely pulled her foot through before it snapped shut. Huge thuds and shrieks sounded from the other side as the birds flew into the wall.

"I—will *never*—look at birds the same way—again," panted Lawrence as they hurried through the piano room. "Did you *see* the way they chomped with those teeth?"

"Shush," Victoria said, putting out a hand to stop him. They had reached the hall of mirrors Mrs. Cavendish had led Victoria through on the way to the hanger.

"We don't want to go this way," said Victoria, but when

she turned to leave, Lawrence stayed put. "Lawrence, come *on*, this goes down to the hanger."

But Lawrence didn't move. He was staring at something in the mirrors and started to walk toward the nearest one.

"What are you doing?" said Victoria, squinting at the mirror to see what, precisely, was so fascinating. She saw only Lawrence's reflection waving him forward.

"*Come on,*" the reflection said, winking. "*It's safer this way.*"

"Oh, I'm sure." Victoria grabbed Lawrence's arm, but he threw her back, and she stumbled.

"What do you think you're—?" Victoria stopped. Lawrence's reflection was changing. He was growing taller, thinner. His hair grew into a brown, roiling sea, his face grew red lips, and his fingernails shone as they waved Lawrence forward, closer, closer. . . .

"Oh, no you don't," Victoria said to the Mrs. Cavendish reflection. She ran up to Lawrence and slapped him hard across the face. He blinked and staggered back, and as the dozens of Mrs. Cavendishes in the mirrors howled with rage, Victoria pulled Lawrence back through the pianos, into dark rooms they'd never seen before.

Lawrence put his hand to his cheek. "That really hurt, you know."

"Well, next time, don't go looking into strange mirrors, how about that?" Victoria snapped.

"Wait—"

"I mean, really. Haven't you been here long enough to know not to trust—"

Lawrence clapped his hand over Victoria's mouth. "Vicky, look."

In front of them, through a doorway that looked like it led toward the terrace and outside, peered several gofers. Their eyes—and each of them had only one of those—were as yellow and round as the butterscotch candies Mrs. Cavendish kept in her kitchen. They chewed on their lips. They dripped drool onto the carpet. They waited.

"Lawrence," Victoria whispered. She couldn't stop staring at the gofers' yellow eyes. "Do you think . . . ? Their eyes . . . and those candies she keeps in the kitchen . . . they look the same."

Lawrence gulped. "That's not possible . . . right?"

"No, you're right, surely not." Victoria wasn't so sure, though. It made an awful, horrible lot of sense. Mrs. Cavendish hated the gofers. They were her slaves. Would she *really* go so far as to pluck out their eyes, though?

"I ate two of those candies," Victoria said. She leaned hard against Lawrence to catch her breath, her palms sweating.

"I did, too," Lawrence said, grimly. "When I woke up in

the parlor, there were some on the floor. I was so hungry, I couldn't help it!"

Victoria somehow resisted the urge to scrape her tongue raw with her fingernails.

"Do you think we can go past them?" asked Lawrence.

"We can try," said Victoria. She wasn't sure she believed that, but what else could they do? Carefully, they crept toward the door. The closer they got, the quieter the gofers became.

Victoria tiptoed through them, holding Lawrence tightly by the hand. She squeezed her eyes shut and gritted her teeth. Several unblinking yellow eyes followed them, but the gofers did not move or make a single sound.

Lawrence sighed, as they cleared the room. "Well, they give me the creeps, but at least they didn't—ow!"

Lawrence fell to the floor.

"Lawrence?" Victoria gasped, but then something pulled her down—a gofer, its brown, bony hands clutching her feet. Another gopher had Lawrence, and both of them were being dragged back to where the other gofers stood, waiting, bouncing up and down.

"Greedle," they muttered, "greedle, greedle," and smacked their toothless mouths.

"Stop it!" Victoria reached back and hit her gofer's ears,

but it wouldn't let go. Beside her, Lawrence scrabbled at the rug, trying to pull himself away. His gofer bent over and started gnawing on Lawrence's foot.

Victoria flushed with rage. "Get away from him!"

"It's eating me," Lawrence cried, clawing at the wall in a panic.

Victoria's gofer grumbled something and started rolling up her pant leg. Yellow drool dripped onto her foot, but as the gofer bent over, its shoulder gleamed. Victoria narrowed her eyes and saw an oozing scab—a wound from Mrs. Cavendish, perhaps.

"Not if I have anything to say about it," said Victoria. She twisted back with all her strength and pounded her fist against the gofer's shoulder.

It yelped and jumped away toward the others. Victoria jumped to her feet and kicked Lawrence's gofer, aiming for the scabs on his back.

"Greedle," it said mournfully, and hopped away clutching its backside.

"Come on, come *on*," said Victoria, helping Lawrence to his feet. Together, they staggered out toward the terrace, the gofers whining in a heap behind them.

"Are they locked?" asked Lawrence, pointing at the terrace doors.

"If they are, we'll just have to break them down," Victoria said, but when she tried the handle, it turned at once, and they were outside. Lawrence fell against the door, panting.

Victoria wiped the drool from her leg. "How's your foot?"

"It's okay," Lawrence said, pale and sweating. He gave her a weak smile. "At least they don't have teeth. You all right?"

"Yes. But those gofers won't be if they come near me again. Ugly, stupid things."

"What do you think they are, exactly? And how did Mrs. Cavendish get them?"

"I don't know," said Victoria, although she had a bad feeling about those gofers. A *very* bad feeling. When she peered back through the terrace doors, the yellow eyes were gone.

They stood for a minute to get their bearings and catch their breath. The fingernail moonlight was enough to make out what Victoria remembered from that first night: winding, well-kept gardens; a mess of overgrown tree and wild bushes in the corner; the two tiny cottages.

"Come on," Victoria said. "Let's go look around."

"What are we looking for?" whispered Lawrence as they crept through the crooked twists and turns of shrubs and giant, reeking flowers.

"I don't really know. There has to be something out here, though. Something important. Why else would there be these giant gardens? I can't think Mr. Alice likes to garden just for a hobby, you know."

As they crept on tiptoe through the gardens, an awful rotting smell started to sting their noses. It was worse than the stink of the ceiling birds. It came from one of the cottages, back where the grounds and gardens changed into thick trees and briar patches. Rusty piles of tools and equipment littered the ground.

"What's *in* there?" said Lawrence, bringing his collar up over his nose.

Victoria thought she might be sick. "I don't want to know. But we have to check."

They tiptoed through the tangle of growth at the edge of the gardens until they reached the stinking cottage. Grime and dirt covered the windows, but Victoria rubbed her palm against the glass until she cleared away a spot. Together, she and Lawrence peered through. Silver things glinted in what little moonlight there was—knives, saws, curved blades, scythes, hooks hanging from the ceiling.

Tiny biting things hit Victoria's neck. She swatted at them and realized that the air was full of flies.

"What . . . what do you think that's all about?" Lawrence whispered.

Only then did Victoria realize how close they had pressed

together to look through the window; their cheeks had touched, so close that she could hear Lawrence's noisy, nervous gulp.

She stepped away, hurriedly, brushing flies from her pajamas. "I don't know, but we won't go in there unless we absolutely have to. Agreed?"

Lawrence grabbed for her hand once more. "Agreed."

Victoria bit back an irritated comment and allowed him to hold on. They headed back into the maze of the gardens. The shrubberies seemed to crawl. Victoria ignored them, pushing past thorns and brambles and suspiciously roachlike leaves, concentrating not on them but on the pinching grip of Lawrence's fingers. *Hmm*, she thought. *I suppose this is actually somewhat useful.* She didn't so much mind holding his hand from that moment on.

"Look." Lawrence pointed at the second cottage, a little ahead of them. "There's a light on in that one."

Amber light shone through the windows. It moved, like someone was carrying a lamp around. Lawrence pulled away, but Victoria tightened her grip on his hand and moved toward the cottage. "We have to see," she whispered to him, and he set his mouth in a determined line and nodded.

At the window, they crouched and peeked inside. Victoria made sure to keep her cheek in its own proper place this time.

In the cottage, a pair of lamps on a pair of tables provided the light, but that was not the first thing Victoria and Lawrence noticed. The first thing they noticed was that the cottage was filled with puppets—hanging from the ceilings, tacked up on walls, sitting propped up on tables and chairs, covering every last bit of flat surface.

"What . . . ?" Lawrence murmured.

Victoria narrowed her eyes, trying to count the puppets, but there were too many of them. They were the kind with strings; "marionettes" was the word, and they dangled by their strings from the ceilings, swaying a little bit from side to side. At the ends of the strings were wooden lattices. That's where the puppetmaster would control them, Victoria knew.

Lawrence realized it first; he pressed a shaky finger against the glass. "It's them," he whispered. "Look. They're puppets. They're *all* puppets."

It was true; inside the cottage stood a model of Belleville. Victoria saw it all—the tiny red Academy, the library, Town Square, the pretty neighborhoods with their green hedges and black gates, Lawrence's house . . . *and my house*, Victoria noticed, getting a hard knot in her throat. And everywhere, dotting the town, placed here and there as though they were simply walking around running errands, stood puppet Bellevillians.

"My parents," came Lawrence's strangled voice. "They're right over there."

Victoria saw them—perfect likenesses of Mr. and Mrs. Prewitt, with shining, hard, wooden faces, and shining, hard, wooden smiles. Their dead puppet's eyes stared wide and unblinking.

"It's everyone," Victoria said grimly. There was Dr. Hardwick, standing on the steps of the puppet Academy. There were Mr. and Mrs. Everett hanging from the ceiling. Their heads turned as they spun slowly from their strings.

A horrible thought pierced Victoria's heart. *Mother*, she thought. *Father*. She searched through the forest of puppets for a bald head, for a bright, penny-colored head. . . .

In the corner of the cottage, someone moved.

Lawrence cried out. Victoria moved quickly and clapped her hand over his mouth again, but she could not even be angry with him, because there, walking out from the corner with a puppet in one hand and shining silver cutting shears in the other, came Mrs. Cavendish.

"What's she doing?" Lawrence asked. His lips scraped Victoria's hand when he spoke, and she pressed down on his mouth harder.

"Quiet," she hissed. *Wonderful*, she thought. *Lawrence slobber*.

Together, they watched Mrs. Cavendish working, for that was surely what it was—she moved here and there, arranging a puppet over there in the corner, and tying that one back up to the ceiling. Every now and then, Mrs. Cavendish would put the tip of the silver shears to her mouth, tapping her blood-red lips with the blade. Then she would smile a horrible smile of white, gleaming teeth and resume working—tying strings here, retying them there, settling this puppet in Town Square just so, rearranging all the puppets everywhere in Belleville to her delight.

Victoria's mind whirled around and around with one desperate thought: *What does this mean?*

For some reason, this thought decided to manifest itself as a sneeze. Victoria sneezed a large one.

Lawrence stared at her in horror.

Inside the cottage, Mrs. Cavendish froze. She opened the blades in her hand. She began to turn.

Immediately, Victoria and Lawrence hurried back into the gardens. They reached the darkest place—the overgrown corner in the Home's shadow.

"Why did you sneeze?" Lawrence whispered frantically.

"It's not like I meant to," said Victoria. She kept looking back over her shoulder at the lit-up cottage, but Mrs. Cavendish remained inside, the windows still lit up. They waited a few more minutes, watching the cottage, hardly able to breathe. Lawrence grabbed Victoria's hand again, and she didn't even mind. In fact, she was glad of it. In fact, she found herself shrinking toward him without really planning to.

"What was she *doing*?" Lawrence said at last. "All those puppets . . . and they were all real people! They were people we know, people from town!"

"Playing with her dolls? I don't know! How am I supposed to know what she was doing?" said Victoria, licking her dry lips. If she let go of Lawrence's sweating hand, she would surely start to cry. Or worse, scream. She took a step back.

Crack. Something beneath Victoria's foot broke.

"Ow," she said, pulling her foot away. Something made of glass shone back at her. She picked it up.

"Eyeglasses?" said Lawrence.

"I know these," whispered Victoria. She bent over and started scraping through the dirt.

"What're you doing?"

"Wait a minute, wait a minute—agh!"

Victoria leapt back from the gnarled hand she had just uncovered in the leaves.

Lawrence caught her before she could fall. Together, they followed the arm up into the wall of the Home, where a familiar face gaped out at them from the mess of brick, tree roots, and climbing vine.

"Professor *Alban*?" said Lawrence. Victoria was too busy trying to wipe hand slime off her skin to say anything much just then.

Somehow—impossibly—Professor Alban had grown into the Home. He was *part* of the Home, slumped on the ground and tangled up in brick and mortar. His skin looked like tree bark and mud. When he blinked, his eyelids creaked and groaned. Flakes of brick snapped off and floated to the ground.

"Mrmph," said Professor Alban.

Victoria regained herself somewhat. "I found your eyeglasses, professor," she said, holding up the limp, broken frames.

"Mrrrrmph." Clumps of burrs and little white moths spilled out of Professor Alban's mouth.

"What has she done to you?" Lawrence knelt in front of him. "Is this because you tried to help Victoria? Tried to help us?"

Professor Alban's treeish throat jumped. It looked like he was trying to speak again, but his eyes were rapidly losing their shine. They were hardening. So was what remained of his skin. He was becoming part of the gardens, part of the Home. He was dying.

Somehow—impossibly—Professor Alban had grown into the Home.

"Professor Alban," said Victoria. She snapped her fingers in front of his face. "Don't you know who I am? I'm Victoria Wright. Remember? From the Academy? And this is Lawrence Prewitt, and we need your help. You can't just turn into a useless pile of bricks on us."

A tear of sap pooled at the corner of Professor Alban's left eye. Victoria dug in her heels to keep from running away in horror. She wondered if it hurt, being soaked up into a house like that.

"Professor?" she whispered. "Stay awake, please. We need to get out of here. There are *lots* of us, and we're all alone."

Victoria turned away to fight her tears in private, unable to say more. She tried to tell herself that it wasn't her fault Professor Alban got snatched, but it wasn't really working. Dry crackling noises popped behind her, like a tree zipping itself shut. Victoria bent over and put her hands on her knees, trying not to get sick.

"He's gone," said Lawrence quietly, his hand on Professor Alban's frozen knotted, leafy shoulder. "Well, I think so, anyway." He wiped his cheek on his sleeve and took Victoria's hand. "Vicky, are you—?"

But Victoria was already staring at something else—that big, wild tree in the corner, so overgrown it seemed like five trees in one. There was something familiar about it. In the center of its trunk, the bark formed a distinctive shape. It looked almost like a—

"There's something in the bushes," said Lawrence, pointing to a rustling pile of leaves all knotted up in the big tree's roots. He grabbed Professor Alban's eyeglasses and thrust them out like a sword. "Don't worry, Vicky, we'll get out of this somehow."

"Yes, with broken eyeglasses, I'm sure," said Victoria, but she wished she had something to hold out too, because the bushes were *growling* now. She ducked behind Lawrence's arm just in time for something to come flying toward them.

"Gallagher!" Victoria whispered, holding out her arms. Gallagher jumped into them and slopped a whiskered kiss on Victoria's nose. He was absolutely covered with muck, but Victoria didn't care. "I've never been so glad to see something so smelly."

"Isn't that Mr. Tibbalt's dog?" said Lawrence.

"Yes, his name is Gallagher. But why is he all the way out here?"

Lawrence kicked around the bushes Gallagher had been hiding in. "Looks like he's been here for a while. He's brought a bone. Lots of bones, actually."

"Right there at the base of that tree," said Victoria. She put Gallagher down to inspect the tree more closely. He followed, whining and sniffing along the tree roots.

"Maybe he could lead us out of here, back through the grounds," said Lawrence. "I mean, he had to get in somehow, right?"

As if in response, a cold wind swept around them, flinging dirt and leaves into their faces.

Lawrence spat a snail from his lips. "All right, never mind, maybe not."

"This marking," said Victoria, running her finger over a knot in the bark. "What does it look like to you?"

"It looks like a heart," said Lawrence. He put his fingers on the knot too. They brushed Victoria's, and he drew back. "I mean, not that I think about things like that, or—well, you know."

"And doesn't it sort of look like a face, up there?" said Victoria. She pointed up at the branches, the knots of bark between them, the swirling leaves.

"Actually, it does," said Lawrence. "That's weird." He paused. "Do you think . . . maybe there are *other* people like Professor Alban here? Other people who tried to help before she caught them?"

Victoria backed up to get a better view of the great tree. The moonlight illuminated what was clearly a face in the bark and leaves. The branches looked like wild, black curls.

And the heart-shaped marking sat exactly where a neck would be, exactly where Victoria had seen that heart shape before. Mr. Tibbalt's gnarled finger had caressed it in the photograph on his lap—a heart-shaped locket.

"Vivian Goodfellow," Victoria whispered. Gallagher whined louder, looking away into the gardens. "I don't believe it. It can't be."

"Who's that?" said Lawrence.

Just then, Gallagher started yapping so angrily that he tipped over.

"Look," said Lawrence, pointing back toward the lit-up cottage. The door opened, becoming a bright yellow rectangle. Then the lights went out. The door slammed. Something dark, long, and thin slithered into the gardens.

"Go!" said Victoria. Hand in hand, she and Lawrence dashed around the corner, across the terrace, and through the doors (which thankfully, ominously, had remained unlocked). They ran through the gallery and up the staircase with the snake banisters (they writhed and hissed golden tongues; "Don't look at them!" warned Lawrence), back through the hallway of golden smiling faces, and to the wall where they'd come down the fireplace staircase.

"Come on, let us in," said Victoria, pounding on the wall as loudly as she dared.

"Someone's coming, Vicky," whispered Lawrence, craning his neck back down the hallway. Candlelight bobbed on the emerald-snake stairs. Shadows flickered up across the golden metal faces, and their smiles melted into frowns and toothy snarls.

Victoria dug her fingers between the wooden panels and tugged hard, but the wall didn't move. "Um," she said, her voice shaking. "Um, right." She started to hum. It was a very disjointed song. It didn't sound like much. She was afraid to hum too loudly.

Lawrence backed up, putting himself in front of her. The candlelight grew brighter. Whoever it was, they were almost up the stairs.

"Vicky . . . Vicky, hurry. . . ."

"I can't find the door!" Victoria whispered, but just at that moment, the floor opened beneath them, and they fell into darkness. Above them, the floor snapped shut.

Lawrence screamed as they fell, but Victoria found him in the tumbling dark and jabbed his side. "It's all right," she said. "This is what happened last time."

"This . . . is *not* . . . all right," Lawrence gasped.

They hit soft, mushy ground, and then they were rolling down a slope of stone and crumbly dirt. When they came to a stop, it was in the hearth of the boys' dorm.

"*Angry*," those whispering voices rushed down after them, ruffling their hair. "*So very angry. Run. Run.*"

"Hurry," said Victoria, pushing Lawrence toward the cots. "Go back to bed. And if anyone asks what we did, for goodness' sake, don't *tell* them. Not yet."

"But what did we find out?"

"I don't know, I need time to think. Go!"

Victoria turned and ran-crawled through the fireplace passage, scrabbling along the walls for a grip. The floor rumbled but stayed in place. *I hope that doesn't mean* Mrs. *Cavendish is angry*, Victoria thought.

"*Hurry, hurry*" whispered a voice, but this wasn't a child's voice; it was a man's, and for a wild moment, Victoria thought it was Professor Alban.

"Professor Alban is gone," she told herself, but her teeth still chattered. Once in the girls' dorm, she smoothed down her hair and brushed off her clothes, just in case someone came looking for her, and sat down on her cot to think.

"What happened?" said Jacqueline, hurrying over. "Where did you go? Did you find out why the Home was moving like that?"

Victoria told Jacqueline about sneaking through the Home, the birdies, the gofers and their eyes (Jacqueline looked a bit ill at that point), the gardens; the stinking cottage (Jacqueline definitely looked ill) and the puppet cottage (Jacqueline gasped and shivered), and Professor Alban (Jacqueline covered her mouth). When Victoria got to the part about Gallagher and the big black tree, and about Mr. Tibbalt and Vivian Goodfellow, Jacqueline said, wide-eyed, "What do you think that means?"

"I'm not sure." Victoria's brain had never worked so fast in her entire life. "But that tree—its roots go all over the place, even up against the Home, where Professor"—Victoria gulped down the sick feeling in her throat—"where Professor Alban was. I think Mr. Alice tries to keep it all nice and under control, but . . ."

"Maybe he can't," whispered Jacqueline.

"Maybe there are *others* in the gardens," said Victoria, remembering what Lawrence had said. She swallowed hard. "It sounds crazy, but . . . what if it's true?"

Jacqueline's eyes got even wider. "Others? Like Professor Alban?"

"Yes. But what we can do about it I don't know. I wonder. . . ."

They went on whispering for a while, but they kept hearing noises and feeling things watching them from the shadows. Jacqueline couldn't stop shivering and went back to bed, and Victoria kept wondering about everything for a long time, till the moonlight in the high window changed to sunlight.

She was still wondering as they headed down for breakfast through hallways that were actually normal for once. Nice pictures of nice people doing nice things hung along the walls. None of the people in the pictures had horns or leathery wings, and they weren't smiling nastily at the children as they passed. The banisters weren't made of snakes, the birdies were quiet, and the shadows weren't crawling with bugs.

"I don't like this," whispered Jacqueline as they entered the dining hall. "It's too quiet in here."

"Hmm," said Victoria, deep in thought—till she caught sight of Hyena Harold's empty seat across from her. She frowned harder. "Jacqueline, look. Harold's not—"

Victoria caught sight of Lawrence's horrified face down the table. He was staring at a gofer—a gofer shoveling eggs and meat onto Caroline's plate. A gofer who, when he got pepper up his nose, sneezed in an awfully familiar way—loud and harsh, like a hyena's laugh.

"No," said Victoria, staring at the gofer's dumb, yellow eye, the drooling, tongueless mouth. It had only one hand, stubs for legs, and chunks missing from all over its gnarled body.

At the head of the table, Mrs. Cavendish scratched the side of her mouth with one shining fingernail.

The gofer grunted as it spooned casserole onto Victoria's plate. The steaming meat chunks looked fresher today—plumper and juicier. It smelled like the scabby kitchen and that stinking cottage in the gardens.

Victoria watched the gofer hobble to Jacqueline's seat. She looked at her plate and back at the gofer, over and over.

Mrs. Cavendish began to cut into her own casserole, primly. She wore a terrible smile. Meat juice dripped from her lips.

Victoria didn't believe it. It was nonsense. It was too horrible to be real. But nevertheless . . .

She turned Harold into a gofer, Victoria realized. All the gofers were children. And all the bits missing from them—their tongues, their hands . . .

Victoria looked down at her plate. Her stomach flipped and shriveled.

. . . she feeds us with them.

19

TWO DAYS LATER, VICTORIA, LAWRENCE, JACQUELINE, Donovan, and Caroline huddled together at the fireplace in the girls' dorm. Victoria had led the boys over from their own dorm. It was late, and pitch black. The moon was barely a sliver.

It felt strange to talk; Mrs. Cavendish had made them stay silent for two days straight. If anyone had talked, unless they were called upon, if anyone had laughed or coughed or cleared their throat too loudly, they were hit and whipped and slapped. All of them bore the welts and scratches to prove it, even Victoria. "No one wants to hear you," Mrs. Cavendish had shrieked after Lawrence had coughed during supper just that very night. "No one, no one!" She had hit him across the face. The Home had shifted and groaned, and Mrs. Cavendish had paled and hissed at them all, "Eat your food, eat your meat," her eyes wild.

Now they whispered together in a little knot. It was strange how thrilling it felt just to whisper. Just that little action felt like a triumph.

"So, let me get this straight," said Lawrence, ticking off points on his fingers. "If you don't get out of here by the time you're thirteen, Mrs. Cavendish chops you up and feeds the other kids with you."

Caroline hid her face. Donovan covered his mouth like he wanted to vomit. Jacqueline couldn't stop shaking. Victoria allowed herself to do none of this. Someone had to keep her head. She swallowed hard and took a deep breath.

"Right," she said.

"And then she turns what's left of you into a gofer, to help her run everything."

"Right."

"And anyone who tries to help, like Professor Alban or Mr. Tibbalt's friend, that Vivian lady—"

"Vivian Goodfellow," said Jacqueline.

"Yes, her. Any grown-ups like them who try to help get swallowed up by the gardens, which Mr. Alice tends."

Victoria exhaled. "Right. I mean, unless anyone thinks I'm wrong?"

There was a heavy silence. Caroline started to cry into Jacqueline's sleeve. Donovan mumbled, "No," and wiped his clammy forehead.

"Well, now that that's all cleared up," said Victoria, "we've got to do something. I mean, we can't sit around and let her chop us up into gofers, can we?" She started pacing. "We can't let her use us like that—cut us up and make us too afraid to stop her."

"And what about those puppets you and Lawrence saw?" said Donovan. "What are those all about?"

Victoria had been thinking about that. She had pictured the puppet cottage in her mind a hundred times and pictured Mrs. Cavendish tying strings and setting them here and there, just *so*. When one wasn't allowed to talk for two days straight, it was very easy to think and gather one's thoughts. Victoria smirked. *You didn't plan on that, did you, Mrs. Cavendish?* she thought.

"Here's what I think," Victoria said, leaning in close. "You know how everyone forgets you once you're here? And people don't care enough to come find you? And people act so strange, like your parents, Lawrence, and mine, too, and Mr. Waxman and the professors at the Academy. . . ."

"And my sister, Jill," added Jacqueline.

Caroline sniffled. "My big brother, Adam. He was acting like he hated me. But he had always called me his 'little goober' before. *Before*." She sniffled again.

Everyone nodded. Everyone remembered how it had been, just *before*. Victoria imagined her parents smiling coldly at her, how they had stayed in their bedroom, how they had not come when she called for them, that day the bugs took her away.

"Right, so," she continued, "I think that's how she makes everyone act that way, how she gets everyone to do what she wants. How else could everyone *really* forget about us like that? Simple: She controls her puppets, and her puppets control the town."

"But—but—" Donovan spluttered a bit. "*How?* How is that possible?"

Victoria remembered back to what Mr. Tibbalt had said: "There are magic tricks, like pick-a-card and white rabbits, and then there are other tricks. Nasty ones. I'd guess that's what Mrs. Cavendish is all about. But I surely don't want to find out."

She shook her head. "It doesn't matter how she does it. What matters is how we're going to stop her."

"Lawrence's birthday is tomorrow," whispered Jacqueline, out of the blue.

Another silence fell. Donovan solemnly clapped Lawrence on the back.

"Yes, well, we're not going to think about that, are we?" said Victoria, although it was, as a matter of fact, all she could think about. She couldn't stop imagining a Lawrence gofer with a streak of gray in its greasy, matted hair.

"Instead, we're going to focus on this—I've got a plan," Victoria said.

"You do?" Caroline said, sniffling.

Victoria kept herself from wrinkling her nose at the sight of Caroline's messy face. Instead, she wiped it with her sleeve and patted Caroline's shoulder and tried to smile. She would not think about Caroline snot on her sleeve; there were more important things.

"Of course I do," she said briskly.

Lawrence tried to smile, too, but it looked a bit sick. Victoria wondered if he was also imagining a Lawrence gofer. "Vicky always has a plan up her sleeve."

Victoria flushed with pleasure and tossed her curls without really thinking about it. This was good. This felt like school, taking charge of group projects and doling out assignments. She could do this. She straightened her dirty pajamas.

"Yes, I do," she said, "and this one should work, but everyone has to help."

"Everyone?" Caroline squeaked.

"Yes. But don't worry, it'll be okay."

"But how do you know?"

Victoria raised an eyebrow. "Because my plans always work. Now listen. . . ."

As Victoria whispered instructions, other children crept up to listen—a couple of the girls, and also three boys Lawrence recruited from next door. By the time they all gathered at the fireplace to leave, they were a dozen.

"You're sure Peter's still asleep?" Lawrence said to the boys.

"Didn't even move when I tripped in the dark," said one of them.

Victoria was worried about that. Out of everyone, Peter would be the likeliest to go find Mrs. Cavendish and ruin the plan. But it was a risk they would have to take.

Victoria crawled in first, Lawrence just behind her, everyone else behind them. ("Stop *grabbing* me, Caroline," Jacqueline snapped.)

"Well," said Victoria, coming to a halt, "that's new."

A black door with a dark, curving handle stood in front of them, far back in the fireplace's shadows. She hadn't even had to hum or whisper to the Home for help.

"A door," whispered Lawrence. "Well, that's awfully convenient, isn't it? What if it's a trap?"

"It could be," said Victoria, but then she saw that the handle was a knobby little tree limb, and the hinges were, too. They reminded her of Professor Alban's dried-up face and arms, and she smiled sadly. "But we can't turn back now. Come on."

She reached for the handle. Two beady-eyed roaches fluttered up from the handle and burrowed into the wall. Caroline shrieked.

Just remember the plan, Victoria thought. She turned the handle. The door creaked, like something old and rusted opening its mouth for a yawn. Beyond the threshold stood the gallery.

"Well, at least it put us out in the right place this time," said Victoria, trying to smile.

"Don't worry, I'll be out there with you as soon as I can," whispered Lawrence, peering over her shoulder. "We'll cut them all free."

Victoria nodded, but she was beginning to feel the first hints of panic. "But what if cutting all the puppets loose doesn't do anything? What if Mrs. Cavendish just gets angrier and we're all trapped here just the same?"

"We'll run for it, or else we'll fight her. We can't just sit here till we're all gofers, can we? We've got to at least try." Lawrence squeezed her hand. "It's a good plan, Vicky. No one else has ever had the guts to try anything like this. No one has ever even had the guts to go outside, like you did." He squeezed her hand again. He stepped a little closer, and his face got all funny, with a small, wobbly almost-smile.

Victoria looked away, her throat full. If anything were to happen to the others because of her—if anything were to happen to Lawrence . . .

"Your collar's all messy," she said, clucking her tongue and refusing to meet his eyes. She fixed it and turned. "Well, let's go."

Victoria drew herself up as tall as she could. Then she whispered, "Go!"

Everyone scattered. Some went to the left, some to the right, some up the first staircase around the corner, some up the second. Victoria watched Lawrence till he disappeared down the gallery. Once he was gone, she was alone.

It didn't feel as nice as it used to.

Victoria balled her fists and crept forward into the gallery. Was it her imagination, or were the gallery walls closing in on her? She paused to listen and look around, holding her breath. Once she focused hard enough, she could feel it—little ripples beneath her bare feet, and a slow, low rumbling from the ceilings, the banisters of the nearby staircases, the hallway behind her. The walls *were* closing in, and then opening back up and then moving closer again.

Then everything went quiet. Victoria inched toward the nearest wall and raised a finger to poke it.

"Hello?" she whispered. No one and nothing answered. The wall felt normal enough. She waited a little longer and then scolded herself and made herself focus on the plan. Being the one in charge helped her feel more like herself again, like the old Victoria who would never believe that walls could move or mirrors could talk. It was a nice feeling, a familiar, strong feeling, but she didn't let it come back all the way; walls *could* move here, and mirrors *could* talk; she had to be ready for anything.

In the gallery, Victoria heard the other children whooping from upstairs in the classrooms and throughout the hallways. They shattered windows, smashed paintings, and ripped curtains off the walls. A drop of blue fell on Victoria's foot as she raced through the dark gallery. Jacqueline and Caroline were flinging paint balls down from the Classroom of Art. Two of the new boys stampeded through the dining room, knocking over chairs and screaming as loudly as they could. Hopefully, this would be a good enough distraction, and Victoria could sneak out without anyone stopping her.

But, despite the noise, everything else was quiet. Victoria saw no gofers come out of hiding to attack them, no Mr. Alice with his rake. No Mrs. Cavendish with her smiling fingers. Even the birdies were quiet, Victoria noticed, glancing up at the high, pointed ceilings. Here and there, she saw a nervous flutter of feathers and a shiny black eye, but the birdies stayed put in their painted trees.

But are they painted? Victoria wondered. Above her, the trees waved and rustled as though their branches were real, but they didn't sound like normal trees. When the leaves brushed against each other, a faint rattling noise, all clicky and sharp, floated down to where Victoria had paused beneath a darkened lamp.

From upstairs, one of the boys let out an earsplitting cheer. A smash of glass followed that, and then, far down the gallery, something dark, thin, and leggy fell from the ceiling.

She ran for the terrace doors, but a dark shape stepped in front of her. She jumped back, too frightened to scream. It was Peter, staring at her with a lean, hard look on his face. He smiled.

"I followed you," he whispered. He nervously pulled at his sleeves. "I did, I followed you, through the fireplace."

Victoria opened and closed her mouth, too shocked to speak.

"Mr. Alice," Peter shouted suddenly. "There are kids out of bed!"

As Victoria burst out onto the terrace, Peter kept yelling for Mr. Alice and ran back into the Home. Victoria could barely hear him, though, her heart was pounding so much.

In the dark gardens, without any lights on, it was hard to find the puppet cottage. Everywhere Victoria turned was a tree or a tangle of bush. The wind pushed her this way and that way, the beginnings of a storm.

From her right came a scratching noise: *Skritch skritch*.

Victoria spun around and gulped. "You don't scare me, Mrs. Cavendish."

The *skritch* turned to a whine. A wet, whiskered nose poked into the moonlight.

"Gallagher!" Victoria ran to him and put out her hand, but he wasn't in the mood for kisses. His fur stood up everywhere, and his tail wagged uncertainly. His ears pricked toward what he'd been scratching on—the door of the puppet cottage.

"Oh, what a good doggie," she said. She scooped Gallagher up into her arms and put her hand on the door latch. Gallagher started growling, which gave Victoria goose bumps. The door stood a little ajar, which made Victoria pause, but then she gritted her teeth and slipped inside. She had to try. She could not give up, not with everyone else crashing around the Home so she could do what she needed to do, not with Lawrence's birthday so close.

Victoria opened the door and fumbled for a light switch. There wasn't one, but there was a table, and a lamp and matches. She put Gallagher down and grumbled, "I hate matches. Very imprecise." It took a while to light because her hands were so shaky, but when it was lit, and she turned around and looked—

—she saw all the people of Belleville hanging from the ceiling, in that same puppet forest from days before. The police chief and his officers, her professors, Mr. Waxman, Dr. Hardwick, Mr. and Mrs. Prewitt . . . and near the center, dangling happily by silver strings, her parents. One bald head, one copper head, two bright smiles.

"Mother," Victoria whispered. "Father." She balled her hands into fists and stepped into the grinning, puppet-filled lamplight.

All around her, shining wooden faces stared at her, too many to count.

ICY WIND BLEW IN FROM THE OPEN COTTAGE DOOR AND BIT Victoria's ankles. She shut the door behind her. There was no lock, not that she could see, anyway.

"She probably never thought anyone would get this far out," Victoria whispered. She would have felt much better with a lock on the door.

Gallagher started sniffing around. "Yes," said Victoria. "That's right. Investigation." She took a deep breath (it was hard to do) and started searching through the marionettes. It was a thick puppet forest. Some hung from the rafters, tiny as dolls, and some stood or sat around the model Belleville. Curious, Victoria peeked inside the library; yes, there stood Mr. Waxman, at the reference desk. Strings trailed from his hands, legs, and head, ending in a lattice propped up against the miniature library wall. All around her, shining wooden faces stared at her, too many to count. They wore bright smiles, clean and perfect.

"Jill," whispered Victoria, seeing Jill Hennessey's shining red hair. "Professor Carroll. Mr. and Mrs. Baker. The *Prewitts.*" Lawrence's parents smiled at her, black eyes shining. Victoria stopped just before her parents, who hung from the ceiling. She reached out a hand toward their four dangling feet. Her mother wore glossy red shoes. Maybe if Victoria touched these puppet parents, they would come alive.

She stretched her hand farther, closer, farther *still*—

A whine from Gallagher interrupted her. She found him in a dusty corner, nosing through dust bunnies. He had found another puppet, a dirty one, all tied up in knotted strings.

"Mr. Tibbalt?" said Victoria. She knelt to clean off his face, but a terrible vision flashed before her eyes—the marionette coming alive, chomping off her fingers with strong wooden teeth. It wasn't such a ridiculous idea where Mrs. Cavendish was involved.

She knelt and sat back on her feet, looking around at the hundreds and hundreds of dangling puppet feet. From across the room, the Dr. Hardwick puppet grinned at her. *Puppets,*

Victoria thought. *Puppets have strings, and the puppetmaster moves the strings.*

She swallowed hard. The air was cold and thick and sharp. Mrs. Cavendish was the puppetmaster here. She had tied up the whole town.

As horrifying as it was, a part of her brain approved. It was an efficient plan. Hadn't Victoria herself always taken over group projects at school, to make sure they were done just *so*? Uncomfortably, she remembered what Mr. Tibbalt had said: "You like things to be just so, no matter what the cost. So does she. So does everyone around here."

Victoria clenched her fists and thought about Lawrence never playing music again or Donovan never eating cake again or Jacqueline painting boring pictures. They wouldn't be better; they would be *someone else.*

"I'm not like *her*, I'm not," she said, and the sound of the words gave her courage. "I'll never be like her." She reached for the Mr. Tibbalt puppet and glanced at Gallagher, who sat watching, waiting. "Do you think it'll bite off my fingers?"

Victoria could have sworn Gallagher raised his doggy eyebrow.

"No, right, of course," said Victoria, and she wiped the marionette's face clean. It was Mr. Tibbalt, all right. There was no mistaking him. Whoever made these marionettes was very good. But Mrs. Cavendish had apparently not been able to properly string up Mr. Tibbalt. She had tried; the piles and piles of string proved it. And yet here he was, hidden in the corner.

Victoria smiled, wondering if those dust bunnies carried to Mr. Tibbalt his never-ending nightmares. "She never *could* get him all the way, could she?"

Gallagher licked Mr. Tibbalt's frazzled head.

In the corner, cabinets and cubbies stood in a line, with blank marionette heads, buckets of paint, spools of thread—and a long, perfect pair of silver cutting shears. When Victoria caught sight of them, they winked at her in the lamplight.

Victoria did not want to touch those shears; Mrs. Cavendish had tapped them against her red lips; Mrs. Cavendish had held them and used them to work her puppet magic. But Victoria had no choice. She reached for the shears carefully. When her fingers brushed a nearby thread spool, it stung like she had been bitten. She backed away and turned to her parents. Her fingers trembled around the shears' handles. Each of the two long blades was as long as her arm. They seemed to smile at her. When she flexed her hand as if getting ready to cut, the scraping metal sounded like someone faraway, screaming.

Gallagher's hair stood up again.

"Well, that's just unnecessary, don't you think?" said Victoria through her teeth, almost too frightened to breathe. "A bit dramatic." Her hair stood up too, along her arms and neck.

She raised the shears to where the strings ended at her mother's shoulders. A draft from outside, coming in through the cracked walls, made the marionettes twirl slowly. Their smiling mouths were too big, their arms and legs too long.

"If I cut them free," Victoria whispered, "will it hurt them? It will just ruin her magic, won't it? They won't . . . *die*, will they?"

Gallagher's ears and tail pricked, but Victoria wasn't watching. She could see only the sharp blades and her mother's shining head. If this was how Mrs. Cavendish controlled everyone and made them do what she wanted them to, what would cutting the strings do? *Without strings, a puppet isn't a puppet*, Victoria thought. *It's only a doll. What will that do to them?*

But there wasn't time to stand there and think. She raised the shears to the closest string and opened them, ready to cut. Surely her mother, going through her catalogs at home, wouldn't drop dead once Victoria started cutting the strings?

"No, don't be silly," said Victoria, but tears burned her eyes. How *dare* Mrs. Cavendish make her have to worry about whether or not saving her mother would in fact kill her.

That burst of anger did the trick. Victoria tossed her curls.

"*Honestly*," she said. "Focus." She closed her eyes and made the cut.

With a tiny plunk, her mother's arm dropped to her side.

Victoria opened one eye. She waited but heard nothing . . . at first.

Then she heard a *plop*. Something dark fell from the ceiling. She followed the *plop* down to her feet, where a roach waved its ten legs in the air, flipped over, and scuttled away under the cabinets.

Victoria groaned. "More bugs." But she raised the shears and cut again—her mother's other arm, her right leg, her left leg—*plop, plop-plop*. Three more roaches. The only string left was the big one attached to her mother's head.

But before Victoria could get to that one, more *plops* sounded from behind her. More roaches scuttled out from the shadows in mad circles, dropping from the ceiling, the walls—

Gallagher began to yap like he'd never yapped before. They weren't alone anymore, or maybe they had never been alone.

Victoria had never *not* wanted to do something so much in her entire life, but she turned around anyway. Out of everything that had happened to her at the Home, this was the absolute worst.

Rearing up out of the shadows of the doorway, so tall that her shoulders hit the ceiling and her head hung low, snake-like—was Mrs. Cavendish.

"I'M VERY DISAPPOINTED IN YOU, VICTORIA," SAID Mrs. Cavendish, her voice sweet and thick. She reached out a long arm that shone as if with scales. "You could have been great, you know. One of the best. A triumph. I thought I could help you, maybe even *keep* you. Mr. Alice won't last forever, and you're so talented, Victoria. So accomplished. So . . . *good*."

Victoria stepped back. She couldn't keep her mouth from dropping in horror. Mrs. Cavendish's beauty melted away like a snakeskin, and now she looked like a great white roach herself, black tongue flitting out over blood-red lips, her eyes never blinking, her long arms and legs stretching, curling.

"One—one of the best?" Victoria wanted to run, but Mrs. Cavendish blocked the only exit.

Mrs. Cavendish traced her lips with her tongue, gurgling deep in her throat. Her cheeks sharpened, her hair grew even shinier. It was almost too bright to look at.

"Do you want to know what your sickness is, Victoria Wright?" said Mrs. Cavendish. "Do you want to know what's *wrong* with you? Why you're here?"

Victoria tried to look around without being too noticeable. "My sickness?"

Mrs. Cavendish kicked the table by the door, where the lamp had been. "Don't repeat what I'm saying. I really don't have the patience, *Vicky*."

"Tell me," said Victoria, shaking. She could throw the shears at Mrs. Cavendish, but they were so long, she didn't trust herself to throw them right. "What's wrong with me? Why am I a degenerate?"

Mrs. Cavendish danced back and forth, ready to pounce. "Why, you're just like her, Vicky."

Something silver glinted at the corner of Victoria's eye—the strings holding up her father. "Just like who, Mrs. Cavendish?"

The slithering word was too low for Victoria to hear clearly, but she heard enough. It sounded like "Vivian."

Victoria had never been more terrified in her entire life—but she had also never been more sure of herself, and that was saying quite a lot, really. Her hand tightened around the shears. "What's wrong with us, Mrs. Cavendish? With me and Vivian?"

Mrs. Cavendish grinned. It took up more than half her face. "You don't know when to stay *quiet*."

Quickly, Victoria swiped upward with the shears. They sliced through too many strings to count. Distant screams filled the cottage, and a dozen marionettes clomped to the floor. So did a cascade of writhing, *plop*ping beetles.

Mrs. Cavendish shrieked and fell to her knees, scraping, clawing, trying to gather up the fallen marionette bits into her slithering hands. Victoria scooped Gallagher up in one arm and ran for the door, slashing at whatever strings she could reach. More marionettes fell with loud wooden clatters, and as Victoria dashed into the night, Mrs. Cavendish screeched behind her, "What have you done? What have you *done*?"

As fast as she could, Victoria ran back through the gardens. The furious wind tossed up brambles and dirt clumps into her path. It was hard keeping her balance, with the long shears in one hand and Gallagher in the other. Even over the wind and trees rattling, Victoria could hear Mrs. Cavendish in the cottage behind her, screaming. The cottage door flew open and broke off, flying away into the night. It raced

Something long and dark tore through the gardens after her, right on her heels . . .

close by Victoria's head; she had to duck into some shrubbery to avoid it.

Something long and dark tore through the gardens after her, right on her heels, panting, gnashing its teeth. It grew closer, closer. Hot, stinking breath hit Victoria's neck. Someone who sounded like Mrs. Cavendish, but with a lower, growling voice, hissed, "*Victoria.*" She ran faster, but it was so difficult to see. If she could just get out of the gardens, out of the maze of rosebushes and black, thorny bushes, and—*Oh*, Victoria thought, *What if the gardens are full of dried-up people, like Professor Alban in the Home, like Vivian in the tree? What if they reach up and grab me, keep me here forever?* Or at least until Mrs. Cavendish caught up and sliced her into pieces.

"No!" Victoria shouted as she tumbled out of the gardens and onto the terrace. She was so frightened, the word burst out of her. She whirled around to face Mrs. Cavendish and opened the shears, thrusting them up into the dark.

With a whine, Gallagher jumped out of Victoria's arms and ran off to the left.

At the gate to the gardens, Mrs. Cavendish crouched on her fingers and toes, dancing back and forth once more, flicking out her tongue. Her pretty white dress flew around her like wings. Her eyes were so, so blue, her smile too large, snapping and clacking. Her arms were far too long to be real, snaking up the terrace steps toward Victoria's ankles.

Victoria jabbed with the shears. "Stay away from me!"

"Oh," said Mrs. Cavendish. Roaches fell out of her mouth when she spoke, and out of the ends of her sleeves, fluttering. "I wouldn't do that if I were you."

That voice made Victoria blink. It was so sweet, so kind. Perhaps if she just lay down for a moment, she could get some nice, restful sleep. . . .

Somewhere in the storming shadows, Gallagher barked. It woke up Victoria a bit. She raised the shears higher and gritted her teeth.

"Don't talk to me like that," she said, putting her chin up. "I'll do what I want."

"Oh," said Mrs. Cavendish. Her head turned around till it was hanging low, upside down. She laughed a sweet, upside-down laugh. Roaches slid out of her collar and into her hair. "You'll do exactly as I say."

"And why's that?"

"Vicky," came a strangled voice—Lawrence's voice. Faint with dread, Victoria glanced toward the Home, never lowering the shears.

There, gathered in a frightened knot, was everyone—

Donovan, Caroline, Jacqueline, the others who had helped her. Peter, looking smug and a bit unbalanced.

Lawrence.

Mr. Alice had him by the collar, his rake at Lawrence's throat. The rusted prongs dug into Lawrence's neck, but there wasn't any blood—yet. Holding the children in place with fireplace pokers were the gofers. Their eyes blinked yellow moonlight. They smacked their mouths stupidly. They seemed uncertain even as they held the children in place.

"Don't hurt them," Victoria said. She couldn't think of anything else to say, and Mr. Alice looked far too happy, his rake ready to strike. Victoria could maybe throw the shears at Mrs. Cavendish, taking Mr. Alice by surprise, and grab Lawrence and run away. But any wrong move on Victoria's part and Lawrence would be—

Victoria thought she might pass out from the fear. On one side, Mrs. Cavendish inched closer, pulling herself up the terrace steps, flat on her belly. Spitting and crooning, roaches spilling from her clothes, she slid closer and closer.

On the other side were Lawrence, Mr. Alice, and all Victoria's friends—*All my friends*, Victoria thought, surprised. *They're my friends. I have* friends *now. How strange*.

"I have something special planned for you, *Vicky*," said Mrs. Cavendish, her face growing longer and thinner and distinctly *not* human. "Oh, yes. You're going to stay with me and help me, for a very, very long time. I would've treated you well, I would've taught you things you'd never believe . . . but you've ruined that now."

Victoria held out her shears. The gofers shifted restlessly. Lawrence made a choking sound as Mr. Alice pressed the prongs closer against his throat. Some of the younger children were crying.

"Why do you do it?" asked Victoria. She stared down at Mrs. Cavendish through the open blades.

Mrs. Cavendish's long black tongue flicked out to release a single roach. It crawled toward Victoria's foot. "Do?" she said, laughing.

"Why do you bring us here? Try to fix us?"

"Because they want me to," said Mrs. Cavendish, laughing sweetly, reaching up with clawed hands, following the roach up toward Victoria's legs. "Your parents, your teachers, everyone. They want me to make you perfect, and I do. I keep their town beautiful, I keep it perfect. And they're happy. Or they were, till some people got too nosy, like that professor of yours, like you yourself, *Vicky*."

Over the laughter singing Victoria to her doom came frantic little barks—Gallagher, in the shadows by the overgrown tree. The tree that was Vivian Goodfellow, kept in the garden for years, forever a part of the Home because she didn't keep quiet. A part of the Home, which had vines and tree roots growing up its sides.

Victoria thought quickly, remembering Lawrence's coaching. She had hummed and sung as he played the piano, and he had pounded the silent keys, and the Home had moved, and it had kept moving all night, in waves, like something was *beneath* it, rumbling awake. She had hummed and talked to the Home, and it had helped her get from place to place. And tonight, it had kept the bugs from swarming through the walls and snatching them away, and with all of them running around and shouting and breaking things and banging things, it had moved even more. Even now, the ground beneath them quivered like gentle water lay beneath it.

And Mrs. Cavendish, ugly and horrifying and beastly, was still flicking nervous white eyes toward the Home's gray walls. . . .

Inside Victoria's mind, everything clicked into place—the shifting, restless Home, the bugs in the walls, the tree roots that had caught her as she fell; Professor Alban growing into the brick wall; the Vivian Goodfellow tree; the sad, whispering voices.

"Of course," Victoria said. She slapped her forehead. "Oh, for heaven's sake. Why didn't I think of this before? *So*

obvious. Professor Alban would give me a B for this, and I'd deserve it."

"What are you saying?" said Mrs. Cavendish, sliding closer. Her hands opened. Her claws scraped Victoria's ankle. "Speak up, speak up, little Victoria."

"Um," said Victoria. Then, she began to sing the same tune from the other day, from Lawrence's coaching—the Fauré duet. She remembered what it was now. During his coaching, he had pounded it across the silent keys. They had played it together the morning before Lawrence disappeared.

Everything was suddenly clear, especially the soft, friendly, Lawrence-y place in her brain she tried to ignore. Focusing on that soft place, and on Lawrence's face and Caroline's and Jacqueline's and Donovan's, helped her sing past the terrified jumps in her throat.

"Ba-dum-dum-dum DUM. Ba-da-dum-dum-dum DUM. Ba-da-dum-dum-dum-dum-dum-DUM-DUM-DUM-DUM-DUM!" sang Victoria.

This didn't take long to sing, because it was a fast piece (Victoria remembered Lawrence's featherlight fingers flying), and Victoria didn't have a good voice, either.

But it was enough. Everyone froze.

Immediately, something rumbled quietly beneath their feet, beneath the stone of the terrace and the mud of the gardens. Stupidly (or perhaps not so stupidly, considering the circumstances), Victoria thought the storming air around them suddenly seemed a little bit friendlier.

Mrs. Cavendish shrank back, spitting, frantically looking around into the night. "Quiet," she snapped. "*Quiet!*"

Lawrence joined in, smiling at Victoria from Mr. Alice's arms. His voice was strained because he could hardly breathe, but he sang a few notes along with Victoria, till Mr. Alice choked him quiet.

"Sing," Lawrence managed to gasp out as Victoria kept *bum-bum*-ing and carefully backing away from Mrs. Cavendish. "Sing something, anything!"

"Scream!" Victoria shouted. "Yell! Just make noise!" She remembered the voices whispering, "Lonely, so lonely." "It likes singing, it likes noise!"

The other children looked at each other in confusion. Mrs. Cavendish saw their fear and grinned. She darted for Victoria, three black tongues and three sets of gleaming teeth ready to strike. . . .

"Er. Row, row, row your boat, gently down the stream," sang Jacqueline, her voice a bit rusty. The gofer beside her pinched her arm, but she kicked him and went on anyway. "Merrily, merrily, merrily, merrily, life is but a dream."

Then she started again, and the other children started

to sing too, and scream and holler and whistle and whoop like sirens. They sang all sorts of things, like rock songs and nursery rhymes, and the Impetus Academy school song, of all things, and little Caroline, trembling, piped up with an opera aria, much to everyone's surprise. The notes soared on the air like golden birds. One of the smallest boys, who couldn't have been more than five, started zooming around the terrace like an airplane.

"Stop it," Mrs. Cavendish shrieked, her face drooping in horrified flaps of skin. She tried to lunge for Victoria again, but this time, the terrace lunged too. The stone rippled, and an enormous tree root broke up through the banister, whipping at Mrs. Cavendish. Clinging to the root were rotting, bark-covered arms and tiny bare feet. But that was only one root, and the terrace wasn't moving enough yet; the Home wobbled but stood tall.

"Sing louder!" said Victoria, waving the shears wildly. "Yell! Scream! As loud as you can—it's waking them all up!"

As it turned out, seeing a giant tree root lashing out at Mrs. Cavendish was quite an inspiration. Caroline trilled louder, and one of the new boys made guitar motions with his hands as he belted out his rock song, and Jacqueline kept rowing merrily, a wide grin on her face. More kids crept out of the Home, those who had been too afraid to help. The doors were falling; the windows were collapsing. Everyone started running around and screaming their heads off, banging on anything they could find, hollering out war cries. Songs turned into an angry din of shouts and chaos.

"What's happening?" said Mr. Alice, clapping his hands to his ears and releasing Lawrence. Some of the gofers clapped their hands to their ears like Mr. Alice, but some of them started grunting and banging their fireplace pokers along the terrace walls. One fat-bellied gofer smashed a window and squealed.

"BANG BANG BANG," it shouted. The other gofers began echoing him, their voices so loud and hoarse that Victoria's ears rang.

"Bang!" repeated the smaller children, and they and the gofers began pulling up the terrace stones, helping to free the gardens underneath.

Mr. Alice's face started to crumble and writhe, like things were moving beneath his skin, and when Lawrence let out a bellowing roar, Mr. Alice moaned horribly. His skin broke open, and he collapsed into a shining pile of confused roaches that spilled everywhere. Lawrence danced away, kicking cascades of them toward the Home. They swarmed across his legs, and Victoria ran for him, but Lawrence waved her away.

"Go, Vicky!" he yelled, and Victoria ducked just in time, because Mrs. Cavendish had come crawling toward her, through the mass of whipping roots. There were lots of them now, coming up through the terrace and the Home itself. Victoria threw the shears at Mrs. Cavendish's face, but Mrs. Cavendish dodged them and leapt at Victoria with arms outstretched.

"But I can *fix* you," Mrs. Cavendish cried at Victoria's heels, tearing through the gardens like a giant beast. She didn't even look remotely human now, just shining and spiderlike, a monster skittering closer and closer, too horrifying to look away from. Her clawed fingers tore through the mud for Victoria, reaching, reaching . . .

"I don't *want* to be fixed," Victoria shouted, and finally, she reached the great, wild tree. She darted behind it and pressed close to the bark, panting. Gallagher was there, his paws on the trunk, yapping like mad. Victoria picked him up and peeked out.

The gardens weren't even gardens anymore. The children's singing and screaming and chaos and noise, and the ruckus of the gofers, had woken them up and brought them to life. Branches waved through the air, the ground rumbled like an earthquake, and here and there, the groaning ground erupted into hills and ridges. Victoria also saw hunched-over *things* rising up out of the gardens. Shaped vaguely like people, the *things* crawled up brokenly out of the twisting gardens, their heads tilted weirdly, their movements sharp and unstable. Victoria saw rotten arms and legs and angry, gaping faces in the tangle of writhing trees and flowers, but she didn't look too closely at them for long.

"Vivian?" Victoria whispered. The tree groaned, its branches and roots snapping free into the air. "Please help us? I know you've tried before—and you've been trying, haven't you? You and the others. But now you really can help the most of all. Please, please . . ."

Mrs. Cavendish dodged the tree's whipping branches. She leapt over the roots that popped and twisted up out of the dirt. Behind her, the Home began to collapse, the chimneys swaying dangerously in the air, bricks and bugs and dried-up arms exploding in rattling cascades, but Mrs. Cavendish didn't seem to care. She lunged at Victoria, her mouth opening wide, wider than a window, wider than a door.

Victoria hid her face in Gallagher's fur. *Well, so this is the end*, she thought. After everything else, it seemed easy to let the end happen.

But if Victoria had thought the tree was alive before, it was nothing compared to what happened now. The tree sprang taller, so many roots and branches flinging themselves up into the air that it became a forest, surrounding her. And the rest of the gardens reared up, too, and the Home was a mass of shining, clicking things. It wasn't a Home at all anymore, and all of it surged toward Mrs. Cavendish in waves of roaches, angry branches, and eyeglasses and fingers and boots and other things that had been on the people fed to the Home over the years, including one ugly heart-shaped locket. Black with rust and mud, the locket popped up out of the great tree's roots, and Victoria grabbed it before it could tumble away. The lashing roots stung her hands, and she gritted her teeth in pain, but she just couldn't let that locket disappear.

One of the tree's branches shoved Victoria away, and she took the hint, running as quickly as possible in the opposite direction from the collapsing gardens, right into Lawrence and the other children.

"Vicky, you're all right," Lawrence whispered, and he hugged her so close she couldn't breathe, but Victoria had never felt anything so wonderful. Together with the other children, they watched the Home and its gardens swallow Mrs. Cavendish into the ground. She shrieked in rage, darting this way and that till the black sea of thorns and mud swarmed over her, swallowing her up. None of the children covered their ears to block out her screams.

When it was over, there was no Home, no gardens, no stinking cottages. They stood in an empty, naked-looking clearing in the middle of an empty, lonely woodland. The ground rumbled softly a few times. Dim lights flashed from deep underground like lightning. Then all was silent. The only thing left was a black spot on the ground where Mrs. Cavendish had gone under.

The breeze became nice and cool, and the remaining trees throughout the grounds rustled peacefully. Everyone looked at each other, dazed, shivering, and tried to smile. After all, they were free now, weren't they?

"Look, Victoria," said Peter, stepping forward. He kept blinking, like he was waking up, and maybe, Victoria thought, he was. "I'm really sorry about—I mean, it wasn't *me*—"

"It's all right," Victoria said, although she didn't altogether believe him. It hadn't always been Mrs. Cavendish making Peter do things. Just like it hadn't been *only* Mrs. Cavendish doing bad things in Belleville. People had let her. They had *wanted* her to, at first, all those years ago.

Victoria didn't like thinking about that, but she made herself anyway. It would not do to forget. Luckily, Victoria never forgot anything.

Everyone poked around in the rubbish for a while, but there was not a lot to see—only shriveled bits of garden, like something had burned all the little twigs and thorns to a crisp.

"What about the gofers?" squeaked little Caroline. "What happened to them?"

Lawrence shifted uncomfortably. Victoria put her hands on her hips and kicked her foot around Mrs. Cavendish's black spot. Ash flew up, and dirt, and specks of what Victoria dearly hoped was *not* bone.

"Mrs. Cavendish made them," she said, "so when she went, I guess they did, too."

Some of the children looked away. Others lowered their heads. Donovan looked as though he might lose whatever Mallow Cakes were left in his stomach.

"So, we can't forget about them," Victoria said. She heard her voice sounding bossy, but she didn't care. Sometimes it was all right to be bossy. "And we can't let it happen again. Agreed?"

Everyone nodded, their faces suddenly fierce and solemn. The night around them was very quiet and cool and barely silvered with moonlight.

"Well," said Lawrence at last. He took Victoria's hand.

"Well," Victoria agreed. She squeezed Lawrence's fingers and didn't let go for a long time.

Gallagher trotted away toward the street, barking happily.

A light bobbed toward them, and when it got closer, Victoria saw that it was Mr. Tibbalt and a flashlight.

"Hello, everyone," he said. He looked around where the Home once stood, his eyes lingering over the spot where the big, black tree used to be. It was strange to see him out in the real world, outside his house. He looked small beneath the trees, and lost.

"Mr. Tibbalt," Victoria said, hurrying toward him. She dug around in her pocket until she found the dirty, half-shattered old locket and pressed it into his hand. "This is yours now."

Mr. Tibbalt's purple-tinged, wrinkled fingers closed shakily over the locket. He did not look up for a long time. Victoria wondered if she should say something else but decided against it; enough had been said—and done. Mr. Tibbalt would understand.

Finally, he looked up. Beneath his glasses, his eyes shone and his mouth trembled, but he stood a little taller now. He could straighten his hunched-over shoulders. After a moment or two, and for the first time in Victoria's life, he even managed a smile.

"Would anyone like to come over for hot chocolate while you call your parents?" he said, and they did.

EPILOGUE

SEVERAL YEARS LATER, VICTORIA HUGGED HER PARENTS good-bye at the train station five times before they would let her go. They had been excessively affectionate ever since that storming night when twelve-year-old Victoria came home in dirty pajamas they had never seen before. They had even started saying "I love you" on occasion, although not in public. It wasn't the most dignified of things to say, after all. But for Victoria, it was enough. She knew that they would never again forget her, and she would not let them.

"Well, good-bye," she said, and then she said, "I love you," and hugged them one last time, and then she got on the train, took her seat, and pulled out her notebook. Her luggage had already been sent ahead to the city. That's where

she was going, and all she had to worry about on the train was finishing this postcard to Lawrence.

"Hello, Lawrence," it began, and then Victoria went on to talk about how she was so excited to go to the city at last, and yes, she'd gotten his letter, and she wanted a tour of his fancy music school this weekend, and she was very much looking forward to his autumn recital.

It had been almost six years to the day since Lawrence had disappeared, when they were twelve and only had each other.

Victoria looked out the window as Belleville sped by in reds and golds. In a moment, the train would pass near the street that took her parents back to Three Silldie Place.

"I'm so glad you've found what you want to do, and that you do it so well," Victoria wrote. "I don't know what I want to do yet, but I think maybe I'd like to be a professor—a good one, like Professor Alban. Or a journalist, so I could investigate things. Or maybe a detective." Then she proceeded to list the pros and cons of these and several other potential careers and to write out a few hypothetical scenarios of the rest of her life, depending upon which profession she ended up choosing. When she was finished, her tiny, clean handwriting filled up the entire back of the postcard.

Victoria nodded briskly, stamped the postcard, and smiled, running her fingers over Lawrence's name. She would send it to him from the city train station, and he would receive it the next day, right before she showed up to surprise him, and he would pick her up with the force of his hug and whirl her around, and she would scold him to not *do* that, for goodness' sake, but she would know—and so would he—that she did actually very much want him to do that.

Victoria smiled again. She sat back and watched the trees fly by, too quickly for her to see where they were, and anyway, she was far too busy thinking over the lists she had just made, and of how nice it would feel to be whirled about in the air.

But as a matter of fact, the trees by the train tracks stood at the outermost limits of the old estate at Nine Silldie Place, near the bare, run-down gate of which, at that very moment, stood three people.

One of them was the realtor, with all the proper papers, smiling brightly because he really wanted to make this sale. It was a tremendous property. It would be an extravagant commission.

"Never been developed," the realtor said, leading his clients through the rickety old gate and down the tree-lined drive. "Real shame, too. Lovely property, don't you think?"

The woman, who had bright red lips and seemed to be in charge of things, smiled. "It's perfect. Don't you think, darling?"

The man, dressed in black gardener's clothes, said, "It's perfect, yes, perfect."

The realtor looked uncomfortably at the man in black, who held a puppet in his hands. He was carving a face into its head, a face that looked somehow familiar. The realtor rubbed his nose. The man in black began carving the puppet's nose.

Trying to be polite, the realtor said, "So, where are you from?"

"Oh, very far away," said the woman. "We've . . . had a long trip. But it's time to settle down again."

"I see," said the realtor. He narrowed his eyes at the puppet's face. It was really quite extraordinary, that nose. "Is that a toy, or what?"

The woman smiled wider. "I plan to open a children's home here. It's a puppet. For the children, you see. They love to play."

"Oh," said the realtor, relieved. "Yes, I see. Well, fantastic. That's really great. Now if you'll look this way—"

"No need," said the woman. Her hair shone, and the realtor suddenly felt very fond of her. She held out her hand for the gate key. "We'll take it."

"It's a puppet. For the children, you see. They love to play."